Manhattan Passion

'Wouldn't it be great to have a dick?' said Zoë.
'I mean apropos of nothing.'

'You mean apropos of this morning.'

'Mmm. I guess that thought didn't come
completely out of the blue.'

'I can't imagine having a thing that I'd
want to stick into all manner of pussies. That's
what's so disgusting.'

'Just for a day. I don't want to be a man all
my life,' said Zoë. 'And I didn't say I wanted a
man's mind. Just the dick, to sort of find out
what it's like.'

'It'd be weird.'

'I just wonder what it would feel like to
have it inside of, well . . . inside someone like
me, for instance. I mean, would it feel like the
inside out of what I feel?'

'Imagine the kind of mind that wants to
just go dipping it in here and in there – in
women.'

Zoë arranged the waffles on two breakfast
plates.

'Weird shit if you think about it,' she said.
She turned off the cooker.

'Let's not think about it. Sausage?'

Manhattan Passion
Antoinette Powell

BLACK LACE

Black Lace books contain sexual fantasies.
In real life, always practise safe sex.

First published in 2002 by
Black Lace
Thames Wharf Studios
Rainville Road
London W6 9HA

Design by Smith & Gilmour, London
Printed and bound by Mackays of Chatham PLC

ISBN 0 352 33691 9

Which one of us is not suspended by a thread above carnal anarchy, and what is that thread but the light of day?

John Cheever

1

'Why are you fucking me differently?' My voice rang out of the pitch dark at him like a church bell tolling on a cold rainy night. I hoped I'd stung him. I hoped I'd caught him off guard.

He didn't say anything.

For a long while I'd suspected. Suspected my husband was having an affair. Oh, I don't know who with. I had no evidence. He continued sliding in and out of me, his heavy breath in my ear. What was he trying to prove? Still he said nothing. But my question would not disappear. I could barely remember when we'd last made love. My question – not so much a question as an answer – occupied the room like a dead body on the floor, a wretched stolid truth that was not going to get up and walk away. David's whole life was a lie. I could tell. There was something. Something subtle, something a woman's intuition couldn't fail to pick up. The perfunctory way he had licked my pussy wasn't even subtle. Now his steady, slow, throbbing movements were just an imitation. The harder he tried to prove there was only me, me, me, the more I knew there was only himself, himself, himself. And someone else.

He came.

I felt the hot jet spurt into me. I came too. But it was just a shallow imitation of passion. How ironic, I thought, that some women fake orgasms because they love their husbands, whereas I didn't want this traitor to know he'd brought me to a real one. He rolled off me on to his side of the bed and fell asleep. Not another word. Not even asking me what I'd meant by my question. I lay there staring up into the dark, not moving, my short nightie still up over my belly, feeling my skin grow cool in the night air of that spring, not a sound except the shambling, sleep-rhythmed breathing next to me, heavy and pathetic.

That was that. And I don't call that being a man.

I am not a woman accustomed to passivity. I was not going to stay in our flat another minute. I did not even want to stop and peel off that wretched nightie: stumbling through the huge rooms, hearing my heartbeat reverberate through my skull and echo back at me from the hollow darkness, I took what my hands grabbed first. I threw on my fur coat, slipped on the first shoes my hands found in the dark – my treasured Prada heels – and then I stuffed his travel money, mostly US currency plus a couple of thousand in major European and Asian currencies, into my coat pockets. I grabbed credit cards. Should I take my birth-control pills? What difference does it make if I'm leaving David? These were the elements of freedom. Just these few moments to gather them up had taken too long. I couldn't stand another minute within these oppressing walls. The cash, the credit cards, these necessities of freedom weighed me down: the pockets of a woman's fur coat should always be empty. I considered whether or not to take my house key. I left. Didn't even lock the door. As I exited the building, the doorman was not at his post. I stepped out on to the Manhattan street at an unknown time. I wandered around the Upper West Side aimlessly as the pre-war apartment blocks looked down on me impassively, not a face in a window, not even a light. I smelled the wet bark on the trees along Central Park West. It was the deadly dark part of an unseasonably warm late-April night; a rain some hours earlier had left the city glistening wet; an unearthly silence blanketed New York, a silence snapped apart with each crack of my heels upon the pavement.

I walked along the low wall of Central Park, the forms of trees and ragged bushes in the gloom looming like savage men. I thought about all the crime and death in the city: I could see the tabloid headline for me: MILLIONAIRE'S WIFE FOUND DEAD IN CENTRAL PARK *Wears Only Nightgown and Fur Coat in Grim Mystery*. You could expect to be found dead the next morning in the middle ages, when people lived in walled cities, if you didn't get back within those walls before they shut the doors for the night. Our time is not so different.

I was ripped away from my tabloid reverie by one of those epiphanies that leaps up at you only in this city. My footsteps multiplied and echoed. No. My footsteps were joined by another set. The loud clack-clack of leather soles rushed up to me and I turned, expecting to confront an attacker. Instead, a petite blonde dressed in black leather was almost upon me, a little white dog running before her. The two of them barrelled towards me as if an unstoppable Great Dane tore her forwards rather than the snow-white poodle that bounced ahead of her with maniacal energy. She ran fast, the dog's rhinestone leash sparkling as it thrummed, pulled taut ahead of her, the animal more a cloud of electrons than a dog. The blonde wore a white blouse, leather jacket with studs, leather skirt, black stockings and black patent flats. She laughed at me, a lightning flash of white teeth and flying blonde hair as she whooshed by.

I watched her recede: she just kept on running until she disappeared from view. And it was over, as if she had never been there. No explanation.

I don't know what that running girl in leather meant. She laughed when she saw me. Does she do this every night? I had never seen her before, but then why should I? It's a big city, and I have only walked around it at this hour once before in my life. I wished I could be her.

Maybe she wished she could be me: it would be no more absurd if we were to exchange our clothes on this spot and continue on in each other's lives than the absurdity that our paths should have crossed in the first place. Did she wonder about the sad, nearly naked woman in the fur coat as I wondered about her?

She had hardly vanished into the night when a sense of having a future returned to me. With this returning sense, which I had not felt for so long, I realised I had forgotten how numb my life had become without ... without a sense of direction, or even the sense that there was a possibility of direction. I could be free; I could choose to be free after all. The hopeless sense of endless struggle could be stepped out of, as easily as I had stepped out of my front door. Until this moment I had not even an illusion of direction. How many other lives besides mine did the laughing girl in black leather, on a hell-bent chase led by a white puff of a dog, touch this night? I felt free, wildly free. I still cannot make sense of the events that happened to me: I set them down here exactly as they occurred. My life has not been what I would describe as a series of events, one following the next like so many pearls on a string. Rather, my story is more like pearls fleeing across a polished floor in a hundred hell-shot directions when the string has broken, perhaps when the strand was

4

pulled too hard in a moment of passion. These events, then, have formed the diary before you.

I hailed a cab.

Did you see me? If you think Manhattan is a sprawling urban jungle, you're wrong. It's narrow. It's a long, thin island that reaches up snugly between the Hudson and East rivers, sort of like a penis lying in a vagina. I find it constricting. It is constricting. I walked around for I don't know how long; sorrow and doubt conflicted with happiness and freedom. Maybe you saw me that night, at a time when all but a few drunks have struggled home. Maybe you were that first cabbie, who passed me by thinking I was a common whore, as if I were a lower life form than him. There are no life forms lower than you, Mr Cabbie. There is only your belief that there are, which is the last refuge of those who know they will never rise. Maybe you were the cabbie who picked me up, who kept looking at me in the mirror. I never got your name, not caring to look close at your picture bolted to the dashboard.

You thought I was a whore too. Or a crazywoman. A crazy housewife maybe, out on some nervous-breakdown nightwalk, a delicate greenhouse-protected orchid of a woman in need of a good round thrashing of raw blue-collar sex, your Fabada-laden sweat thrilling my nostrils. No. You are not sophisticated enough to have imagined that. You are one of those ignorant men. All women are either Madonnas or whores to you. You will never learn otherwise. You could not imagine that I grew up in a good middle-class family, had a good education. As cliché as it sounds, I was the senior prom queen in high school. Yes, me, the sluttish woman you see in the back seat of your cab. Went to Columbia, have a good job (that's what you would call it). And I am highly aware of the fact that my husband is the only man I have ever had sex with. I have always been a good girl. Look at the happiness I've got as a result. Hah! And I – looking at your leering eyes in your rearview mirror – am highly aware that I can change my one-man-only-ever-in-my-life right now, with you, if I wished.

I leaned my head back and looked out the rear window of the cab at the lights of Manhattan flitting by unimportantly. The sky was turning light, to the glowing electric blue of a satin evening dress. Soon we'd be downtown. This wasn't supposed to be the deal. It was supposed to be: be a good girl, get voted prom queen, everything will fall into place. I thought of a life insurance ad I saw in a magazine when I was a little girl: it showed this kindly looking, youngish Caucasian man with his cute blond kid and an attractive young wife on the lawn of their wonderful house in a place like Connecticut and the kid is playing with a dog and his wife wears an apron and the man has just finished raking up leaves into a little hill and it's fall and the man is smiling proudly and the man has a big grey X painted over him. Somehow I'd always expected to live that life. I was too young to know what that big X painted over the man was meant to indicate in a life insurance ad.

I got out of the cab at Broome Street and the cabbie cursed me when I paid him. He had expected me to pay my cab fare in trade – no doubt that was why I had come to forlorn, defunct, sweatshop-façaded Broome. He was indignant that I would not fuck him to cover the $9.75 cab fare or give him a blow-job or whatever whores customarily paid for such livery services. His eyes glowed with hate. It is always the people who have no reason to expect something who feel the most wronged when they don't get it. I did not tip him. As I walked across the wet bluestone cobbles I heard his whining stupid voice volatilising to the empty air something about 'some fuckin' nerve to dress that way if you don't mean business'. But it didn't seem that he was referring to me. The cab evaporated into the lightening sky along with the dew on the wrought-iron railings, rubbish-bin lids, fire hydrants. It was a cool, beautiful morning that would develop into a warm spring day. The air was clean and the street was empty, the sky, grey as iron, an anvil sky. A church bell tolled drearily.

The door to Zoë's building was propped open. I hadn't called her; I wasn't even sure she was in town. I got into the black steel cage of the rickety old lift and slowly, very slowly, rose to the fifth floor.

Zoë answered her door wearing only a bathrobe. She stared at me as if I were a stranger, her arm bent upwards, stopped in the midst of towelling her head.

'It's Julia,' I finally said, wondering if I had stepped into a parallel universe where nobody knew me. In my present state I was, I suppose, a stranger, even to myself.

'Come in,' she said. 'What happened to you? Is David all right? Jack just left for work about four minutes ago. I thought he'd forgotten something and come back.' A set of wet footprints led across the wooden floor to where she stood.

Zoë and Jack Grove's loft took up the southern half of the fifth floor in a 110-year-old cast-iron building. A spacious place, to say the least: one unpartitioned room, rectangular, with no walls except for the walls added around the bathroom. Five cast-iron Corinthian columns, painted glossy white, stood in a widely spaced row right down the middle of the place, reaching up to hold a classic tin ceiling. The building had been a sweatshop for most of its existence; one wall was almost all windows, reaching from waist high up to the fourteen-foot ceiling. The Groves had no curtains or blinds. Curtains are not fashionable. Besides there was no need for curtains; an abandoned building stood across the street. You wouldn't know from the rubbish scattered along the streets in this neighbourhood – all the streets in this area looked like decrepit back alleys rather than streets – and you wouldn't know from the terrifying ancient lift, which looked more like a nine-teenth-century execution device that was just too cruel and unusual to use on capital offenders, that the lofts themselves cost in the high six to low seven figures and were exquisitely decorated, in many cases with art on the walls worth more than the loft. Walking along Broome Street it was difficult to tell which buildings were abandoned and which were the residences of wealthy artists, actors, restaurateurs and so on. The Groves had painted their three walls art-gallery white. The Pop silk screens they had hung on their walls had risen in value to about $6.2 million over the last five years.

'I was getting ready to spend the day shopping,' said Zoë, stepping into a pair of white silk panties and pulling them up into her bathrobe.

'It's kind of early, don't you think?'

'Here, let me get your coat. God! You've got nothing on!'

'I wouldn't say "nothing" –'

'What the hell happened to you, Julia?'

'It's terrible: I've left David.'

'Oh God! You've been wandering around the streets? You could've been mugged. Killed! Raped!'

'What am I going to do? I don't have anywhere to

stay; I couldn't even get my clothes. It just came apart all at once.'

'Sit down. Everything's going to be OK. Sit down. You can crash here till you get on your feet. As long as you want.'

'I can't do that. What's Jack going to say? Oh God, I'm practically naked.'

'Never mind Jack. What good are friends if they can't help you out when you need it?'

'If I can just take a nap or –'

'Don't be silly. You can *stay*. Want some coffee?'

'Yes. That'd be nice.'

'You were out all night?' said Zoë, rattling around in the kitchen area of her loft.

'It's a long story. Not much to tell, really,' I said.

'Here, drink this,' said Zoë.

'Holy – What time is it?'

'A quarter past seven,' said Zoë.

'I've got to get to the museum! I'll be late for work.'

'Your going to go like that? In your nightgown?' Zoë giggled. 'With people looking at your pussy on the bus?'

I looked at myself. It was a *short* nightie.

'Have you even got bus fare?'

I felt sad and tired suddenly. 'Oh God, I am so fucked up. How did I end up this way?'

'You'd better call in sick.'

'But I've got to –'

'You *are* sick. You've got to get your life in order.'

As Zoë took off her bathrobe she momentarily rose on the balls of her feet, as if that would somehow help lift the robe off her shoulders. I was struck by her gracefulness, like a swan about to take flight: I cannot say that I was struck by her image in the platonic sense of a heterosexual woman knowing that another woman is beautiful. I desired her and I could not turn my head away and pretend otherwise. How much easier, in my fatigued state, to stare at the brave vibrations of her naked form, her perfect bare breasts glowing before me, her pussy indicating itself as a dark and nebulous mound beneath the stretched thin silk of her panties. I looked up into her face, fully expecting to find poisonous-snake rebuke in her expression. This had been an inexcusably awkward moment in which my gaze had lingered on her for far too long. But I found her face looking upon me kindly, knowingly. We searched each other's eyes in explicit wordlessness. I had to say something, something to redeem myself, break the tension.

'God, do you think this means I'm ... bisexual?' I said.

'I don't think so,' she said, chucking her damp robe on to a chair. She stood before me glorious, fresh from her morning bath, rewrapping her towel on her head. 'Don't worry about labels so much: a rose by any other name would smell just as sweet. Or some such cliché.'

'Still ...' I said.

'I think you're bi-curious.'

'Bi-curious?'

'Yeah. That doesn't mean you're bisexual. It just means that you're bi-curious,' said Zoë, opening her closet. 'Why don't you pick out something you'd like to wear.'

'What a lovely spring dress this is. But I won't wear any of your panties.'

'Not bad,' said Zoë, once I had her dress on. 'It almost fits you.'

'You don't think it's too short?'

'It's beautiful weather outside; how could it possibly be too short?'

'Well –'

'It isn't *that* short.'

2

Later that morning I bought two dresses and some panties with Zoë at Bergdorf's. After a nice lunch, we browsed art galleries on 57th Street. On the way home that afternoon we bought gourmet groceries at Dean and DeLuca.

Zoë put the groceries in the fridge and opened up a cupboard: 'I think extra virgin olive oil for the pasta puttanesca tonight, don't you?' On the counter next to the olive oil she set out garlic, tomatoes, broccoli, sprigs of fresh oregano, parsley, basil, red peppers, olives, fresh penne, a package of capers dried in salt, and the can of anchovies; and so on. Her efficient yet complex series of actions reminded me of someone playing a game of solitaire with groceries instead of cards.

'What do you think, sauté the broccoli?'

'Do you mind if I try on your white heels?'

She opened the package of nickel-sized, salt-encrusted capperi de pantelleria and shook a good many into a small glass bowl full to the brim with water.

'What do you think?' I said. I knew I looked good in the sky-blue summer dress with a white-flower print I had bought.

'You could probably get David down on his knees begging you to come back if you wear that,' she said.

'You know, Jack isn't going to let me stay. You're not going to have any privacy here in your loft.'

'What do you mean?'

'Look around. No walls – except for the bathroom,' I said.

'We haven't got anything you haven't seen before. Jack and I are very liberated,' said Zoë.

'But I'm not liberated. What if he wants to kiss you or something? You won't have any love life.' Measuring by intuition, Zoë poured about a third of a cup of the olive oil into her Le Creuset pot to heat. The delicious scent floated through the room and made me feel grateful – not about anything specific, I just felt grateful. I was very tired for not having slept last night, and the fatigue heightened my emotions – in this case gratitude – and senses.

'I'm sure Jack'll be glad you're here. Just keep your panties on. I don't want you sleeping with Jack.'

'I won't sleep with Jack.'

'I was *kidding*, silly.' In went three cloves of garlic. 'Let's see you in that pink shift.'

'But you know – this is serious here. I have to confess that I'm a lot more naïve than I look.'

'Oh, come on; how many boyfriends have you had?' Zoë was washing and chopping tomatoes.

'It's not that … Oh, I can't believe I'm telling you this. David is the only one I … actually.' It was hard for me to tell this to Zoë.

'That's … uh …'

'You needn't be polite,' I said. 'I'm quite aware of how awful it is.'

Into the olive oil went about four cups of tomatoes.

I looked out the window. Broome Street was unholy with desolation. 'Nothing at all. No one,' I said as the emptiness of the street drained away the thankfulness that had only moments before filled me.

Zoë turned sad, lost in thought, as if something contagious had just entered our bodies.

'What is it, Zoë?'

'I was just thinking about something.'

'You look so sad.'

'Sorry. I was just remembering something sad.' Then cheerfully: 'I hope you don't mind that I'm not cooking meat tonight. Do you think one rocoto pepper is too hot?'

Zoë prattled on about cooking and I didn't pay attention. I leaned against the window sill and felt the afternoon sun catch my face. Zoë worked in her kitchen. 'Do you know I've never seen anybody do it?' I said. 'I mean, besides me.' I was open now; I needed to confess things.

'I think other people probably look the same as you.'

'You can't really see *yourself*, though.'

'I have a confession to make. There's something I've always wanted to do,' said Zoë, taking a jar of non-pareille capers out of her fridge.

'Oh God, Zoë, I'm afraid to ask.'

'I've always wanted someone to watch me. Is that weird?' said Zoë. She tossed in about a tablespoon of chopped oregano and two tablespoons of the non-pareille capers. Zoë was the sort of cook who did not use recipes and who did not measure things, tendencies that applied to the rest of her life as well.

'Yeah, it's weird,' I said. 'Say, Zo, there's something I've never told anyone about my marriage. About David. I've kept this a secret so long. You're going to think this is weird because of his high position in the firm ... I don't know what to say –'

'Are you going to tell me he's a closet gay or something?'

'I wish. I wish my marriage could end over something that straightforward. Did you know David used drugs?'

'No!'

'I always needed to cover it up. I didn't want people to know. What would happen if they knew?'

'But I'm your friend! If you can't count on your friends –'

'As long as it wasn't too much, it didn't matter. But lately he's gone psycho. I spent so long trying to convince myself he was having an affair, but it's deeper than that – far more all-consuming. I don't mean to exaggerate. Maybe "psycho" is too strong. He has become strange and difficult. You know our vacation last year? That wasn't any vacation. David went into rehab and I hung around the flat pretending to be in Europe.'

'Whew. I don't know what to say. I know a couple that went bankrupt; I know couples in which one or both of them were having affairs. But drugs ... What does he take?'

'What does it matter? He's not an alcoholic, except sometimes he binge drinks. He can be sober for weeks. He takes pills, opiates like Dilaudid. He intensifies it by taking the Dilaudid with ulcer drugs like Zantac. He doesn't snort coke any more. He snorts heroin. I don't think he shoots heroin, but I haven't had much opportunity to look for tracks. It all started three summers ago when David picked me up in a pair of company limos. He and a friend from work were in the back. The friend had this boorish fashion-victim girlfriend with a thick Brooklyn accent who worked in the trading department of another firm. The chauffeurs put our suitcases in the second limo and we all headed off for the Hamptons. The girlfriend handed around a white powder that I thought was cocaine. The three of them took snorts. I refused because I'd never had coke and I heard some people are allergic and can die. Anyway, it was heroin. I didn't think anything of it. I know that sounds strange, but I didn't know it was heroin and nothing really happened. Then, when I found out what it was, it seemed like a one-time thing, and it was over with. I don't think David had any more of the stuff until the next summer, when the market was sagging and shorting stocks, and snorting heroin was so popular in the Hamptons. That girl is dead now.'

'This is heavy, Julia. Is David . . . dangerous?'

'I don't think so. He's been able to hang on to his job through all this. As long as he keeps his job, he can afford his habit.'

Zoë hugged me.

'There's nothing left I can do,' I said. 'I spoke with his firm's chemical-dependence consultant. I have no idea what they did, if anything, because the consultant wouldn't violate David's confidentiality. There's a lot more of this on Wall Street than most people imagine. Who thinks a guy in a grey suit is snorting horse? Pills, maybe people can imagine that. Uppers. Coke. The next move is up to David, and no one else.'

Zoë knew as little as I did about where to turn next.

'Hey, Zo. Why don't we do something? I mean, let's have a girls' night out.'

'Are you sure?' Zoë uncovered the pot of puttanesca sauce and let it continue simmering.

'I've been in such a state, I'm torn between wanting to curl up on your couch and forget that there's a world out there and . . .'

'And?'

'On the other hand, I want to go out there and paint the town red. I've been working long hours at the museum to avoid going home. I even hung out there on Sunday. I've been cooped up in my flat pretending I can hold things together. I'm going buggy. You know, a girls' night out like in the summer when we were in college could be just the thing.'

'Could be,' said Zoë. 'You know, Julia, there's a place I've wanted to go. A club. I'd never have dared go alone, and I've been deathly afraid of mentioning it to Jack. It's actually one of Jack's clients.'

'You don't know the meaning of "deathly afraid".'

'True. How scary could it be?'

'You make it sound like some kind of den of iniquity. Do people smoke drugs there or something?'

'Heavens no! They'd get busted for that. I've mentioned it to you, and now, now that I think of it, maybe I shouldn't have.'

'Come on, let's go.'

'But you don't know what it's like. I don't know what it's like. I've just heard about it from Vivienne, across the hall.'

'Does Vivienne go? Let's all go. Don't tell me your nerve is failing you now. I must go – you've gotten me all obsessed with this. Do they play loud music your husband hates?'

'Frankly, yes.'

'Not country and western I hope. Don't let me down now that you've mentioned a great place to go out to. Do you know how dull my life has been these past five years with David?'

'We'll go already. You can tell I used to be in public relations. I've got you all hyped up about something that can't possibly meet your expectations. It's just a disco.'

I sat on the couch in my new dress reading *Vogue*; Zoë added the anchovies, stirred, re-covered her pot and turned off the heat. She put on a pot of water to boil, adding salt and olive oil. Since he wasn't answering his office phone, Jack would be home soon, barring a national state of emergency.

'How are you going to break it to Jack about me?' I said.

'Don't be silly; Jack'll love to have you stay,' said Zoë.

'Lofts sure don't have any walls, do they?' I said.

'We've had people stay over plenty of times,' said Zoë. I heard a key going into the front door.

'Uh oh.'

'Don't you worry about a thing. I'll handle him.'

'I'm home,' said Jack.

'Dinner's almost ready,' said Zoë. She gave him a big hug and a kiss. 'I'm making a puttanesca like you wouldn't believe. How does that sound?'

'Hello, Julia.'

'Julia's having dinner with us tonight,' said Zoë.

'Hi, Jack.'

'You've got to keep this a secret,' said Zoë. 'We'll explain everything later, but you can't tell anyone Julia is staying with us.'

'Staying with us?'

'It's a long story. All in good time.'

Zoë tossed the penne into the boiling salt-and-olive-oil water.

Jack took some casual clothes out of his closet and went into the bathroom to change out of his suit, where I gathered he did not usually change his clothes after work. I could already tell that my staying with the Groves in their loft was turning into a problem. Zoë heated a saucepan of olive oil and drained the capperi she had been soaking. Then she tossed the capperi into the saucepan to fry.

The phone rang. Zoë picked up the kitchen extension. Immediately I knew who it was.

'No ... Really! Gosh, I have no idea ... I'll certainly

tell you if she calls. I hope she's all right ... Have you checked with the police? ... And they won't even start until it's been twenty-four hours? ... When did you last see her? ... Uh huh ... Do you need me for anything? ... OK ... Yeah ... Take care, David.' She hung up. 'That was David. The strange thing is he seemed more angry than worried.'

'That's David all right. Maybe I should call him. Maybe I should call the police and tell them not to look for me. I intend to go to work tomorrow. I don't want my face in tabloids all over the city as a missing person.'

The puttanesca came together in an instant of clanging pots and pouring hot water, with Zoë looking like a multi-armed Indian goddess lost in the clouds of heaven as the steam billowed up from the sink. She tossed the penne in the puttanesca pot and then spooned hills of it on to three plates, quickly sprinkling on fresh parsley and basil and topping it with the fried capperi.

I would have to sneak back into my flat when David wasn't there and get my clothes. Of course the doorman would see me. And when I left with suitcases I would have to tell him something. I wondered if my neighbours knew yet that I was missing. No. David would not have told them. I thought about my neighbours. I would never have known if any of their spouses were missing; so, what would they know about me? I never knew whether our neighbours were home or away anyway.

Around seven that night I sat in a huge leather armchair watching as Zoë and Jack laid sheets and light blankets over their big leather couch. I was so tired I felt like I was having an out-of-body experience. I had, after all, been up since two or three that morning. Zoë ordered Jack to the bedroom end of the loft. He turned his back on us without being asked. Zoë helped semi-conscious me slip out of my new dress and into one of her old nighties. I floated on to the couch, where Zoë tucked me in. Instantly I was asleep – my too-long day had come to an unconscious end, devoid of all sense, devoid even of darkness.

Later that night, I have no idea when, I awoke to hear Jack and Zoë whispering. I knew they were arguing in the dark, trying to keep it down so I wouldn't know. Jack was dead set against having me stay with them, I was sure. The only words I was able to actually make out were Zoë saying, 'You've got to keep this a secret. If David calls you, you can't tell him Julia is staying with us. She just needs a while to cool off.'

I listened, hoping to hear them make love – which I could take as a sign that they had settled their argument for now. But after their whispering stopped there was a tense silence, the vicious sound of a couple not arguing aloud. I knew they were in no mood for pleasure. And I drifted away again into my sleep.

3

I awoke and looked across the vast floor of the loft. From my position on the couch I could see that Zoë and Jack were still asleep. Morning light lent a grey-blue volume to the room. I could hear the chirping of the birds perched on the abandoned building across the street. Zoë stirred awake. I shut my eyes and pretended to sleep. There were no further sounds of movement. I opened my eyes again and saw that Zoë was watching her husband sleep; then she gently kissed him. Jack awoke.

'Did I wake you?' said Zoë.

'No,' said Jack. 'I was awake.'

'You were not,' said Zoë.

'I was. I was wide awake,' said Jack. He reached down the front of Zoë's nightie to massage her breasts as they kissed. He stopped. I shut my eyes.

'What?' said Zoë.

'She'll see,' said Jack.

'Look at her. Sleeping like a baby,' said Zoë.

I wondered when I might dare open my eyes again. I listened to them whisper and their bedsheets rustle.

'*Oh*,' said Zoë.

'I've been waiting for you,' said Jack.

'Liar. This is just a morning soldier, standing to attention,' said Zoë. I burned with envy at the sounds of their playful lovemaking. I knew I had lost so much – missed out on so much – if this is what other couples did and I almost never had. The wild sense of freedom that had seized me along Central Park the night before sank out of sight like a weighted murdered body dropped into the East River. I had a long way to go before my life would ever resemble theirs. I was not free.

I opened my eyes and saw Zoë giving her husband head. In the hushed silence, Zoë's eyes shut with calm; the only sound was that of Zoë's lips slipping over and over again around the bulb of her husband's cock, her fingers caressing his shaft. Jack's hand was buried between her legs, pushing the cloth of her nightie against her pussy as he rubbed her clit through the material. Her nightie came over her head and I caught a glimpse of her rosy-lipped little flower as she climbed astride Jack, his fingers refinding their position, clinging to and exploring her pussy.

I saw her feed his cock into her as she sank herself upon it. There was an absoluteness in the gesture: woman sinking her cunt over a cock.

I don't know what I imagined other people's sex lives would be like. Somehow, I guessed, they would have to be much better or much worse than mine. Watching Zoë and Jack, I didn't see any advanced new techniques or anything physical that I hadn't done with David. But there was one thing that was totally different. Something, I knew, I was missing from my life. In their simple progression of acts, they had a joy that I longed for. I knew they loved each other; I knew they were making love, not just having sex. It wasn't the acts so much; something arose out of the purity of their openness. There were souls here, souls meeting, with that extra sense of aliveness that can never quite be put into words, something like the difference between live theatre and a movie – there are some things that movies and books and other dead media can never capture from the living. As she rocked on him I heard rhythmic sighs from deep inside her. Quiet at first, then louder, more resonant and primal, then Jack too. When they came – I am certain they were simultaneous – he let out three shouts that *no one* could have slept through. I pretended to stay asleep. They had totally given in to their ecstasy. Then, I could tell they were whispering, but too quietly for me to make out words.

It was not until Jack had gone to work that I pretended to wake up. They were taking such care to tiptoe, I knew if I awoke they would wonder if I had been faking sleep. Zoë was taking an after-sex bubble bath. I knocked on the bathroom door.

'Come in,' said Zoë.

She was stepping out of the tub.

'Oh, it's you,' she said.

'I wanted to thank you this morning,' I said, interrupting myself. 'I mean, thank you *for* this morning. Isn't that funny? I almost said, "I wanted to do you this morning".'

'Is that so funny?'

'Sorry. I just wonder if that's some kind of Freudian slip.'

'Could be,' said Zoë, who was lost in preoccupation with her thoughts.

'Jack left early.'

'Not so early by his standards. He has to see a client. Another client, another dollar.' Zoë towelled herself dry. I noticed something glittering in her pussy, two jewels hanging suspended from chains. I was so intrigued I spoke before I could stop myself.

'What's that?'

'Girl, don't you know what *that* is?'

'No. *That*. You didn't get yourself *pierced*, did you?'

'This? It's a clip-on.' She rested one foot on the edge of the bathtub. More quickly than I could properly see, her fingertips disappeared under her and reappeared holding a piece of jewellery. 'Kind of a trippy thing I got to please Jack.' I looked at the golden device and tried to imagine how it fit on her. 'Want to try it?'

'That's OK.'

'Even I haven't had the nerve to get anything pierced down there. Good thing you saw it; I might've left it on all day.' She threw on her robe.

'Sorry, we're out of regular cream; Reddi Wip OK?' said Zoë, bending over me and splurching a glop on to my coffee.

'OK,' I said, although it was already too late to say no. She was close enough that I could feel her body heat against my cheek. She splurched a glop of Reddi Wip on to her coffee as well.

'What would Dean say if he saw me do this to his coffee? Or DeLuca for that matter?' she said, setting the can of Reddi Wip on the counter and turning her attention to the noisy frying pan on the stove.

I daydreamed, imagining myself having sex with Jack that morning, myself in Zoë's place. Jack's method – his entire vocabulary of movement and touch – was different from David's.

'Do you suppose every man is different? Or do you suppose there are just three or four categories?' I said.

'I don't know,' said Zoë. 'I wonder if every man is unique, yet at the same time they are all the same. Interchangeable even.'

'I wonder what it would be like to have two men.'

'I could *never* do that,' said Zoë. 'I *want* to. But I'd never get Jack to share me with another man. Do you suppose men think about that sort of thing?'

'You mean about sharing their wives with other men?'

'That and the idea of having multiple women, like three or four, or even two.'

'I don't know,' I said.

She concentrated on the breakfast she was cooking.

'Wouldn't it be great to have a dick,' said Zoë. 'I mean apropos nothing.'

'You mean apropos this morning.'

'Mmm. I guess that thought didn't come completely out of the blue.'

'I can't imagine having a thing that I'd want to stick into all manner of pussies. And to *want* to, that's what's so disgusting.'

'Just for a day. I don't want to be a man all my life,' said Zoë. 'And I didn't say I wanted a man's mind. Just the dick, to sort of find out what it's like.'

'It'd be weird.'

'I just wonder what it would feel like to have it inside, well ... inside someone like me, for instance. I mean, would it feel like the inside out of what I feel?'

'Imagine the kind of mind that just wants to go dipping it in here and in there – in women.'

Zoë arranged waffles on two plates.

'Weird shit if you think about it,' she said. She turned off the cooker. 'Let's not think about it. Sausage?' She speared a sausage and put it on my plate, then took one for herself.

'Zoë, what am I going to do for money?'

'You took the credit cards, right?'

She set the plates of waffles in front us.

'What if he cancels them?'

'What's wrong with your job?' said Zoë.

'I have never had a job for *money*,' I said. 'I can't imagine actually having to live on that salary.'

'You're not paying rent,' said Zoë.

'I've never paid rent. I know I can't stay with you forever. All of a sudden I have to deal with my future.'

'You'll find a flat.'

'I can't afford rent. I'll need a room-mate. David used to buy me everything —'

'Your lawyer will make David pay support. You'll be OK,' said Zoë.

'But I'll still be dependent,' I said.

'Julia, I'm not sure you're ready to make a decision. Are you going to separate? Are you going to divorce? You need to talk with a lawyer immediately. I can recommend somebody.'

'Oh, Zoë, I can't even *think*.'

Zoë dipped her finger into the golf ball-sized blob of Reddi Wip that floated on the surface of her gourmet coffee: 'This cream came from somebody's breast, one of our cow sisters. All you can get from a dick is come and piss.' She held up her cream-slicked finger: '*This* is useful.' She licked it off. 'Tastes good too; not like that other stuff. Aren't you glad we have breasts instead of dicks?'

'I have to get a part-time job. But what? It can't conflict with my regular job,' I said.

'I think you'd better consult with a lawyer.'

'It was all so crystal clear when I walked out and now it's all so complicated.'

'Jack's clients own businesses. Maybe he could find you a position.'

'Oh hell, I don't actually hate David. If he ever quit getting loaded, he'd be a nice guy. Do you know how intelligent he is? You'd have to be to do all that financial manoeuvring — I don't even understand it,' I said.

'Your master's was in art history,' said Zoë. 'If you'd majored in financial manoeuvring instead, you'd be

25

every bit as good as David. Every bit as intelligent. More so.'

'I suppose,' I said.

'Better to have breasts than dicks,' said Zoë thoughtfully. 'And thank heaven men don't have two dicks hanging on their chests.'

'I should call David and really lay it on the line. Either he goes clean or I go – for good. Is using drugs a ground for divorce?'

'Julia, was he abusive? Is there something you're keeping back?'

'He's psychologically abusive. He has episodes. There were times when we stayed up arguing all night about such crazy shit you wouldn't believe it. I'd get so tired I'd be cross-eyed and stuttering the next day at work. I'd be a wreck. And I'd be thinking, This is it; never again; he's had it this time; he's crossed the line.'

'Oh God.'

'Well, finally he crossed the line and here I am. He didn't hit me ever. Not in the face; sometimes on my arm; or he'd grab me and twist my arm. But it was the psychological shit that got me. I thought I was going crazy. Do you know he once threw a chair through the living-room window? Of course not; we didn't tell anyone. He could've killed someone on the sidewalk below. Finally, I knew I had to get out. I can go, I can move, I can change the channel on this shit.'

'Julia . . . I know a therapist.'

'No. Not yet. I want to breathe. I want a few normal nights of sleep in a row.'

'Yeah, of course. You poor dear.'

'The thing is, I have to call David. I can't just sit here and let things happen around me. I can't let him decide everything.'

'Maybe after you've had a chance to think things over –'

'No! I'll call him now and meet him. For once in my life I must act first. I must have the upper hand.'

Chez Céleste was one of the two or three fanciest restaurants in Manhattan. It looked like a doll's house: a quaint 120-year-old townhouse at the foot of a suite of mirror-glass towers in Midtown – the owner had refused to sell his building to developers, who had offered him millions. I walked up the flight of steps to the front door, which like most old townhouses was on the second floor. I saw David's profile in the bay window. From his table he was watching people walk by below the restaurant in the bright midday light. He had to have seen me walk up to the place, but his profile was oblivious to my existence.

I told the *maître d'* that someone was waiting to have lunch with me. When I rounded the corner expecting to find David, he was gone. I had seen him in the window not one minute earlier. I stared in disbelief at the empty table.

'There you are,' said David, appearing out of the interior of the restaurant behind me. He kissed me tepidly on the cheek and then sniffed rather as if he had caught a cold. I knew better. He had sneaked away for a snort.

David elbowed the waiter aside and helped me with my chair. He then retook his seat at the table and surveyed the room, like a king in his court, which, I suppose, was how he thought of himself. David's eyes looked right through me as he scanned the scene. This was his kingdom: tablecloth, nice flowers, solicitous waiters, a brandy. He was dressed to the nines in a cream-coloured suit with a vest and tie. In stealing a snort, as he had, he had already outmanoeuvred my whole point for seeing him.

'You're late,' he said.

'You're right.' And I could kick myself for what I did next: I checked my watch – and realised I didn't have my wristwatch any more. Why the fuck should I care if I'm late! He should beg me for forgiveness, not the other way around. He should wait here for hours until I show up whenever I feel like it.

The waiter handed me a menu and asked me if I wanted something to drink. Another waiter poured me a glass of water. Any chance for my entrance to be pregnant with drama was drained away by the mundanities of waiters.

'Who was he?' David said – a typical peremptory accusation.

'None of your business,' I said – why not confirm all his worst fears? He never believed me when I told the truth.

'Aha!'

'Shut up,' I said.

'So you're already seeing someone.'

'It's none of your fucking business.'

'I knew it; I knew it.'

'If you knew it then what are we doing here?'

'I have a few specials today,' the waiter said.

'I'll have the lobster and she'll have fettuccini in pesto,' David said.

'Any starter? The soup today –'

'Just bring what I ordered,' interrupted David.

'Just a Caesar salad, thank you,' I said.

'Very good,' said the waiter.

'She'll have the fettuccini,' David said. 'No Caesar salad. It has garlic.'

'Perhaps if you need some more time to decide –'

'I will have the Caesar salad,' I said. 'No fettuccini.'

'That's not what she wants, waiter. You will bring the fettuccini.'

'No! No!'

'Julia, I'm paying for this meal.'

'No! Goddammit.'

'Now, now, Julia. You're becoming shrill, and that's never pleasant.'

I looked the waiter right in the eye and, in a voice I didn't recognise as my own, I coolly, and cold-bloodedly as I might stab my husband one day, said, 'You will be so kind as to bring me the goddam motherfucking Caesar salad or I will throw such a fit as you've never seen before that you will most likely shit your pants.'

The waiter headed worriedly for the kitchen.

'I'm sorry. I wanted to talk things over and I guess – Let's not get off on the wrong foot,' David said.

He wiped his forehead.

'Hi, my name's David, what's yours?' In an instant he was the charming long-haired David I had gotten to know at Columbia. Immediately I felt drawn to him. David's instantaneous ability to manipulate me made me hate myself even as I saw myself drift under the spell of his charm.

'My name is Julia.' I was willing to give him a chance. I believed in myself; for the first time ever, I had stood my ground on something and he had backed down. The lunch was back on my terms. 'I should warn you, I've just broken up with my boyfriend, so I might not be very interesting company,' I said.

'I think you're very interesting company. What boyfriend would be crazy enough to let *you* get away?'

'Sometimes I wonder; it was so great for so long.'

'I understand. I mean, I'm sort of in the same situation.' He shifted in his chair and looked at me with what I interpreted as a note of pleasure. 'That's a very pretty dress. It shows off your figure nicely. New?'

'Yes. It's like the sort of thing my boyfriend used to surprise me with,' I said.

'Oh? He must have had good taste,' said David.

'He did. There were a lot of things good about him, David,' I said.

'Do you think there's any hope for him?' said David.

'Yes. I do,' I said.

'That's good to hear. I mean, for him,' said David.

'All he has to do is clean up his act,' I said.

'Doesn't he have a job or something?' said David.

'Oh, he has a job. He heads a department at a Wall Street brokerage firm; but I was thinking how if he would just quit taking drugs . . .'

'I'm clean and sober,' purred David.

'Then why are you so defensive!'

'I'm not defensive –' Suddenly he held up his hands, as if a mugger was relieving him of his wallet at gunpoint.

'What is it?' I said.

His eyes bulged with surprise.

Oh, fuck, not here, I thought.

'*Ahghgh.*' He puked all over his chest with a ferocity and concentration that made it look as if ruining his expensive suit had been intentional. The expression on his face, which was now calm and contented, and the aiming of the stream of vomit at his chest, with his hands held up about head height to keep them unbepuked, all looked to be the final stage of a well-executed plan.

'You fucking shit!' I jumped up from the table.

Our waiter emerged from the kitchen, his hands

loaded with another table's food, just in time to catch sight of the disgusting scene already accelerated to full thrust. The poor man set down his tray and rushed over.

'Is there something wrong?'

'Leave us alone!' said David. '*Bleaughghgh!*'

I headed for the door. The nerve of that bastard. David reached out and flipped up my dress as I tried to pass him.

'I want to see what I'm missing.'

I stopped in my tracks, angry enough to kill. I grabbed David's face and wrenched it towards the window.

'You see that?' I said.

'What?' said David.

'That! That's the world out there; that's the universe. *That's* what you're missing.' The rotting-Parmesan-like stench of his barf made me gag.

I stalked out. My stomach was churning: I was dizzy with anger and the smell of David's puke was inordinately strong.

'Oh yeah! I'm high on life, babe, higher than you'll ever be,' I heard him saying. The waiter doubled over the back of my chair and barfed where I had been sitting.

When I went out on to the street I saw Gavril sitting at the wheel of the Rolls – the car and driver the firm provided for David. Gavril saw me and I know he recognised me. I shook my head and headed towards the Avenue to hail a cab for downtown. I would have loved to have left David stranded, taking the Rolls and leaving him to hail a cab in his stinking, puke-soaked suit. But the last thing I wanted was for Gavril to find out where I was staying and tell David.

* * *

When I reached Fifth Avenue, I was too mad to go back to Zoë and Jack's. That would have meant defeat. To go home and sulk and stew would be exactly what David would want. A couple of blocks up the way, Bergdorf's gleamed like a rainbow after a storm. I resolved to replace my spring wardrobe and have it delivered to Jack and Zoë's loft for me. No. Now that I had had a chance to collect my thoughts and saw that my marriage was over, I would check into a suite at the Four Seasons – their closet space is better than the Plaza's and the Pierre's – and pursue my divorce. I could not impose on Jack and Zoë any more, and they didn't have any space to put the clothes I needed.

Skip Bergdorf's. I called Barney's. Kate, my favourite shopper, was surprised to hear from me, and that I needed to see her immediately. I told her I realised she might have another appointment booked. But she said no, no, she'd be there for me. I told her I needed a full wardrobe this afternoon.

Kate knows my figure, my tastes, my needs. I told her I needed a couple of conservative suits (I did not tell her I wanted to present myself well when giving depositions and testifying in court). I told her I needed some *prêt-à-porter* for work – not too conservative, not too sexy – and a couple of signature pieces for evening (I knew that was always risky, but I did not intend to go to any social events – I needed something appropriate for going out to dinner with friends). I needed a couple of sexy summer dresses for daytime, and let's include at least one fashion-slave piece. I like to be done up to the hilt for at least one moment in a season. It's always fun to be a fashion victim, but only if you do it on purpose, and only if you go over the top once per season. There is nothing so unfashionable as to be a permanent fashion victim and not even realise that you are – it's a sheer sign that one is a member of the *nouveaux riches*.

'Sorry. I need intimates and accessories as well,' I added. 'Please pick out a nice – and expensive – wristwatch.'

'Wonderful!' said Kate.

I hung up the phone and hailed a cab.

Kate met me up in one of the showing rooms on the top floor of the store, a large, oval room with vanilla walls and a bright-white, domed ceiling that was supported on a tasteful, simple moulding. Kate wore a very sharp suit.

'Kate, I love your hair!'

'It's my spring do. Do you like it? I just got it today.'

After two hours we had picked a full wardrobe and Kate's assistant rang up my purchases, which came out at a little over $73,000. I am not a clothes horse, although I had now and then run up a bill of this order of magnitude.

There was a problem with my credit card, Kate's assistant said. She was on the line with the credit card company.

'Is there a problem?' I said, taking the phone from Kate's assistant.

The credit card woman asked me the usual security questions – my husband's mother's maiden name, my birth date and so on. When she was satisfied I was me, she informed me that my card privileges has been suspended.

'When?' I said.

'Today,' the woman said.

'There must be some mistake.'

'No. No mistake. The database says the card is suspended.'

'I didn't authorise that,' I said.

'It is a joint account,' the clerk's voice said.

'Did my husband authorise that?'

'I don't know. The account has been suspended.'

'Never mind,' I said. I hung up and gave Kate another credit card.

That one failed too.

'Kate –' I said. I couldn't try a *third* card in front of them and risk that one also not going through.

Kate smiled pleasantly. Not a hint of tension. She had spent a major portion of her day with me and a rack of clothes that retailed for more than her annual income, and most of it was marked up with pins and chalk to fit me and no one else.

'Kate . . .' How to graciously exit? 'I would like this delivered to a different address.' I wrote down the address for the Groves' loft. 'There has been a mix-up at the credit card company. I can't straighten it out right at this moment.'

'Think nothing of it,' said Kate graciously. Kate's assistant looked glum, but Kate was as cheery as she was the moment I first set foot in the showing room that afternoon.

I looked at my new watch as if I had an appointment.

'I've got to get my hair cut today too,' I said. 'There won't be any problem delivering this?' I looked at the rack of extravagant clothes: what was mine a moment ago now might as well be a million miles away. So, David had decided to cut off my credit cards!

'I'll sort out my credit cards first thing tomorrow.'

'It's no problem at all,' said Kate.

Kate's assistant shot my wrist a look. Without a word, I took off the $12,850 Cartier and handed it to Kate, who had betrayed no concern in the least that I might try to walk out wearing an expensive watch that wasn't mine.

'See you,' I said, and left.

I wondered how Kate had interpreted what she had just seen, whether she believed I had gone broke or that there was a simple mix-up with the credit card company.

Kate had given no hint – and her assistant would never be promoted to Kate's level unless she could learn to keep as cool.

When I got to the Groves' loft I called David to demand an answer. The phone rang and rang. I thought it odd that the answering machine did not activate.

I called David's office and left a voice message.

I called all my credit and charge card accounts. The accounts were not 'closed', but they were all suspended until their past-due bills were paid.

'What?' I said to one clerk.

'When the past-due level reaches a certain point, we cannot authorise further charges until the balance is paid,' was the answer.

The bills were astronomical – and I knew most of the charges could not be mine.

Back in Zoë's loft that evening I realised that I was not at all as cool and composed as I had told myself I was. The brave, commanding front I had presented to David at lunch was stripped from me now and I was shaking. I was nervous about my future, angry about my lost past. It all came home to me how big and mean and cold this city was and that I was nothing more than one woman, tired and homeless, just one woman with hardly more than the clothes on her back, a cup of coffee in her shaking hands, and her wits. I wondered seriously whether I should just go back to him. Perhaps David would simplify things and quietly OD.

'Julia, you're staring into space,' said Zoë gently. She wasn't sure what to say, or whether to say anything at all.

'I actually do care about the guy,' I said.

'You do, don't you? I know how it can be.'

'To see him so weak, so vulnerable?' I said. 'You should have seen it; God, what a mess.'

'I'm glad I didn't,' said Zoë.

'Zoë, do you think I'm fucked up?'

'No. Why do you say that? I mean, no more fucked up than the rest of us.'

'I suppose.'

'Well, I mean, you might actually be fucked up.'

'Yes. I just wish I could run away to another world and play hookey from this one for a while.'

'You're not really going to find another job, are you?'

'I don't even have my chequebook. What if David closed the account? A couple of handfuls of cash that I stuffed into my coat pockets is all I have. I can't pay a divorce attorney.'

'Why don't you work at a club downtown? It's not intellectual, not like legal proofreading or something. Nothing to do with Wall Street, nothing to do with art conservation, and it can pay well,' said Zoë.

'But where? Would I fit in?' I said.

'I can get you in someplace. One of Jack's clients runs the Where It All Happens Club, in the East Village,' said Zoë.

'You keep harping on about that place.'

'I've always wanted to go. Now's our chance. It'll be the girls' night out you wanted. We'll see if Vivienne wants to go. She's been there dozens of times. You'll love Vivienne. She's a real hoot.'

'Julia, I'd like to introduce you to my friend and neighbour Vivienne.'

'Hi,' she said. 'I'm Vivienne Li.'

'Nice to meet you,' I said. 'I guess you get a lot of comments about how you aren't *the* Vivien Leigh.'

'Yes. Although I do tend to think of myself as *the* Vivienne Li, just not the famous dead actress Vivien Leigh.'

The very much alive and wholly original Vivienne Li had straight black hair that ran down to the hem of her waist-length black leather jacket. Her skin was an unblemished shade of gold, impossibly smooth, not unlike the radiant smoothness of a Robert Graham figurine that Zoë and I had admired in a 57th Street gallery yesterday. And though she was little over five feet tall, and carried herself with the nonchalance of a devastating beauty – as opposed to the haughtiness of attractive women who wished they were beautiful – there was no mistaking Vivienne for a figurine. She had a flash in her eyes that caught me off guard every time we had reason to look at each other, which for many minutes after I met her had the effect of making me halt mid sentence if I looked at her while trying to talk. I was sure that her effect on me led Vivienne to suspect that I was Zoë's imbecile friend, perhaps a country girl who was overdue to be sent back to some sleepy Midwestern backwoods like Cincinnati.

'Zoë tells me we're ditching our husbands tonight,' said Vivienne.

'Are you married?' I said, regretting the imbecilic question as soon as it had left my lips.

'*Of course* I'm married,' said Vivienne.

What astonished me was not so much her married state but that any husband would knowingly let his beautiful wife out of the flat dressed in such a short black skirt, black stockings, black heels and so on; in other words, with an inconceivably powerful ability to attract men.

'And you're married?' said Vivienne.

'Yes. *Of course*,' I said, emphasising the same words she had. It was a warm night and people who had been cooped up all winter were out and about. We decided to walk it. Even though I was all dressed up and looked quite sexy in my new pink shift, I felt dowdy and married walking alongside Vivienne towards the East Village. All eyes were upon her. Men whistled and made stupid whooping noises. They made sucking sounds in their cheeks. I suppose men think this is sexy for a woman, although it sounds like they are about to spit or are trying to clear wedged food particles from between their teeth. Sexy. Oh, why couldn't they all just go off to a war and die or something and leave us alone? I guess that's too harsh: Why can't all those men be at home recovering from diarrhoea and leave us to ourselves to enjoy this night?

We found ourselves at the intersection of four abandoned blocks of buildings. There the tenements stood, eyeless with their bricked-up faces. It was not so many decades ago that landlords abused their tenants here for not paying their rent on time. Now the buildings were so worthless it was too expensive to tear them down. The sullen, soot-scorched cubes represented so many bribes and schemes and deals and political favours woven together by such a long succession of incompetent popular mayors that the land was more valuable occupied by the empty brick hulks than any economically productive purpose.

The exception was down at the end of East 8th Street, an address well known to the sub-subculture, and previously unknown to me. A doorway glowed in the distance, lit by one thin blue neon tube – the faint cobalt glow would have been overwhelmed anywhere else in Manhattan, but here, where there were no shops and most of the streetlights had been shot out, this frail light was a blazing beacon not unlike a single candle in the window of a farmhouse in the dead of night in the country.

Here, this light was an indication of life of some sort, among the moonscape-like desertion. Music permeated up through the sidewalk from deep within the crumbling brick edifice, not so much as music heard but as a vibration below the threshold of perception felt by a sixth sense.

The Where It All Happens Club: Zoë proposed that I try to secure part-time work here because it wouldn't interfere with my day job at the museum. Zoë's husband was the owner's accountant. Yes, though it was supposedly trendy beyond most mortals' comprehension, its deepest darkest secret was that its books were well kept and its taxes were filed on time by a man who wore starched white shirts and conservative ties and lived in an expensive loft condo with original art by famous artists on its walls.

Fear rose within me as I stood on that abandoned street. Where had everyone gone? Signs of life: someone had fit together an intricate pattern of tiles and ceramic shards, coloured glass and mirror fragments, filling the cracks of the sidewalk with a gleaming mosaic that wended its way in all directions in gleeful psychedelia.

In the interstices, where the shoddy sidewalk of the City Public Works Department cracked apart, florid mosaic filled in like a colourful opal patina creeping across ancient Roman glass.

Zoë tried the door; the rusting old thing didn't budge. Instinctively, Vivienne pulled Zoë back, just in time to keep her from being hit as the bouncer swung the door open as easily as if it were a screen door. His arms were thicker than my legs. He was a tough, solid wall of a man, and at the ends of his huge arms were thick muscular fingers that were fatter than erect penises.

'Yeah?' said the bouncer. There was no expression on his face.

'Don't be an asshole!' yelled Vivienne.

'Hey, Viv,' he said, smiling. In a miraculous instant, a warm, welcome look overtook his face and his mannerisms were immediately courtly and deferential. 'Didn't see you there, standing behind your charming friend.'

'This is a girls' night out and we don't want to talk to any men,' said Vivienne. She marched past the bouncer, Zoë and I in tow. A dimly lit hallway led to a courtyard and, beyond, the entrance to another tenement building. A hundred years ago desperate immigrants lived too many to a room, worked seven twelve-hour days a week for just enough money to subsist on and gave each other tuberculosis and syphilis and died in these cramped, damp rooms or in knife fights in bars. The woman taking admission looked up from her till and, recognising Vivienne, waved the three of us in, *gratis*, without so much as a word.

The place was dimly lit with coloured lights, mainly red. The music was some sort of weird modern pop that I had never heard before. A DJ with a bone in his nose played records in a booth above the floor, rather like a priest in a pulpit. Couples danced here and there. Strobes flashed. Vivienne handed me and Zoë each a tequila, a drink I very much dislike. We downed them.

Zoë gave me a pouty, apologetic look that said, *I know I promised you a den of iniquity, but I guess this darkly lit bar will have to suffice.*

'Well,' said Zoë. 'This certainly is way out.'

'You think so?' said Vivienne. 'Because if you think this is way out, maybe I shouldn't show you the basement.'

Zoë noticed the horror in my expression: 'Oh, come on, Jule, it'll be fun.'

The basement was a sub-club called the Willard Room, named after the rat movie, I supposed. It was crowded down there, a lot like the crowded smoky bar upstairs. There was another DJ in another booth playing different music from what they had upstairs. Vivienne threaded us through the crowd towards a fountain that projected away from one wall and poured into a wading pool that encroached into the middle of the room. Spilling into the wading pool was a hot tub. Six naked people were up to their knees at one end of the wading pool, soaping themselves up. There was a very fat young woman, three ordinary-looking young men, a shapely, incandescently pale Caucasian woman and a shorter, thinner, very beautiful young woman with long black hair who looked like she was from India or maybe was Hispanic.

'OK,' said Vivienne, 'five of those people are customers and one is a shill. Can you tell who the shill is?'

'One of the women,' guessed Zoë. 'Two of them are far too good looking to have walked in off the street. Both of them are hired models.'

'Getting warm. Which one is the Don't-Touch Girl?'

'The what?'

'That's what she's called. One of those girls is basically just a stripper. Her job is to take off her clothes and jump into the fountain. It depends on who's working. Some don't mind being touched. Some are just here to get side work. But the one here tonight is a Don't-Touch Girl.'

One of the guys started running his soapy hands all over the huge, luxuriant, globulous breasts of the fat woman.

'She's definitely not the Don't-Touch Girl,' I said.

'Do you want to go in?' said Vivienne.

Zoë and I looked at each other. I'm sure our expressions mirrored each other. She was aghast; she looked as aghast as I felt. Vivienne was slipping off her skirt – not that there was much of it to slip off – and she slipped out of her thong, leaving on, for the moment, her stockings and garter belt and high heels. I saw a silver flash as she pulled her black silk blouse over her head. I stared intensely as time and my mind went ritardando: she had a silver ring in her bellybutton and the sight of it gave me a tingle. I was not supposed to be bi but oh how I wanted to touch my tongue against the ring and oh how I wished the tip of my tongue could wander down from there like a drop of rain to that little thatch of black hair nestling between her legs.

'Come on, let's jump in!' yelled Vivienne, kicking off her heels and looking undignified as she unhooked her stockings and rolled them off. She splashed into the water still wearing her black garter belt. 'Come on. It'll be a blast!'

'Hey!' yelled a man who'd got splashed. He shielded his hand over his martini.

'Fuck you!' yelled Vivienne, laughing and splashing at him again.

'Fuck you yourself,' yelled the man, who was in a nice business suit. He stalked off through the crowd in a huff.

'I really can't,' said Zoë, looking at me pleadingly. She looked helplessly towards the wading pool, the hot tub spilling into it, and the fountain, a grandiose affair worthy of the Trevi that an artist had collaged together from a panoply of stone figures that looked like they'd been collected from the architectural salvage companies that line Lafayette, an eclectic concoction of statuary rescued from demolished buildings from *fin-de-siècle Beaux Arts* to Depression-era American fascism. 'I really . . . This is too much,' said Zoë, who was obviously torn by conflicting desires.

'At least watch my stuff for me,' said Vivienne, smoothing her wet hair back from her face and behind her shoulders. 'I'll show you which one is the Don't-Touch Girl.'

Vivienne laughed at us, her square friends who had wanted a thrill and then frozen in terror when she'd delivered the goods. She romped off through the water, taking the bar of soap away from the fat woman. Vivienne soaped herself up. The fat woman helped her. Then they hugged – I was very struck by what a soapy, slippery conglomeration of flesh it was. Vivienne winked at us. Oh how I wanted to join her. I longed to be as free as her. I saw her hug the others one by one in the shallow end of the pool, where the fountain was, until it was clear whom she did not touch. And if she *did* dare touch the Don't-Touch Girl? Would a bouncer stride into the water and grab Vivienne, a soapy slip of a naked woman, nothing on her but a garter belt and a silver bellybutton ring?

The soapy people in the pool started splashing each other and dancing under a spout that poured into the wading pool out of a coil of copper tube carried over the shoulder of a square-featured fascist-style labourer, a nude nineteenth-century marble odalisque reclining against his limestone knee. The crowd within splash range cleared away pretty quick. Water struck me. I let it. I knew that I could not yet have that pure joy. As fun as it looked, I knew if I was in there laughing as much as Vivienne and the rest of them, I would only be imitating having a good time. I was sure my self-doubt would suck away all their vitality. Oh how I wanted to join them; oh how I knew if I did then there would be eight depressed people in the pool feeling conspicuous and naked and wanting to leave.

The tequila was already making me feel relaxed, but there was no escaping myself.

'That was clean fun,' said Vivienne when they'd all got tired of splashing around and the soap was off them. Somebody dumped a box of bubble bath into the fountain and it was producing enough foam to overflow on to the dance floor.

The dark girl – the Don't-Touch Girl – emerged from the crowd and gave Vivienne a towel.

'This is Lata,' said Vivienne.

'Do you do this every night?' Zoë asked.

'It's a job,' said Lata, with a light New York accent. 'I do it every hour.'

The two girls sat on the edge of the pool and towelled their hair.

'Lata's from India,' said Vivienne.

Lata laughed. 'Sure,' she said. 'The same way that you're from China, right? Did she tell you I was the

Don't-Touch Girl? That's what Viv calls me, the Don't-Touch Girl. But I let Viv touch me, don't I?'

Oh, the two of them sitting side by side like that, dripping with water; the drops of water on the black hair of their pussies made it look like they'd spilled caviar in their laps. I wanted to get down on my knees, first Vivienne, then Lata, then Vivienne again, then Lata again, eating up the caviar.

'Oh, fuck! I lost my bellybutton ring,' said Vivienne, pawing at her tan belly in disbelief. 'It's in the pool somewhere. We'll never find it. Guess I'd better go for an actual pierce if I don't want to keep losing them.'

'I gotta go up and blow-dry my hair,' said Lata. 'That's show business for ya. When I'm on again, I've got to do this as if it's completely spontaneous.' I watched her slender naked form cut through the crowd unimpeded, like the parting of the Red Sea before her: nobody, not even the drunks, touched her.

'Aren't you going to put on your clothes?' I asked.

'I feel so refreshed,' said Vivienne. 'Let's go up to the lounge on the second floor and get a drink.'

We followed Vivienne. I carried her clothes in one hand and her leather jacket in the other. The crowd parted for her too. Strangely, by now I found it perfectly normal to be with a naked friend in a crowded bar. I couldn't get over how people didn't seem to notice Vivienne very much except to get out of her way more readily than when we'd squeezed through the crowd fully clothed. She was invisible here, a far cry from the way she had been treated in the street on the way over, with badly dressed ugly young men constantly injecting comment. Nevertheless, I feared for Vivienne: people were smoking and not necessarily careful about how they held their cigarettes.

Up in the second-floor lounge people stood around sipping from a variety of odd-coloured drinks, bright blues and reds and greens. Zoë bought us a round of adult drinks, asking me and Vivienne what we wanted: gin and tonic for me, straight tequila for Vivienne, and she got a scotch and soda for herself. Though most of the Where It All Happens Club was dark, we found ourselves seated around a tiny disk of a table that happened to be directly under a bright pin-spot casting down its slim pole of light through the smoky bar air. Vivienne sipped down half her tequila and put on her clothes, leaving her thong, which was about the size of a crumpled blindfold, on the table.

'You looked like you were having a lot of fun,' I said finally.

'Why didn't you come in then?'

'You know full well. It's just too goddam weird.'

A man tapped Vivienne on the shoulder. She turned and smiled at him and turned away, as if her smile had the magical power of suddenly vanishing him from existence.

'Yeah, I know. That's what I thought the first time I came here,' Vivienne continued, as if uninterrupted.

The man – he was attractive I might add – tapped her on the shoulder again.

'Can't you see I'm talking to my friends?' Vivienne snapped.

'Are those your friends?' the man said. This idiot is in every bar in America right now, I thought. Like Santa Claus, able to be everywhere in the world in one night.

'Yes. These are my friends. And they're not your friends.'

'Can I have you?' asked the man.

Vivienne thought for a moment. She had a look of superiority on her face, that flash in her eyes again, like she was coming up with a great retort to put this attractive dimwit down with.

'All right,' she sniffed, handing her drink to Zoë. Vivienne stood up and tossed her head, as if doing an impression of a bored aristocratic lady. She bent over our table and pulled up her skirt. Barely two feet from my face, Vivienne's pussy hung between her legs like a delicious ripe plum ready to drop off the tree. Zoë and I were petrified. We sat there helpless, too stunned to move. How many drinks had Vivienne had? Just two, I was sure, one and a half. Was she really this slutty? What had Zoë got me into? Should I rescue Vivienne from this drunken, horrible mistake? I just sat there.

The man had his erection pointing at Vivienne's slit within moments. She was wet and she was aroused. This was wrong! Wrong, wrong, wrong! What was happening?

The man eased his cock in and out of those luxuriant folds of pussy lips. This was in full view of everyone, under the spotlight that shone down from its recessed position in the ceiling. I had always thought of a pussy as being irredeemably ugly. This thought was based on never having really gotten to see one. Now I could see what it was that men were so turned on about, its convoluted shape, its colours, the density of its textures – rough, soft, smooth, hairy. I sat in fascinated horror at the scene before me. I was alternately flush with envy that I did not have a cock to probe that soft, fleshy beauty, and I was revolted at the wrongness of what I saw. I never would have guessed that Vivienne had such a poor sense of self-worth that she would allow herself to be publicly degraded this way. And still those reddish-purple Asian lips of hers, the deep black of her pussy hair ... I wanted her. The horror; the beauty.

'Just a moment,' said Vivienne, standing up. The man

casually withdrew his cock; it waved in front of my face. 'You know, I just remembered something. You stay here and keep yourself hard while me and my friends go and put in our diaphragms. Is that OK?'

'Sure! Wow!'

'I mean, you can fuck all three of us.'

He caressed himself in a most disgusting manner, standing there lovingly massaging the shaft of his cock, stimulating the head every third or fourth stroke, a glazed distant look having overtaken his face.

'You sure you're going to be here?' said Vivienne, a look of doubt crossing her face that the man was any longer capable of being reached by human speech. 'Because me and my girlfriends will be very disappointed if we come back and find you're not here.'

'I'll be here,' said the man, rousing himself momentarily from his trance to look at us.

Vivienne turned to a black transvestite: 'You keep an eye on him and make sure he doesn't go soft.'

'I won't go. I promise!' said Vivienne's erstwhile sex partner.

'Good. One of my biggest turn-ons is men who keep their promises.' With that, Vivienne winked at him sexily. 'Come on, girls, let's go to the powder room.'

'I refuse!' I said, when we were out of earshot. 'You don't seriously expect –'

'Calm down,' said Vivienne, leading us through the courtyard to the exit. 'Let's get out of this place.'

We were back on the street. The bouncer had set up velvet ropes around the door, making it look like the entrance to a club. My knees were shaking. I realised I still held Vivienne's thong in my hand. We walked west through the empty street.

'Sorry, gotta piss,' said Vivienne, descending into a

squat, feet wide apart. Zoë and I squatted down too and we pissed on the sidewalk with her.

'Bet my husband would like to see this,' said Zoë. 'Three women pissing.'

'*Attractive* women,' scolded Vivienne. 'We are attractive women, and I have no doubt that your husband would get a charge out of watching us piss in unison.'

I watched the piss splatter out of Vivienne and Zoë's crevices. Beneath Vivienne her stream beat against a patch of mirror and bottle-glass mosaic, the arching droplets splashing between her high heels looking like a golden anemone caught in the streetlight. Though I knew my pussy must look exactly the same as theirs in this instant, I watched transfixed by their gushes of piss, having never seen a woman do this, not even myself. I fought hard with myself to resist the temptation to reach my fingertips into their duelling streams and feel the rushing hot wetness: I wanted the experience to be that much more complete, and that much more indelible in my memory.

'How could you stand to let that guy ... *Ughgh*,' I said.

'I got my revenge, didn't I?'

'Yes. But. He was inside you. I *saw* it.'

'You make it sound like fucking a stranger in a club is something bad. I think it's one of the charms of the Where It All Happens Club.'

'Who's got Kleenex?'

'I do,' I said.

'I hope you've got three. I'd prefer not to share,' said Zoë.

'That guy's probably still up there hungry for these snatches,' said Vivienne, wiping herself and standing up. 'I bet you he's *still* there jerking off.'

'Let's go back and check.'

'Zoë!'

'Come on, Julia. Don't be such a stick in the mud.'

'You're fucking crazy,' I said.

'Come on, it's a girls' night out.'

'It's disgusting. It's insane.'

'Come on, Jule. I gotta know if he's waiting for us.'

We went back into the club. I had to know. I followed them upstairs.

He was still there, still jerking off.

'What a pitiful man,' I said.

'Don't tell me you feel sorry for him,' said Vivienne.

'I do, actually.'

'Why? A minute ago you were complaining that I fucked him. He's already had a lot more than most of these other guys here are going to get all night.'

'I suppose you're right,' I said. 'But he does look wretched and pitiful.'

'Good!' said Vivienne. 'Let's scram before he sees us.'

Vivienne was mad at me.

4

I had decided to wear my Thierry Mugler suit to my appointment with the divorce lawyer. I had bought it on Old Bond Street, in London, for £1,600, and I resented that David had it in my closet. The suit was black, with a corset-motif around the waist that showed off my figure, very sharp. It was a suit that made men lose their composure and stare inappropriately when they saw you at intermission at the opera. The hard part: returning to my flat to get it. I put on my new sky-blue knee-length dress with the white-flower print and headed out. I turned down Zoë's offer to accompany me. She wished me luck. I was on my own.

David usually got to his office by 7:30 each morning so he could finish scanning *The Wall Street Journal* and checking the wires before trading opened. At 9:30 a.m. – a safe time since that's when the market opened – I called his office from a pay phone one block from my flat.

His secretary answered.

'Is David LaFleur there?'

'Is this Mrs LaFleur?'

'Is he there?'

'Is this a client?'

'This is a prospective client. Mr LaFleur was recommended to me by one of his current clients.'

'And who would that be?'

'Is he there?'

'Perhaps you'd like to leave a message and he or someone else could give you a call –'

I hung up.

I called my flat. The phone rang four times and the answering machine came on. Having failed to determine whether my husband was at home or at work, I bravely pressed on towards my former home, each step filled with dread. I had decided to approach my building on foot. On this spring morning my neighbourhood of only days before, my former neighbourhood, looked utterly alien and foreboding. Columbus Avenue in the morning, on the Upper West Side, trilled with the voices of West Indian nannies and the little white children they shepherded. As I approached Central Park West and steeled myself to turn the corner I prayed that it would be Enrico the intelligent doorman posted today rather than José, the stupid one, who gossiped worse than an old village woman and who couldn't keep a secret even if you bribed him to.

Fortune smiled on me for once: Enrico snapped to attention in the brass doorway the moment he saw me.

'Good morning, Mrs LaFleur. Had a good trip?'

'Oh, yes. Excellent.'

He walked swiftly ahead of me through the lobby to press the lift button, something stupid José failed to do for me even when my arms were full of packages.

'I hadn't seen you around for a while and Mr LaFleur said you had to go to Europe to look for some paintings.'

'Yes. It was a business trip but it seemed like a vacation.'

'When did you get in?'

'Last night, actually. I'm still quite jet-lagged.'

Enrico abruptly turned serious. 'I hope everything is all right.'

'Yes. Everything's fine,' I gushed, too much, I realised.

'I know everything will work out OK for you,' he said, not taken in by my pretence.

I dropped my act: 'Is he in?'

'No.'

'Are you sure?'

'He left this morning at the usual time.'

'Is the maid in?'

'She ain't come this week, far as I know.'

'Enrico, Mr LaFleur doesn't need to know I was here this morning.'

'As far as I know, you're still in Europe, Mrs LaFleur.'

'I'm not much of a liar, am I?'

'I've been here since four o'clock yesterday afternoon. José, he call in sick. I'm working a double shift.'

'I just need to get some clothes and get back to ... Europe. If my husband should suddenly return, you will do me the courtesy of ringing the intercom?'

'I'll do it. Sure, Mrs LaFleur.'

I walked through the twelve spacious rooms of the flat I had once known as home. I looked up at the high, moulding-edged ceilings and it seemed nothing more than a dim memory that I had once worked with decorators, architects and contractors to make this a source of pride that I showed off to dinner guests sometimes two or three nights a week.

The flat looked like a ghost-filled mansion. I felt like a ghost, drifting through the stale rooms, the occupants having only just departed for my funeral moments before my astral arrival.

The library. David had always wanted a wood-panelled library. To him that was proof that he had succeeded on Wall Street. Not that he was well read. He didn't much care for reading at all except for the *Journal* and analysts' reports. And he skimmed those. Well, he was successful. The curtains had been left open and the sun poured on to the oriental rug. The maid knew better than that. I drew the curtains shut. I had always thought of this as a comfortable room, with its dark-wood panelling and plush leather chairs and couches. The panelling, shelves and cabinets were antique, and obviously from an earlier era than the building. David and I had found this woodwork in an architectural-salvage place downtown on a tip from a decorator friend, whom we ultimately hired to oversee its installation in our flat. The woodwork had originally been in a nineteenth-century mansion built by one of the lesser-known robber barons. No craftsmen alive today could re-create this ornate hand carving. The columns, mouldings and panels had been lushly grandiose for over 100 years, and then been summarily removed at the request of a *nouveau riche* couple who had moved to New York from Texas and who had thought it looked old-fashioned, and who a year and a half later went famously bankrupt and went back to Texas. Maybe they were right, I thought just now, it is old-fashioned.

This library is the room where my husband and the men would retire after dinner to smoke cigars and tell juvenile jokes about women's breasts and the like, which they would have felt just plain stupid telling in the presence of women. How I longed to join them, with their boyish jokes and cigars in the wood-and-leather room. Now it looked more like a giant coffin. The jokes had long fled, as quickly as sound waves absorbed into the leather bindings of the old books that lined the room. The cigar smell lingered, stale, and the room was all the sadder for its bygone good spirits, as airless and lacking in vitality as the library on a sunken luxury liner. I could not in this moment specifically recall any happy moment occurring in this room or witty comment spoken that would contrast it in my memory with the lifelessness that yawned mustily before me now.

Anxiety flooded me like a door flung open: I had to get my safe-deposit box key and Mugler suit and get out while I could, for I felt like I was on a sinking ship, on the edge of a whirlpool that was about to suck me down with it to the bottomless depths.

I debated between my Anya Hindmarch and my Mulberry purses. I went for the Mulberry, black, its sharp corners complementing my suit, and the metal buckle looked very businesslike. I pulled open the drawer where David kept the cash. Damn! Nothing. I got my passport; I scooped up all the chequebooks and thrust them into the Mulberry. I took David's passport too, out of spite. I couldn't find the safe-deposit box key. Mentally I wrote off all jewellery right there. I could have kicked myself for not taking the advice Zoë had once offered: be sure to keep an account of your own. I told her that I thought that would be a sign of mistrust and that I couldn't bear to carry such a secret within myself and still feel like a good wife. Marriage was about sharing and trust and giving yourself completely to the other person. Zoë's response: 'People don't buy life insurance because they want to die, they buy it because it's the right thing for them to do.' Zoë was too much of a friend to ever raise the subject again. Zoë was my closest friend and I know she didn't even think 'I told you so', let alone say it.

I felt like a housebreaker in my own home – and it did not seem like home. The sight of my walk-in closet depressed me: long rows of dresses that I had bought in happiness and good faith, when I thought I had a future, when I thought it was my moment to live and be young and enjoy a piece of life. Clearly, it was all over. I wanted to run. These dresses weren't any use to me now. I walked along the rows, looking at them, like someone in an up-market used-clothing store. I looked at a black cocktail dress that was now out of style and found myself daydreaming: who bought this dress? What was she like? What were her hopes and dreams? I wonder if she's alive now or dead.

I stripped from the waist down and put on black pantyhose. I knew this wasn't my home any more, because I felt exposed and vulnerable – I *could not* be naked here in what was once my own dressing room. I took off my blue dress. The Mugler was the kind of *prêt-à-porter* suit that could only be worn braless. I had lost weight: God, this fit me well. I had an eerie sense of being The Other Woman. I was in my own walk-in closet putting on my own clothes and, as I furtively delved through row upon row of plastic shoe drawers for an alternative to my black Pradas, I felt like a cheap floozie helping myself to the clothes of my lover's wife. My dressing table: all my make-up weirdly exactly as I had left it. I wanted to whoosh the lot of it into a shopping bag with one sweep of my arm and go. I sat down and did my face. I looked at the tragedy of my dressing table and felt like a god looking down on a village that I knew was about to be destroyed. How could I ever replace all this: the Clinique moisture surge, the Paco Raban XS eau de toilette, the Christian Dior icône, the Hoi Tong talcum powder from Hong Kong, the Shu Vermura eye make-up from Japan, the Shiseido Optune perfect sebum-off, the Estée Lauder Enlighten, the nine Chanel nail polishes and the twelve others, the twelve lipsticks in a row from Chanel, Guerlain, Revlon, Estée Lauder, Lancôme, the twenty other lipsticks standing in the back, the perfumes Acqua di Giò, Fire & Ice,

Pleasure, Acqua di Parma, Miss Dior, Coco, L'Interdit, L'Air du Temps, Chanel No. 5, L'Eau D'Issey?

Miraculously my hair looked good. The perfume? No. Not here. Nails? Not here: stop at Miss Kim's for a manicure.

The intercom buzz shattered the air: could it be? The realisation that I was a criminal in my own home gripped me to the core.

I thrust my blue dress under my dressing table, grabbed my Pradas and ran into the foyer to pick up the intercom.

'Mrs LaFleur, I thought I ought to tell you that Mr LaFleur is on his way up.'

I ran through the kitchen and stepped out the servants' entrance on to the fire escape, a bleak, windowless staircase that ran up through the centre of the building and where the porter loaded our garbage on to the service lift. A fluorescent halo buzzed dimly on the ceiling, in its last throes before burning out. Where was my key? Inside the flat somewhere. David would find it lying wherever I'd left it.

I stood in the grey, shabby fire escape, paralysed with fear. I put on my shoes. I was way overdressed for such a predicament, but I felt strangely comforted by thoughts of outrageous fashion photography. In the world of *Vogue* it was perfectly normal for a woman to be dressed to the nines – nay, dressed to kill – accessorised with a chic and functional bag, her face taut with fear, while she stands tensely in a decrepit, claustrophobic staircase next to a shut metal door whose paint was peeling. This happens every day.

I heard the lift rumbling through the brick walls and come to a stop. I heard its mechanical door clank open. I breathed shallowly and quietly; the insides of my ears grew hot as they strained to pick up the least sound, my own heartbeat measuring off units of silence in which my future hung in the air, waiting to be determined. In this moment my entire life lived up till now lay in the sounds that echoed off the 1920s steel stairs and grey-painted brick walls of that hallway: I placed my ear against the cold steel of my kitchen door and listened, hoping for footsteps, voices, any sound. And then I heard them.

I waited. I was too angry to think – anger had crowded out fear. I would catch them red-handed. I lay in wait, choosing my moment to spring. Would he seduce her right away? Should I wait twenty minutes? An hour?

Oh, I imagined them: David, suave in his Brooks Brothers suit and $775 shoes, and she, a stupid, pretty secretary impressed by his seven-figure bonuses and company-provided chauffeured Rolls limo. I counted the moments, trying to imagine events playing out in their real time, as if my eyes could see through the old fireproof door. And to think that *this* adulterous episode was delaying me on my way to an initial meeting with a divorce lawyer. I hoped he had her down to her bra and panties. The very idea of her bra coming away from her skin entangled in his fingers charged up my anger all the more. I didn't want to catch them in The Act; I wanted to catch them at the exact moment her bra hit the floor. Time enough had passed. I marched right through the door and into the kitchen.

My heart stopped. They were right there; her back was to me. David looked at me wide-eyed with terror. She turned around. She was ugly, a young thin girl with long, greasy brown hair and watery eyes. For a moment I thought she'd been crying, but I was struck by her peculiarly pinprick pupils, as if her eyes had been crudely painted on her. She gripped the top of David's arm tightly and would not let go. Possessive little wretch, I thought. The girl delved into her bedraggled pocketbook. 'It's cool,' said David.

She was really just a girl, maybe 20, not tall, and way too thin. What caught me off guard was not that this grim slip of a girl was someone my husband committed adultery with, or that this creature was something he preferred over me; rather, I was in awe of her *presence*. She was years beyond her age, she was bigger than life, she commanded my respect – and I realised why: she was Evil in its purest depraved form.

'It's . . . It's not what it looks like,' said David. I could then clearly see him pull the used syringe out of his arm and lay it on the kitchen counter alongside a glassine bag and one of my good silver spoons.

'Oh, fuck, David. What do you take me for?'

'Duh yew know huh?' said the girl in a thick New York accent and a husky low voice. She wore a horrid navy-blue corduroy miniskirt, with her bare legs reaching down socklessly into dirty, flayed running shoes. She wore a black-and-white striped polyester top and a loop of green and blue plastic beads around her neck that swooped over the black-and-white pattern. No bra. Virtually no make-up: I hated her. A slight miscalculation and she could have killed my husband. I pitied her so much I loved her.

'Hey, Julia,' said David.

'Is dis duh othuh wuhman?' said the junkie girl.

'Of course not,' said David.

'Who is she then?' said the junkie girl.

'Yeah, who am I?'

'I know this may look bad,' said David, 'but everything's cool.'

'You give huh the good clothes and you don't give

me shit,' said the junkie girl. 'I fuckin' trusted you. You think you hustled me, you don't know duh *meaning* of hustled.'

David smiled broadly.

'Please. Please. There's been some kind of misunderstanding here –'

I waved his heroin syringe under his face.

'Holy fucking shit, David!' I yelled. I slapped down his syringe on the counter and ran out into the welcome bleakness of the fire escape. He didn't try to come after me.

I was shaking with fear as I made my way down the stairs. My knees fluttered like vibrating contrabass strings. What did that girl mean when she said David didn't know the meaning of 'hustled'? Did she carry a gun in her pocketbook? I could just have easily walked into the flat and found David dead of an overdose, or shot. The girl might have been the type to have shot us both right there in the kitchen and then rifled the flat for jewellery and cash. The questions ricocheted around my head: how could everything go so wrong? What have I done to deserve this? To be tossed away like an old rag? How could I have ended up being so unwanted?

When I got down to the lobby, Enrico was not at his post by the door. Outside it was a bright, sunny day and I was wearing an impeccable Mugler suit. The sun goes on shining, the world comprises an infinity of parallel universes.

On the corner I called 911 from a pay phone and reported a domestic dispute. I said I was a neighbour and I didn't want to get involved. I gave my home address as the place where the shouting was coming from. I added that I suspected it was none of my business but that I supposed the people in the flat were dealing drugs.

If the police put David in jail, they'd be doing him a favour. They'd be keeping him alive. I hung up. Gavril was waiting in the Rolls. Oh, this is rich, I thought: David uses the firm's chauffeur and Rolls to go score smack. Gavril saw me coming but he sat motionless. A couple of months ago he would have leaped out of the car and pulled the door open for me. I knocked on the window and asked him to take me to Miss Kim's for my manicure. He was reluctant, and confused, but ultimately complied. When we got to my manicurist I sent him away. What must Gavril know? Everything? What does he think when the lady of the household exits the building after the husband enters with a junkie whore? One keeps up appearances, of course. Just as Gavril had not indicated that he thought anything might be amiss, I offered him no clue that would confirm what he knew. I couldn't ask him any of the questions I was dying to, because then he would know for sure that it was as bad as it looked.

Jane Conch asked me to take a seat in her spacious corner office, whose floor-to-ceiling windows overlooked Rockefeller Center. She asked me the usual questions about whether David or I had had money prior to being married, whether there was a prenuptial agreement, who was my husband's attorney, did we have children, what would the ground for divorce be and so on. As I gave my answers sometimes she clucked or made a serious expression now and then, but I could not tell what she actually thought about anything. She jotted things down on a yellow legal pad.

My personal rule of thumb for such things as shoes,

tailors, hairdressers, kitchen contractors and the like was always to try at least three and pick the best. I had not adhered to this rule in choosing a husband, and I was about to violate it in choosing a divorce lawyer. I had heard of her before because she had handled the big Inman divorce. Zoë and Jack had said Ms Conch was the best, and the woman had put me at ease with her mixture of a businesslike manner and soothing sympathetic comments.

She asked me whether I actually knew what my husband earned. I said I had no way of knowing, although I had twice seen confirmations of wire transfers. Once for two million dollars and once for seven million.

'Wire transfers from where to where?' she wanted to know. I admitted that I had no idea where all the money was or whether David had other accounts. We had a safety-deposit box, I said, but I didn't know where the key was. She asked me what bank that was in. I had no secret accounts, I went on. I admitted that I did not recall signing a tax return at any time during our married life. But then again, from time to time I signed all kinds of papers David put in front of me. Yes, I admitted, I never read any of them – they were dense with legalese and printed in small type. More clucking.

'He cut off all the credit cards I took.'

An unhappy *harrumph*, then; 'I'll see what I can do about that.'

'How bad is it?' I said.

'You know that anything liquid can be sent offshore in the blink of an eye,' she said. 'I assume your husband is extremely sophisticated about financial transactions.'

I recounted the scene I had just witnessed in my kitchen, and that Gavril could probably provide a wealth of detail.

'Let's just hope the police don't find out about the heroin,' said Ms Conch.

'Really? Why?' My heart sank. I could already tell that whatever Jane Conch was about to say would be worse than anything I could imagine.

'You don't want this to deteriorate into a RICO seizure.'

'A RICO seizure?'

'That would be a nasty situation indeed.'

'Oh, God,' I said. 'It's the end of the world.'

'Julia, listen closely to me. It's *never* the end of the world.'

5

I was waiting for Jane Conch to figure out a legal manoeuvre to help me restore access to my bank accounts. I debated how to handle the museum next week: call in sick again? Go in to work?

Monday morning I finally returned to work at the museum. I felt good returning to this part of my old routine. I was grateful that my entire adult life had not been poisoned by David. Maybe my work is what had allowed me to survive for so long. I realised I enjoyed my work very much. I only wished that it paid enough so that I could live on my own.

I thought about enquiring at a gallery but, if I got found out, the museum would sack me for violating its conflict-of-interest policy. Zoë had called me to say I could make huge tips at the Where It All Happens Club on a good night. Lata, Zoë said, had told Vivienne what the club paid her to splash around in the fountain once per hour. Zoë asked Jack if it was true. Jack said he couldn't divulge confidential business information about a client, but went on to add that generally the tips were much bigger than the salary.

I felt ready to apply for work at the club, which had occupied my thoughts without a moment's rest since Vivienne and Zoë had taken me there. Jack got an appointment for me, and that evening, after working at the museum all day, I went over to the club to apply. They hired me.

* * *

It was 1 or 2 a.m. at the Where It All Happens Club, and I wasn't even halfway through my first shift as a cigarette girl. I'd seen a lot of things around the club that night: people snorting coke, drunks throwing up, a topless woman with her pierced nipples connected by a gold chain – the usual. But nothing as outrageous as Vivienne letting herself get fucked in full view of everyone up in the second-floor lounge. This was not, by any stretch of the imagination, a sex club or fetish club or leather bar or any such thing.

My uniform was mostly satin: a bright-red jacket, a short puffed satin skirt, red stockings held with satin garters, red patent high-heel shoes, pink blouse, a ridiculous tiny red satin pillbox hat strapped on to my head, and a tray of cigarettes and matches like something from the 1940s. I circulated, selling cigarettes with my demeaning tray sticking out from my belly supported with a red-satin strap that went around my neck. I saw a few women in see-through tops and sometimes, when a woman danced or sat down, I saw that she wore no panties, the same as any disco in New York. The place was just a club – nothing special, a pickup joint.

The decor was very East Village, which is to say an assault on the nervous system of anyone who believed that taste ought to be confined by boundaries. Besides the architectural-salvage fountain in the basement, there were sleek, wiry 50s-style stools, gold-leafed Louis XIV armchairs and modern Danish tables. The light fixtures ranged from converted autotransmissions to delicate Art Deco sconces. The rooms were rimmed in outrageous quantities of moulding. When the DJ wasn't spinning the turntables live, the piped music could be a man singing 'Volare' pentatonically in a thick Chinese accent or bootleg Grand Funk Railroad outtakes or anything else no one had ever heard before.

I went down to the basement and strolled the floor with my cigarette tray. There were a few businessmen, ludicrously still in their suits and ties, a few transvestites, who were more beautiful than actual women, and a few fuchsia-mohawk punks. At the fountain, a sight of stirring beauty parted the sea of dullness before my consciousness and I felt like a formless cloud of thoughts beholding a vision, devoid of geography and time.

In the corner of the pool of water surrounding the fountain, to the side of a waterfall and almost out of view, a man and woman, completely naked and lathered in soap, kissed and caressed each other, oblivious to all who could see. And the strangest thing, of the people who could see, nobody seemed to care. Hardly anyone seemed to notice that a couple was making love only a few paces away in the half-light. Revealing, though I'm not sure of what, was the way a woman noticed the couple: she waved me over to her for cigarettes, the scene of the lovers registered on her face, and then she bought cigarettes from me. She lost interest in me and the caressing couple and returned to her conversation with a group of young people dressed in extremely East Village haute, which is to say, a mixture of Comme des Garçons, Patrick Cox and the always underrated Tara Jarmon, Paris.

There were even other people in the pool, a few with bathing suits on, and some with the sort of lingerie that could pass for bathing suits, men in black bikini briefs and a woman in bright-red silk bra and panties with white polka dots. The red looked nearly black when it got wet, the dark silk clinging to her every curve as if it was painted on her. A blonde woman wearing just a plain white bra and white cotton panties stood smoking in the knee-deep water at the edge of the pool. She was wet from head to toe and looked like a Vargas pin-up in diaphanous lingerie. She spoke to the young man who had given her the cigarette, her nipples visible in her wet bra and her dark triangle of hair easily visible under the thin wet cloth of her panties. Though their corner was dimly lit and partially hidden, the love-making couple was still within the sight of a dozen people, and yet the couple might as well have been a thousand miles from human habitation, on an island in the Pacific under the moonlight.

I have no excuse for what I did next, except that the passion in my heart compelled me: I took up a position like I was selling cigarettes and watched them. They kissed and their arms were wrapped around each other, sliding across, back and forth, slippery, gliding over each other's skin. They were alive with the ardour of their passion, they kissed indulgently, their eyes closed, as if the world around them had fallen away, her arms slighter, thinner than his, femininely slight, sweeping over him, her hand clutching him on the waist or shoulder or wherever, guiding him in her passion as the need swept her. They were alone in themselves and I was mesmerised. His hand trailed downwards. She gently encouraged his fingers into her pussy. When he took hold, she kissed him harder, in appreciation. When they parted for a moment, I saw that his dick curled up in a big letter C-shape, touching its head against her belly, now standing free in the air, now enclosed from sight by their renewed embrace. I could not see their faces, they were so buried in the passion of their kiss and their long hair tumbling everywhere down below their shoulders. She was thin and dark. Then I saw her face. And though her eyes were shut in pleasure, I recognised her. She was the Don't-Touch Girl. Lata. Lata, creamy, golden, brown, dark. Delicious Lata, her pussy soaped up and a man's hand in it, working up and down gently.

The pleasure had engulfed her as she enjoyed every stroke and guided him for every new stroke. As she kissed him, the motion of her lips upon his guided him in her desire, as if her lips were a map of her whole body, to be read by his lips to find his way across the terrain of her desire, the rocking of her hips arranging her encounter with him. A momentary parting of their two bodies, a shaft of the half-light falling upon them, his dick rubbed against her belly with its C-shape, long, hard and curved. Through his soapy fingertips I saw that in her dark, succulent folds he was sliding a dildo in and out of her, a short one, of a translucent emerald-green material, that went all the way in, and all the while his dick slid up and down her belly. She reached down for his dick sometimes, her hand wandering through space and over his skin in search of it, finding it and stroking its shaft, and sometimes reaching to his hand as he dildoed her and encouraging him more. She stroked her clit and tucked her face into the space under his chin. She stroked at his cock negligently; she was too enraptured to remember him every moment. She fell away from him in passion, like a person about to faint, fading in and out of consciousness. He pulled the dildo out of her and, without even a word, as if they communicated solely in the silent language of touch, she dropped to her knees and took the full length of his cock in her mouth.

It was a glorious blow-job, as natural as ripples on a pond, as pure as the unconscious. The gliding in and out was a fading of one event seamlessly into another, as in a dream. The head of his cock prodded the inside of her cheek, making a bulb shape. I was envious; I wanted to cut in. I wanted to take that glorious C-shaped cock in my mouth – I wished I had a cock to slide into her dark-brown lips and brush up against the inside of her golden-brown cheeks. Her eyes opened and she looked at him. And he looked down into her eyes. I wanted to look into his eyes. I wanted her face to be directed at me with that expression of uncountable happinesses. Their moment was permanent and unsharable, the ritual of all time unfolding before me, helplessly beyond my reach, as it had unfolded an infinite number of times in the continuum of the human story prior to the sliver of time I called my life. She stood again; he placed his hand on her waist, like a dance partner guiding her to turn.

I felt so left out, so remiss in life. I had never really paired off, not the way these two had – in the midst of us, they had departed all the rest of the species. My husband was never really there with me, we were never absorbed into each other, not like this. Not for one minute had I ever been utterly carried away to somewhere outside the edges of the universe. Never had I taken a journey so deeply inside myself with my husband.

Placing her hand on his waist to balance herself, she stood on one leg and raised the other for him, as if about to step out of the pool. He eased himself carefully into that dark luscious entrance. A momentary expression of surprise shook her face, as if she knew how lucky she was, being filled with all the pleasure I envied her for being filled with, and she knew – oh, how fully she knew – what pleasure it was, and she deserved every pulse of joy sweeping through her.

I envied her pussy, that it was hers and not mine as it hung in the shadowy light, being entered. He held the small of her back with one arm to steady her. She placed her hands up on the grotto-like walls of the fountain to steady herself, the one leg up and open in the classic *Kama Sutra* position. Her free foot hung in the air, toes pointed downwards. I could see fully the man's shaft fucking contentedly in and out of her soft, aroused lips. He held her ankle, he held her ass, he held her, held her, held her. She guided him away and his huge C-shape tumbled out of her. She had not yet fulfilled her passionate need.

Lata got down on all fours in the shallow water. The world was invisible to her; I was invisible to her just twelve feet away. He inserted from behind. It was then that I noticed that, although it was cool and dank in this basement room, she was sweating. Drops of sweat poured off her brow and ran down her face as the man probed the lustrous black hairiness of her cunt. A burning red showed through her bronze skin, as if she had a rash or was blushing all over. She waggled her butt and swooped her shoulders and pounded the water with her fist; his face strained with indescribable pain. They came. He thrust at her in a burst of repeated, satiated jolts.

It was over. They held their position, hearts pounding, breathless; the chase was over, the prey was had. Time slowed. He slid out of her and his long, C-shaped dick, still hard, then less so, dipped its spent head into the water, a flagging wand of pleasure. He stayed on his knees, his hand on her waist. She did not move yet, still catching her breath. Her pussy just held its position, semi-open and still sensitive. So aroused was she that I could make out a strip of pink peeking from the folds of her dark slit. A thick glob of come dripped out of her and into the water.

Lata raised herself to her knees and turned to him. They smiled into each other's eyes and she said something to him that I could not hear from my distance. Just two or three words. There they were, knee to knee in the shallow water. She held his semi-erect penis and regarded it for a moment, as if she could not believe that this was the creature that had inspired such heights of passion only a few moments ago. He said something to her and she smiled; her eyes turned bright and laughing. They kissed, sending postcoital shudders through her. His cock slipped away from her fingers as she reached her arms around him.

Then they stood up. They were like friends. They could have been brother and sister standing up after lunch at a picnic. There was something irresistibly wholesome and platonic about them now. He held her hand to steady her, to protect her, as she stepped out of the fountain.

My attention was stolen from this affectionate post-lovemaking scene by a young man who wanted to buy cigarettes. Was this young man so insensitive to beauty that he had no inkling of what had just taken place? Was he completely insensate to the touching humanity of a man and woman holding hands after having just made love?

'Packet of Mild Sevens,' the young man said. I looked at him.

'What?' I said.

'Mild Sevens; you've got them there.' He was pointing at my damn tray.

'Oh, it's a cigarette.'

'Yeah, it's a cigarette. Keep the change.' The slime had given me a fifty-cent tip.

I noticed Lata sitting on a nineteenth-century park bench against a wall. She wore a short terry-cloth bathrobe and was wrapping her hair up in a towel. She pulled up her knees: I am quite sure she had no idea that doing this showed her pussy lips peeking out between her legs.

'Hey, Cigarette Girl! Got any Marlboros?' said Lata.

'Uh, it's $5 a pack, Lata.'

'I haven't got any money. Could I bum one off you?'

I looked around to make sure the manager wasn't watching. I opened a pack and slipped Lata a cigarette.

'I guess you don't have any matches either,' I said. I lit her up.

'Thanks.'

'I thought you were the Don't-Touch Girl,' I said.

'Today's my day off,' Lata said. 'Besides, you act like it's something strange. That happens to be my ex-boyfriend. I ran into him here by accident tonight. And, well, I guess I got lucky.'

'I didn't realise.'

'It's OK. It's your first day working here, right?'

'But isn't that, like, absurd?' I said. 'I mean, he's your *ex*-boyfriend and you're the Don't-Touch Girl.'

'Was it interesting?'

'Pretty busy learning the ropes ... This crazy uniform –'

'That's not what I mean. I saw you looking at us. You know, most people around here are discreet enough not to stare. Or at least not stare too much.'

'Sorry.'

'Why?'

'Why? I didn't mean to stare.'

'Lots of people look. That's perfectly natural.'

'How does it feel ... I mean, for something so private ...'

Lata took a long, luxuriant drag on her cigarette. 'It's a high like you can't imagine, the greatest high conceivable. Most people can only pretend to be blasé when they watch. A few actually are blasé. My favourites are the ones like you: at least you're honest enough to stare.'

'But why do you do it? How did you do it the first time?'

'You mean in front of everybody? You know what's strange about it, there's this heightened awareness. I don't care how loud the music is, I could hear a pin drop – and I know who's watching. And at the same time, I'm in another world. When I come it's like I wake up from a dream and I never knew where I was or how long I was there. You're a funny girl, asking all these questions.'

'Sorry. I'm just ... Wow, if the manager sees me, he might fire me for sitting around talking.'

'Look at your face. I wish I had a mirror. Just one look at you and I can tell you know exactly what I'm talking about.'

'You can read me like a book. I saw you – you were in such rapture.'

'It's so great when you've got men right where you want them.'

'I want to ... But look at all these people. I don't imagine how I could ever ...'

'You know something, I still feel high. I'm sittin' here feelin' cool and relaxed. And right now, there's a guy over there starin' at my slit – don't look. I can read that son of a bitch's mind. He knows I just fucked. He's thinking about what my cunt looks like five minutes after orgasm. He's imagining what it would've been like if it was him in the pool fucking me. Maybe I'll fuck him sometime. Maybe tonight, maybe next week. Probably never. But if he came over here right now, I'd tell him to go fuck off. I'd love to watch him slink away after I said that to him.'

I held my knees tight together and shuddered with pleasure. 'When you say that, I'm almost ready to come.'

'I want to open my legs right now,' Lata said. 'Really give him a hard-on. But I won't, I'd rather not think about him at all.'

'I want him,' I said. 'I want to get laid in the pool right now, with everybody watching.'

'No, don't!' Lata said; I was taken aback by her harsh tone, her deep look of concern.

'Why not?' I said.

'It's all wrong. You mustn't.'

'You just did it five minutes ago.'

'No. You're not ready. If you do it for the wrong reason, you'll be humiliated. Think how embarrassed you'll feel.'

'You've got ten men looking at your pussy right now,' I said.

'Are you saying you think my pussy is ugly?'

'No. It's the opposite! I'm just saying you're not embarrassed.'

'You just told me you want to walk across the room, get a guy and fuck him in the pool,' Lata said.

'That's what you did. I mean, I know he was your ex-boyfriend.'

'What an insulting thing to say! I can't believe you think that of me.'

'I saw with my own eyes –'

'You don't know who I am inside,' said Lata. She was almost in tears.

'I'm sorry I hurt you with what I said. I've blurted out terrible things just because of my own stupid curiosity,' I said.

'When I dress up to go out to the club, I'm not planning to get fucked with a bunch of slime-ball losers watching. How could I have any self-respect as a woman if that was my attitude? I wanna have a good time. I wanna have freedom of choice. This is the kinda club where people do a little fucking now and then. I'm glad – and if I'm in the mood, great. If it happens, great. If I don't feel like it, that's great too.'

'I want to do it.'

'Of course you want to do it. Every girl does. Look, if it happens, you'll know it's right. If you go over to the bar and get a guy and make it happen, then it's never going to feel right. If it doesn't feel right, you won't be able to lose yourself in ecstasy. You've got to be able to let yourself go fully or not do it at all – doing it halfway is the worst way to do it.'

Lata took another drag of her cigarette.

'Hey, Julia, what're you doing here anyway?'

'This is my part-time job.'

'I *know* that, but you don't belong here.'

'I need extra money because I'm separated from my husband.'

'I know how you can pick up some extra money. A friend of mine is a photographer. She's photographed me a million times; she's always looking for a new face. Interested? It's $1,500 if you're right. It's nudity, but no fucking if you don't want to.'

'I don't know . . .'

Lata stubbed out her cigarette definitively.

'Now I gotta find my purse and my clothes.' She stood up. 'I should get a good night's sleep. Tomorrow afternoon I've got an appointment with my trimmist. Then I've gotta take a disco nap and work here all night.' And with that, Lata disappeared into the crowd.

6

The next morning over coffee I told Zoë everything I had seen on my first night of work at the Where It All Happens Club.

Zoë wasn't particularly shocked, but did interpose a 'tut-tut' here and there. In fact, I was not shocked in the least, but still felt forced by social convention, even in an intimate conversation with my closest friend, to pretend that what I had seen was an affront to my sensibilities. I gradually lessened the intensity of my appearance of being affronted. I told my story in every detail and watched Zoë for her every reaction. Lata was wrong: I *did* belong there. The world I was describing – the one in which people such as Vivienne and Lata lived – was a world I wanted to be in. I was ever thankful to Zoë, although I could not tell her, that she had led me to this world, which I had never known existed, and out of the ho-hum, trapped desperation that had previously been my life.

'Do you think we missed the boat someplace?' said Zoë. 'It seems like everybody is living more interesting lives than us.'

'Nothing in my life had even prepared me to know that such a world existed,' I said. 'I had thought about such things from time to time. Not exactly like the Where It All Happens Club. I had vague thoughts: wouldn't it be great if there were an island somewhere devoted to the pleasure of women, where we could go every other year or so without our husbands?

'Zoë, do you know what I mean when I say I grew up in a cloud of ignorance? Was it just my family or is it every family in the world?'

'It's the lives of women. Men don't grow up in our sheltered, fake existence. It's all a foolish conspiracy to keep us from knowing the profound tidal currents that flow through a woman's heart.'

'This is a true story,' I told Zoë, apropos of nothing. As I told the following story I scanned her for her reactions: 'A woman once raised her son to the age of seven as a girl. When they asked her why she did this, she said she *hadn't known* he was a boy. So they said, "Didn't you, um, *check*? You know, just to find out one way or the other?" And the woman said, "One does not look at such things." Somehow I think we've grown up in a version of that world, a wilful blindness to simple truths.'

The doorbell rang.

'I wonder who that could be,' said Zoë.

When she opened the door, it was Vivienne. Her short leather skirt, a different one from the one she wore a few evenings before, was definitely a 2 a.m. outfit, not a 10 a.m. outfit, and it had a playful A-line flair to it that showed off her petite hourglass figure.

'Hi, Zoë. Can –'

'Come on in.'

'Hi.'

'Would you like some coffee? Tea?' said Zoë.

'Actually, I was wondering if I could borrow your stepladder,' said Vivienne.

'Yes. Hang on.' Zoë kept a stepladder in the back of the loft.

'It looks heavy; let me help,' I said. The three of us carried the ladder across the hall into Vivienne's loft, a north-facing mirror image of Zoë and Jack's.

'There's a hook up there and I'm trying to hang something on it.' Vivienne climbed up the ladder grasping a netlike thing that reminded me of macramé sculptures from the 1970s, except it wasn't jute, it was a collection of leather straps fastened together with studs and knots – a downtown Manhattan version of macramé.

'Is that a planter?' I said.

'It looks like a sculpture from Soho,' said Zoë.

'Haven't you ever seen one of these?' said Vivienne. She climbed off the ladder and into the various straps and loops, which formed a harness. 'Help me. There. It's just the right height too.'

Vivienne sat suspended in the air, her legs apart, and Zoë and I could see her white cotton panties. The obvious dawned on me: this leather contraption is a hanging sex chair.

'Is that comfortable?' said Zoë, who had obviously just had the same dawning as me.

'Sure it's comfortable. A lot better than our old one.'

There was a sound of footsteps; the door to Vivienne's loft pushed open. A man carried in a cardboard box full of small and medium-sized empty picture frames. They were dusty and old. Only one of them had glass. He set the box down on the floor and stood there looking rather like an Asian James Dean in a white T-shirt, jeans and work boots.

'Arthur, darling, Zoë's here. And this is her friend Julia. These are the girls I had my girls' night out with.'

'You got the chair up,' he said.

'Say hi to Zoë and Julia.'

'Hi, I'm Arthur, Vivienne's husband,' he said to me, shaking my hand in a very businesslike manner.

'Vivienne was just showing us this chair,' said Zoë.

'Really?' He approached Vivienne and kissed her.

They nuzzled and Vivienne's thighs wrapped around her husband. 'Doesn't she look delicious?' he said.

'Arthur!' said Vivienne, giggling and giving him an affectionate mock slap.

'Yes,' said Zoë.

'I think so,' I added lamely.

Arthur took the crotch of Vivienne's panties in his hand and tore them off her with a swift, strong pull. The panties' stitches tore apart instantaneously, seemingly without resistance. Vivienne's pussy lay open before us like the centre of a flower in the bloom of her open miniskirt. Though Vivienne was experienced – at least I thought she was – she was speechless with surprise, her eyes wide with genuine shock. Arthur kissed Vivienne's pussy and within moments, before Zoë and I could turn to go, he had managed to remove his hard cock from its home in his button-fly jeans and insert it in his wife. Her eyes closed, her breath quickened.

'Perhaps we ought to be going now,' said Zoë.

'Please stay. This is just a quickie,' said Vivienne, opening her eyes. She said it casually, with the tone she would have used if we had stopped by while she was preparing dinner and had said, 'Don't mind me, I'm just rinsing off the snow peas.'

'We don't want to invade your privacy,' said Zoë. 'You're married, and as the saying goes, two's company, four's a crowd, approximately.'

'Don't be ridiculous; we're newlyweds; we do this a lot; it'll just take a couple of minutes.' We stood watching while she left off speaking to groan in pleasure. 'Put on some tea, we'll just be a few minutes,' she said, finally. 'You know, we've only just had breakfast,' she added, giving me and Zoë a knowing look. I wasn't clear what Vivienne's knowing look expected me to know, except that maybe she assumed *everybody* had a quickie after breakfast.

But before we could even move towards the kettle sitting on the stove, Arthur and Vivienne came. Arthur withdrew; Vivienne sat there breathing hard, her eyes half open, her slit wide open to the world.

It was with some struggle, with the three of us helping, that we extricated her from the chair. 'Arthur, this won't be convenient when it's just the two of us,' said Vivienne, one naked leg swinging in the air like a pendulum, the other twisted in straps, and her quiescent cunt swimming openly through the air, perfectly cock-height.

'Oh, Viv, this is really quite undignified,' said Zoë.

'This was a lot easier to get into,' said Vivienne, one foot finally making it to the floor, her other still quite entangled. Arthur held her steady, while her other petite, perfect, golden leg pointed up in a suspended high kick until Zoë and I could slip the last leather loop off her ankle.

'I've got some more work I've got to get done,' said Arthur when we'd finally got Vivienne safely back on terra firma.

'Come on, Art,' said Vivienne. 'Have tea with us.'

'Maybe next time,' he said, an Asian James Dean pausing at the threshold to button up his jeans; and then he walked out of the flat.

Vivienne put the kettle on the stove. 'Men,' she pouted. 'They're all the same. As soon as they fuck they want to go to work or sleep.'

'Yeah,' said Zoë. 'Just fucking and working; they never want to stop and have some fun.'

My days now were a fractured existence. I kept my job at the museum, restoring art, a job that requires infinite patience, painstaking attention to detail and immense concentration. One of my great personal flaws, as I now saw it, had also evolved into my career: I had *too much* patience. This is what it takes to go over a $10 million old master a millimetre at a time. But this had also been the trait that led to my putting up with too much for too long with a husband who was too insensitive to know whether or not he benefited from patience and caresses. Soon after marrying, I had not needed to work. I worked because I did not consider what I did as work, in even the most nominal sense. David is wealthier than Zoë's husband, but the ladies-who-lunch existence Zoë had chosen for herself couldn't compare to my relationship with the art that Western culture has produced. Restoring a tiny fleck of paint to its proper home on the surface of a Manet might not seem like much, but this and a multitude of other techniques are what preserves Manet's intent for posterity. It takes far longer to restore a Manet than it ever took him to paint it in the first place. But Manet isn't humanly alive any more; his art is, at least so long as we have it to view. Their art is all we have of Manet, Corot, Courbet and all my other favourites. Their works are a part of who we are.

I had got my master's in art history because along the way I realised I would never be an old master or even much of a Sunday painter. Now I was making a better living than just about all of the studio art majors I had taken painting classes with. And, as irony would have it, I spent much of my day applying paint to canvas, although the nature of the work requires that it be removable. I was not so different from a snobby conceptual artist I had known in graduate school. He didn't do anything in his studio space at school. He did nothing and everything; whatever it was he did, he had nothing to show for it. And that's what I do now. Just as the art that is indelible in our collective cultural existence is really just temporary, my effort to keep it alive for another century and beyond is even more temporary: everything I do must be undoable. Everything I do must look as if nothing has been done at all.

I took naps in the evening after work at the museum and went to work at the club at eleven, where I only had to work a half shift till three or four o'clock. Then another nap before work at the museum, a pattern my body adapted to. I had gone from barely living one life to living two at the same time.

A lot of the museum staff came from old-money families and were highly educated people. Instead of becoming coke-snorting, fortune-draining scions, they did important work in cultural areas. I was not truly one of them. I had grown up in a modest middle-class suburb and had a good education. I had met David at Columbia. He was a casual, open-minded guy who could make me laugh. And I must say I missed him terribly during the nine months I worked in Italy in a restoration studio as an apprentice. The real apprenticeship was when one of the guys at the studio took me to visit an art forger in Yugoslavia. I learned more about the painting techniques of past centuries – and how to detect forgeries – than anyone ever taught me while getting my master's. My apprenticeship ended suddenly when my parents died in an auto accident. Two weeks later I married David in a civil ceremony at City Hall, which his parents refused to attend. David had just gotten a job at a brokerage house that his parents considered to be beneath him.

David specialised in high-tech IPOs at a time when they were very tough to sell. Investors shunned them. David was looked upon by other Wall Streeters as they might an aluminium-siding salesman, which is the way most people outside Wall Street look at all Wall Streeters.

Then David hit upon a string of successes with companies such as Digital Resources, DatBase, and Thinktronic, which went up hundreds of percent. David was suddenly Somebody. His annual bonuses quickly rose into the seven-figure area. David was not a forgery. If anything, he was too real and fell victim to the excess that surrounded him.

My work had always been too important to me to be what I considered work. I had never before been forced to consider that I dedicate the major portion of my waking day to a labour of love. Now I needed a salary to live. As I looked around the museum studio at my colleagues working as hard and as conscientiously as I did, I could not help thinking that there was a conceptual resemblance between what they were doing and a jobs program for getting people off welfare. Like welfare recipients, my old-money art museum colleagues could just as easily not work. Some of my colleagues came from families that were wealthy enough to buy the art their sons and daughters were restoring. Yet perhaps restoring art was just a thing to do to keep them out of trouble. Although they had every bit as much a sense of the critical importance of their work and its profound value to our culture as I did, I couldn't help thinking that without this day job most of them were just an employment application away from being like their drunk-driving, car-wrecking, civil-suit-fighting siblings who had not found something as worthwhile to occupy their idle hands.

I left work early on a Thursday and decided to do a little restoration on myself. I would meet Zoë at her trimmist.

Zoë had found her trimmist through Vivienne. Trim-mistry was still an underground fad at the time. I had heard it mentioned here and there but I was never clear what it was. I had tended to lump it in with other consuming fads of dubious relevance to intelligent life: aromatherapy, feng shui, channelling and other time-wasters.

'You go to your manicurist, right?' said Zoë. 'Or a seaweed massage?'

I told Zoë that I wasn't the seaweed massage type.

'Well then,' Zoë announced indignantly, 'you obvi-ously haven't had a seaweed massage performed on you by Noriko, over by Carnegie Hall. But that's another matter entirely.'

I stepped out of the Fifth Avenue entrance of the museum. It was a sunny, cool day in May, before spring had geared up to act like summer. The weather was backsliding, if anything, as if it had determined to retrogress to winter. The traffic was nowhere near its annual street-clogging peak, which would progress to its most serious proportions in the dog days of summer. But on this afternoon traffic was light and the cars were quiet and well behaved.

'Julia!' a man said to me, right on the steps of the museum.

'Oh, hi.' Something about his voice and face filled me with joy. I recognised him but at that instant couldn't recall his name. He felled me: I felt happiness light up my face, although I did not know why, and I found myself drawn towards him as if I'd finally found my long-lost lover. This was a feeling that made no sense to me: who was he? I stood helpless, feeling a gravita-tional tug towards this unnamed man who occupied my full consciousness. I felt like a survivor in a destroyed world. I studied his greying temples, his straight nose, his vexing green eyes. My heart fluttered like a schoolgirl's.

I snapped myself back to reality: be sensible! I commanded myself. I looked at him objectively. Of course I knew him, knew him for years, but I felt like Sleeping Beauty awakened by a kiss and looking up at a face I did not know and yet knew with the totality of my soul. There was something sad in his face, not his expression, something more like an aura. He was a handsome man. And like all handsome men, the understanding of how the world really worked darkened – saddened – his soul.

He wore an expensive Italian suit, black with white pinstripes, a blue-and-white-striped shirt with a sleek white collar and a matching tie and handkerchief of ludicrously bright red and yellow. Now I recalled his name: Carlton Westergaarde. This was a Dr Westergaarde his patients never saw, who probably thought of him as shapeless and scientific in his knee-length white lab coat and who only saw him when they felt ill or were about to undergo an unpleasant test. I tried to think of him this way, in a frumpy lab coat, in the hope of keeping my inexplicably roiling emotions under control.

'I see you survived the riot,' he said. 'In fact, Julia, you look radiant today.'

'I'm all out of breath, Carlton. Running down the steps.' I fanned my face with my hand. 'That's when we last met, isn't it, the day of the big riot?'

I had almost forgotten about the riot. It was something poor people in California had brought upon themselves for no particular reason, and so for me it was neither memorable nor significant. Offices throughout New York were closed early for fear that rioting would spread here. It didn't. I had run into Carlton on Fifth Avenue that day.

'I'm glad New Yorkers didn't bother having a riot. It's encouraging that people who can't organise themselves for their own benefit also can't organise their own destruction,' he said.

'Every cloud has a silver lining, I guess.' I looked around. 'This *is* a beautiful day.'

'Quite,' he said, looking around at the perfect sky and the trees around the museum dressed up in the new leaves they had sprung. This looking around was the first moment in our encounter that his attention had wavered from me.

I looked up Fifth Avenue. There was not one cab as far as the eye could see.

'It is very much so a beautiful day,' he said. 'Tomorrow is surgery day, so I'm just getting a breath of fresh air before I go over to the hospital.'

'Oh, I'm sorry. You're having surgery tomorrow? I hope it's nothing serious.'

'You misunderstand. Tomorrow I *perform* surgery.'

'I feel silly now. You're a doctor . . .'

'You shouldn't feel *silly*. Doctors can get operated on too, just not me tomorrow.' A breeze blew from the direction of Central Park, carrying with it the smell of cut grass. 'I met you quite a while ago, but I must confess I don't remember much of what you told me about yourself,' he said. That was true. I had traded cocktail-party chitchat with him a couple of times at the Groves' loft. I recalled distinctly that he had a wife. Dr Westergaarde no doubt saw me in my former role: the pretty, young wife of a young millionaire Wall Streeter, wholly unacquainted with the harsh realities of life.

'There's not much about me to tell really,' I said. 'I restore art. Right here, actually.'

'Right here? At the museum?'

'Right here.'

'Have I seen your work?'

'You have. And if I did it right, you weren't aware of my work. I'm a kind of surgeon too, a cosmetic surgeon.'

'That sounds fascinating. Would you care to tell me more about it over lunch sometime? My office is in this neighbourhood.'

'I think I would. But I've really got to run now. I've got an appointment with … I've got to have my hair done.'

'Your hair looks perfect.'

'Thank you. I really … I expect it'll be just a trim. A cab!'

I rushed away from Carlton and caught the taxi. As I waved goodbye from the back seat I noticed that the mysterious sadness that had clouded his face had intensified. I realised that Carlton might have thought I'd given him the brush-off and that the lunch was never to be. The cab crept mercilessly downtownwards and regret flooded my mood as I pondered how I had thoughtlessly inflicted damage. Here was a man harmlessly saying hello to me on a sunny day and I had brought a dark cloud into his life. Carlton was debonair, courtly; I wasn't sure how many years older than me he was. Having married young to a controlling and possessive husband, I had never had a chance to get to know any other type of man. The idea of lunch with Carlton strongly appealed to me and, in my unthinking rush to flag a cab on Fifth Avenue, I might have ruined that possibility for ever. Carlton must hate me. He probably saw me as flighty, young and rich, more concerned about a hair appointment than anything of importance, or anyone's feelings but my own. I had known too many women exactly like that.

I arrived at the address on West 4th Street where Zoë said she would meet me. It was a few minutes after two and Zoë was nowhere to be seen. I felt nervous since this was my first time and I did not have much idea of what to expect. Of course, nowadays trimmistry establishments have popped up on practically every block of any major city. But back before this trend seized the nation, trimmistry was just a little-known niche among the *haute couture* set. Zoë had warned me that the trimmist didn't have a name and didn't have a sign. In fact, the establishment didn't even have a number on the building to indicate the address – the place was just too chic for anything so gauche as to actually put up a sign. And what sort of sign would the owner put up? It would have to be a picture of some kind since the place didn't have a name.

In any event the place was easy enough to find: on three corners of the intersection were stately town-houses from the early to mid nineteenth century. On the fourth corner stood a neatly kept brick townhouse, probably built sometime in the 1840s, with several large windows facing the street. Clearly this was a shop of some sort, tellingly with no name on it. Nothing much of the shop could be seen from the outside due to the variety of palm trees inside that filled its windows. I peeked into a window: short and tall palm trees appeared to cram the interior of the shop from wall to wall. This must be the place. I opened the door.

I came face to face with what I took to be the previous appointment on her way out. I recognised her immediately. She was a model whom I'd seen in a million fashion magazines, but confronting that famous face came as a shock: I found myself struggling with the apparent impossibility of her face having three dimensions. Countless previous encounters with her had taught me to expect to see her face in the form of ink on glossy paper, the cover of *Vogue* usually. For the second time that day I found it difficult to recall a name on the tip of my tongue. Oh, you know the model. She's the one who is a kind of everywoman. She has a blank look in her wide-set eyes in almost every picture, cheekbones that earn her $10,000 a day for all those make-up ads, and she does all those lingerie and bathing-suit layouts. Oh, what's her name? Something French. Just the one name, not two. The thing is, I saw that she is better looking in person than in all those perfectly lit photographs. In fashion spreads you see one side of her mouth curl up like she's just about to make a nasty remark to the people at the photo shoot.

On this day she was radiant, her eyes – normally blank – sparkled with joy. As she stepped on to 4th Street, never a busy street, an available cab materialised at the wave of her hand. Perhaps every moment of *her* life was a matter of photogenic perfection. How often have I seen her on a tree-lined street, dressed *au courant*, her slightly open lips as if about to kiss, and that delicate, perfect, *casual* articulation of her wrist, her elbow, as she hailed a cab? And perhaps, as the cab pulled away, stirring up a knee-high cloud of dust in the gutter, she left our world for her proper place in a parallel, two-dimensional universe. Perhaps the cab driver looks for the beautiful woman in his rear-view mirror. She is gone, nothing left of her in our world but her face, on the cover of a magazine lying on the back seat of the cab, the cab driver forever after remembering his vanished passenger.

Inside the shop I took my chances and walked down a path that threaded its way through the palms, many of which were taller than me.

'Good afternoon,' said a pleasant-faced man when I had reached a clearing. It could have been a hundred miles into the rainforest rather than steps into the interior of a Greenwich Village townhouse.

'Good afternoon,' I said. 'Wasn't that . . . ?'

'What?'

'Your previous client. The famous model.'

'My dear, there's no such thing as a previous client.'

He was medium height and slender. And he had a *very* neatly trimmed beard and moustache, as one would tend to expect of a man in his line of work. He was very well dressed: his blue-and-white-striped shirt had been hand tailored, as were his black pants. He wore expensive shoes, the kind men bought at Brooks Brothers in the $750 to $950 range. I admit that I remained nervous about the whole idea, even after the reassuring sight of a supermodel emerging radiant from her appointment just moments before.

'I wasn't sure where your shop was, but I knew three of the corners couldn't be it. So, here I am at the fourth corner.'

'There are only three corners,' he said mysteriously. 'Please follow me.'

'I have an appointment,' I said.

'I know you do.'

'And my friend has an appointment too.'

'I'm afraid your friend had to cancel her appointment. She told me she tried to call you earlier but couldn't reach you.'

'You don't even know my name.'

'Are you Julia?'

'Yes.'

'Then I know your name. What did you have in mind for today?'

'You have a lot of palm trees,' I pointed out to him.

He looked around as if he had never noticed this before. 'I like to think so,' he said, a pleasantly meaningless answer to my nervous, stupid observation on the obvious.

'Let's see what we can work out for you today. Please follow me.'

The man, as nameless, I supposed, as his famous shop, led me through the wilderness of palm trees. Although I knew roughly what a trimmist did, what he would trim, I was not quite sure how he would go about it. Was there some discreet way? Or was there really only one way to go about it? My questions were soon answered.

Deeper into the shop, in a clearing of palms growing healthily under a bright, translucent white skylight, stood a very comfortable-looking leather-and-wood chair elevated on a wooden platform. The chair look terribly old, fifty or a hundred years. Because of its rare style I wondered at first whether it had been constructed out of antique furniture into its present configuration. But after closer inspection I concluded it was all of a piece. It was a very old, very comfortable chair. Although the leather had a warm, comfortably worn look and the wood had a weathered farm-furniture look that I found homey and appealing, the design of the antique chair had an anachronistic postmodern flavour, something along the lines of Bauhaus meets Shaker.

I stepped up on to the platform, which seemed to catch the man by surprise.

'Stand right there,' he said. 'Can you describe the look you intend to achieve?'

'I really don't know,' I said. 'This is my first time.'

'First time,' he noted in a way that gave no hint of whether he thought this was a good or bad thing. 'It's not often first-timers are referred to me. Let's have a look.'

He lifted my dress and looked at my panties.

'Do you usually wear panties?'

'Does it matter?'

'It can. Depending on your requirements, whether your hair gets pressed down or remains free has to be taken into consideration. Can I look?'

'Yes.'

I took my hem from his fingers and held it up. He eased down my panties to mid thigh and regarded my pussy thoughtfully.

'We can go a lot of directions here,' he said.

'I really haven't a clue.'

'Are you planning something simple such as a basic trim? Were you thinking along the lines of a G-string? We can do something along topiary lines, or perhaps a fade. And of course there's the whole range of accessories.'

'Accessories?'

'Essentially stringless G-strings, whether they're made out of feathers, rhinestones, leather, black lace – you name it.'

'Jewellery?'

'We can do clip-ons. I can refer you to someone for piercing, which I don't do. I know several jewellers who specialise in this area if you don't see anything on hand to your liking.'

'Wow, that's an overwhelming choice. Maybe I should think about it and come back. How many women ask you to shave off all their hair?'

'A few. I prefer not to. Hair is very enhancing for a

woman, and I see my role as enhancing her hair, not shaving it off. I'll do it, of course, I don't want a woman to try to do it at home and nick herself. But I feel better when it's being done for a reason; for example, if she's getting a tattoo or is going to use body paint. If you intend to apply something and need the surface area, I always suggest maintaining hair if you can.'

'Do you do waxing?'

'Yes.'

'I bet that hurts.'

'You won't feel a thing.'

'Do you think a wax would be better than a trim?'

'I know what you need.'

'Nothing exotic, I hope.'

'Yes, I agree. I suggest neatening your edges, a little neater than seems natural, but nothing that would seem unnaturally geometric.' He pulled my panties down to my ankles and I stepped out of the leg holes. I noticed the floor was spotless, not one hair anywhere to be seen. 'You've got some nicely dense hair in the middle,' he said, indicating the middle of my pussy. 'Rather than leave it in its natural state, I suggest some thinning so that your middle line is partly visible.'

'What about around my lips?' I said, as I felt more comfortable and warmed to the idea of seeing good results. He held a mirror to my pussy so I could see my lips.

'Here is your pussy in a natural, unaroused state almost immediately after taking off your panties. This is what your lover will see. Your lover might prefer you exactly like this.'

'I doubt that,' I interrupted.

'You see a lot of women shave off this hair. Please don't ask me to do that. I'd like to trim out your centre-lying hair and make your lips more visible. You're fortunate because your hair lies in what is called a natural tiger-stripe pattern. Except for a little trimming, I suggest you leave it intact. I'll wax the edges. Shall we get to work?'

'I just sit in this chair?'

'I'm afraid your dress will get creased. Let's hang it up.'

Off it came. It seemed awkward, and unnecessary in the utilitarian sense, to take off my shoes and socks; so, wearing absolutely nothing else I climbed up into the chair and settled in. I felt immensely comfortable leaning back and letting my legs fall open for him. Why couldn't gynaecologists use chairs such as this? I leaned my head back and felt as though I might fall asleep.

The man clipped mainly with a tiny pair of scissors, and I enjoyed his hands placed on me in a careful, professional manner. I suppose every woman enjoys a caring, knowledgeable pair of hands on her pussy now and then. He did some of the work with an electric razor, which initiated stirrings of arousal in me. I knew when he applied his wax, and it didn't hurt when he hove it off. I lost track of how many minutes passed, then he was done, and I found him brushing off my pussy with a big soft sable brush. He held up a mirror for me to see and I almost fell in love with myself while looking at the result.

'How do you do this work all day?' I said.

'It's the shoes,' he said. 'I'm on my feet all day. I long ago learned I had to buy the best shoes or I wouldn't make it.'

'I don't mean that,' I said. 'I mean all these women. Are you gay? How can you stand it? I'm aroused now. I bet a lot of women want you.' He lowered the mirror and my admirable, well-kempt pussy disappeared from my view.

'Occasionally a client wishes to see how the trim looks while it is in use.'

'In *use*? You mean you hold up the mirror so she can see while you . . .'

'We do what we can to service our customers,' he said.

I offered to pay him, but he said Zoë had already covered the bill. He wouldn't tell me what the trim had cost, because it had been a gift. I never found out his name.

7

Early on Saturday evening, I woke up and got ready for work at the club. I had put in a full shift there the night before, and the morning sky had already got light when I got back to Zoë and Jack's. The bathroom door was shut and I could hear Zoë or Jack or maybe the two of them taking a shower. I was wearing my short white nightie and I would take a shower as soon as they were done. I started laying out my cigarette-girl uniform on the big leather couch, but I couldn't find my little red pillbox hat. I ran out of patience. Where could that stupid hat have got to? I crawled along the floor looking under the edge of the couch. I got up and found Jack sitting on one of the big leather chairs looking at me. I hadn't known he was there. How long had he been watching me? I became very self-conscious about how short my nightie was. When I had looked under the couch, had I given Jack a view of my pussy?

'Oh, Jack, good morning,' I said.

'Good evening,' said Jack. He wore Zoë's bathrobe and was drying his hair. I realised it was not dawn outside but sunset.

'I didn't see you there.'

'Looking for something?' said Jack.

'Oh it's nothing really. I was just looking for the hat that goes with my uniform. It's a little red satin pillbox hat. It's about the size of a cupcake. Where's Zoë?'

'I'll help you look for it.'

'No. Don't waste your time,' I said.

'Can I get you some coffee at least?' said Jack.

'That would really hit the spot. Why are *you* sleeping in?'

'Sleeping in nothing. I just got back from squash,' he said.

As Jack spooned beans into a coffee grinder I went into the bathroom, showered and put on my uniform.

'Find that hat?' said Jack, offering me a cup of the freshly dripped coffee.

'No,' I said. 'Everything is depressing. I can't win.' I was dressed now. I tossed my flimsy nightie on to the back of a chair and put on a leather jacket with studs that Lata had lent me.

'It's just a hat,' Jack said.

'It's another loss,' I said.

'Oh,' he said.

I had made him depressed. I didn't really care.

'I'll be moving soon. I don't want to overstay my welcome,' I said.

'You're no trouble,' said Jack. 'Besides, losses reverse. Sometimes.'

Something about his face – it was *sooo* serious – made me laugh. That made him laugh.

'Why are you laughing?' I said.

'You made me laugh.'

'You saw my pussy, goddammit.'

'True.'

'This is a very short nightie.'

'No argument there.'

'I hadn't intended for you to see it.'

'I didn't assume you did.'

'It's embarrassing, you know.'

'It can happen to the best of us.'

'You are never going to see it again.'

'Yes, I'm sure of that.' And all the while we were sipping coffee and laughing.

'You goddam pussy-starer,' I said.

'Nolo contendere.'

I warmed my hands around the coffee cup. A good feeling had come over me for no reason at all. I don't know why, I just shut my eyes in pleasure. It was as if the world was starting to make sense. Somehow in this moment – almost the only quiet moment I could recall experiencing – in this calm moment, I felt I had control of my life and a measure of control over the affairs of the world. I was not a dandelion bobbing in the breeze waiting to get blown apart. I was strong. I was assured. I was sexy. I was me. I opened my eyes and looked at Jack. He had no idea what was drifting through my thoughts. I could not help but give him a conspiratorial smile. His eyes returned a co-conspirator's look. He didn't know what I thought, but he was with me all the way. We had a perfect, perfectly silent, understanding. I started to lift the hem of his bathrobe.

'What are you doing?' he said.

'I want to see,' I said.

'Why?'

'Well, you saw me. May I?' I said.

'If it's such a big deal for you, go ahead.'

'You mean just like that?'

'Don't act so scandalised.'

'This appears to be your –' I was taken in by its slumbering, now waking beauty. 'Your Little Jack,' I finally said.

'That's what it appears to be,' he said.

Zoë would kill me if she knew what I was thinking and for what I knew I was about to do to her husband.

'Can I fuck you?' I said.

'Well . . .' he said. 'I hadn't thought about it, actually. You know I'm married.' I felt my feminine power rip through me; this man, whom I desired, was completely in my control.

I stood very close to him. Was it my imagination, the feel of the heat of his desire warming me like the spring sun warming the earth after winter?

For some reason, in this intensely human moment, as I was about to delve into this man's soul and allow him to delve into me, I became exceedingly aware of the room we were in, the myriad details of this couple's life. I was about to come between them, about to destroy my best friend, and for no reason at all except that I was in a state of deep sadness and hoped that intense pleasure would rescue me. Is that so terrible? Is that such an unforgivable betrayal of my closest friend? Wouldn't I do the same for her?

I cared for this man, this Jack, and yet I cared nothing for him. He was a lovely man, and he was my sex object that I intended to command. He would pleasure me any way I chose, from one side of his damn expensive loft to the other. There were no curtains on the windows and for all I knew the door was unlocked and his wife could walk in on us at any moment. I wished she'd walk in now, right in this enchanted moment of locked gazes, right at this moment when wild horses couldn't tear us apart. Let's see Zoë try to stop us. I'd like to make her watch me riding her man.

He did not take off his bathrobe. In the perfect silence of the room we slowly circled each other towards the bed in a painfully slow mating dance, wanting to prolong each moment of anticipation in the extreme, toying with the very limits of that deep human gorge of a pure hostile urge to fuck for yourself and no one else, the ultimate human bond: sex in its purest form, where body and soul are finally tied together, inextricably.

I could smell his cologne, an old one that wasn't fashionable any more – something like Devon.

My lips felt hungry for him and soft to take him in, anticipating. I longed for his hand to make that journey that not enough men's hands – not enough men's tongues – had made, to get to my hairy patch and discover the wetness awaiting him.

In the distance, on a high ledge, I heard a dove coo.

I liked the feel of Jack's body, the masculine muscle groups, whose design and delineation were so well defined that I could trace their shapes through his wife's terry-cloth robe; I decide what he does and when.

I must have felt a mixture of toughness and softness to his hands, because I wore my leather jacket with studs, my satin uniform, my red high-heel shoes. His hands glided on my red stockings, lingering where the garter strap attaches. My leather jacket then came off.

He unbuttoned my satin blouse and played lightly with my hair, which trickled down my neck and touched the tops of my bare breasts. He had not yet pulled open the sides of my blouse; he had not so much as touched my breasts. Waves of lust roiled in me. I wanted to grab him by the hair and yell in his ear, 'You fucking shit! Stop this! Stop this fucking game and plough me till I scream!' I wanted to grab him in my legs and rip my skirt right over my head, to get his gorgeous cock slamming into my cunt, and now. But the teasing went on. We still had not so much as kissed. I peeled up my skirt and showed him plainly my red satin-and-lace panties. He knew full well that he could slip them off me now or slip them off me later. I wondered what would finally happen when he had to deal with my split peach gaping at him with desire. That's something a woman has to offer a man, a kind of throwing down of the gauntlet: here is a desirous cunt, do your damnedest to please it or you'll never see it again.

Pleasure rolled through my system with every beat of my heart, each pulsing wave of blood touched the inside of my skin in anticipation of his kiss touching me outside. Now I was a wreck. Now it all came together. Now I was whole. Now my losses reversed. I was in a waking dream of a man's hand scooping scandalous pleasure from the slightest touch of my skin, and all the life-destroyers who would call this sinful fell aside, as transient and as insubstantial as cobwebs in an abandoned church. My panties gripped so lightly around my pussy that I could almost brush them off, not even with my hand but with mere wishing; they lay in place daintily and tenuously and perfectly formed so as to cover my well-trimmed triangle. Still Jack teased. I opened my legs, for even an accidental brush of his hand would leave the dainty lace ribbon of a crotch far askew and worthless in its task of hiding the simple gift I so heatedly desired to offer. His face drew closer and closer to mine in a painfully drawn-out ordeal of arising to a kiss.

At last his hands were on my hips – our faces closer, closer still – and his fingers on the waistband of my flimsy panties. We already knew we were going to fuck and yet we had not even ever kissed each other, this husband of my friend and enjoyer of me to be. At last – finally – contact: the kiss was tentative at first, long and delicate, the way a first kiss should be. I was surprised at how innocent it all was. His fingers did not slip the panties off me; they so easily could have. We looked at each other. His eyes sparked with delight; he made me giggle with embarrassment.

'Hey there,' he said, a laugh bubbling through his words.

The next kiss was more important. He held me in his arms and squeezed me tight. I knew I was wrong: we were not about to fuck, we were about to make love.

'How can you do this?' I said. 'You don't even know me.'

'I don't think I can ever really know you,' he said, wrapping his arm around my waist protectively. 'Not the private self who is deep inside you. But I know I want to make love with you.' We kissed again and he held me and rocked me in his strong arms, ever so gently, like we were a couple that had slipped away from a formal party at a large estate and in the darkness of the garden, with the music coming from the house way in the distance, we did our own swaying dance alone.

'Who are you really?' he said. 'What sort of woman will I find when you allow me into your most intimate place, when you make me feel safe, like a ship in a harbour? There is a part of yourself that only a man can know – I'm not sure you can even see it in yourself. You are letting me make love to you. You say I don't know you, and yet you are about to let me give you pleasure at the core of your womanhood, a pleasure that only a woman can feel, and that only you feel in your own way.'

In our kiss we were as one breathing being, his arms wrapping me assuringly, my hands searching over the powerful muscles of his shoulders and back and stealing down to his round, firm buttocks. There was never a moment when he did not pull me to him, like the earth pulling the moon, and I was the moon tugging at his oceans in a whirling dance through space that was set in motion a million years before we were born and would whirl away forever through future generations unknown.

Jack was a man capable of great roughness if he wanted, I knew. Now I had him in a moment of quiescent sensitivity, like holding the reins of a tall horse with hundreds of pounds of rippling muscles that could explode with a strength far beyond mine if he wished. He did not wish; he was all mine.

Jack kissed my neck and shoulders and was laying a row of kissprints like train tracks downwards to my breasts, but he hardly got three quarters of the way to my nipples when he headed up again, up against my neck and to my earlobes and to my lips again. He could fuck me naked on the cobblestone street outside if he wanted; I was completely his. The objective world around me broke up, a shard of reality here, a shard of reality there, like pieces of a ceramic vase flying apart upon impact with the floor – our fusing consciousnesses were all that was left of the known universe, the shape formerly defined by the intact vase. If only he knew I was completely his, and that this gentle kissing man was completely mine.

My blouse, long since opened but not yet pulled off, now draped from view his hand, whose warm palm covered the surface of my breasts. My nipples had been erect since what seemed like hours ago, and it was these hard fixtures that his fingertips found. Now both hands, now his lips; oh how I needed to be pinched on my nipples, caught lightly in his teeth, caught unlightly in his teeth.

I pressed my hips into him. I wished dearly to fuck him.

My little skirt finally got unzipped and taken off me. So often I go without panties. Today, I regretted having put them on, which I had done just a few minutes ago, embarrassed and vexed. Oh how I wanted to feel his powerful hands pull the stupid charade of panties off me. His hands painted me all over my skin, appreciating, I could tell, my every feminine curve. His hand brushed down my belly and I felt sure it would plunge on a direct route downwards to the curved tuft of my triangle, where it belonged. It did not. As his loving fingers wandered closer to my place, I tingled ever more intensely, as if he had me in his thankful male grip already. But his hand took a side route, tumbling towards the top of one thigh and then swept in sideways, through a panty leg hole, coming to rest on my hill; his generous hand held the fullness of my sex. He shuddered and took in an urgent breath with the knowledge that his fingers were upon my clit. How much longer would it take him to get to my fuckhole? How much longer could I stand this torture of waiting? I went weak.

I looked down my front. The waistband of my panties was displaced by the welcome intruding arm. I could see my hair escaping from under his palm. He massaged his fingers downwards and, finding an oasis of wetness, glided his fingers forwards and backwards along my slit.

There is a special feeling you get when you pull open the bathrobe of your best friend's husband and find yourself presented with the forbidden gift of his erect cock.

'Your cock is so – I don't know . . . triumphant,' I said. 'Ahh, look at it there, standing to attention, waiting for a command.'

He said nothing. He kissed me. I traced the length of

his shaft with my fingertips and weighed his balls in the palm of my hand.

'There is a sparkling, beautiful first moment,' I said. I pushed him flat and shimmied down his body to see his cock up close, causing my pussy to slip away from his hand. 'I am mixed with emotions. First, your cock is beautiful to behold. It's stiff, and I like to feel its velvet touch.' I held it against my cheek; it was hot. I popped its head into my mouth like a big maraschino cherry. I wasn't going to blow-job him just yet; I just wanted to give him a big kiss on the end of his penis to show him how grateful I was that he was going to put it in me. I held it in my mouth till it felt like it glowed. I pulled it out and regarded it. 'It's a comical, ugly thing, isn't it? It's like a sad old bald man. And I am intimidated – what a scary thing, this cock; men are so complicated, so scary.'

'No . . .' whispered Jack. I looked up into his face, all the while holding the shaft in my hand. I felt that if I held on to it, it would give me good luck. Jack looked very sincere. 'Men are not complicated,' he went on. 'We only wish we were. You say you are intimidated and yet I feel completely vulnerable just now. Please be kind to dumb animals and men.'

'I intend to be very kind to you today,' I said. I stroked him.

'I need to please you,' he said, pulling me up to him and throwing his arms around me. 'Will you do that for me? Allow me to please you? I have a deep need to give you pleasure.'

'But why?' I said. 'Why should you have any need to give me pleasure?'

'Because we are each other's. At least now, for these few moments. How can I resist you?'

He eased me on to my back and slipped my panties

right off. 'I need you to show me what pleases you,' he said.

He placed his hand on my pussy. We kissed, quickly and lightly. I guided his hand where it lay, making sure he knew what pleased me. He wrapped me towards him with his other arm and kissed me.

'You make me feel safe,' I said.

'You make me feel safe too. I feel relaxed feeling the folds of your lips pressed into my fingers,' he said. 'I probably sound like a fool saying this, but it's really true: when I feel your pussy, you feel so female, so feminine to me. This makes me happy. For no reason at all that I can think of, you have decided to give me this happy feeling. When you let me hold your pussy it makes me feel like you care about me and that you trust me.'

'I do trust you; I do care about you; I feel happy because I know you want to hold me.'

'Guide my hand,' he said – I already was. 'Teach me what feels good to you. We have hardly even started. Please help me explore what you enjoy.' With only the lightest touch, his hand responded to my guidance, over and on and around and inside me.

I came with a shudder, my stomach shaking, my legs squeezing his hand as my body twisted in pleasure. I was so happy then. He turned me on my side and brought me close to him, his thigh nestled up between my thighs.

'Thank you,' I said. We held each other in silence. What a pleasant appetiser, I thought. How thoughtful of him to want to take me up the ladder of orgasms a step at a time.

After a while I stirred out of my deep contemplation. I reached down and held Jack's erect flesh. Jack was going to give me everything I wanted today. I tipped my forehead against his and looked down the chasm between our two interlocked bodies – his leg snuggled up against my pussy, my hand holding his warm shaft. I smiled to myself. He was so good. He deserved everything he could take from me today. I touched the tips of his nipples with my tongue; they instantly stood erect. I pressed my breasts against him.

'I think you're ready for me,' I said. He kissed me again and worked his way down to sucking and kissing my breasts. My pussy had become thoroughly hot and aroused anew. 'I hope you do something to me soon,' I said. He climbed down my body and explored the fixtures of my slit with the tip of his tongue. He placed my hands on his head.

'Make sure you get what you need,' he said. He reached up and held my breasts as he tongue-ploughed my groove. Again I found that with just the slightest shifts of pressure of my fingertips I could make Jack give me ripples of pleasure far out of proportion to what little effort I was making. Jack did things with his hands like caress my ankles and toes and the insides of my thighs and arms, sending tingling chilly waves of electricity through me, while the main work of pleasuring my furrow blissfully continued.

I guided his hand into me. His finger chased pleasure inside me like trying to pin a moving shadow against a wall. I had a wonderful come between his tongue and forefinger. He lay his head on my belly and I thought he fell asleep. I stared up at the white tin ceiling, at the plant and geometrical patterns and thought how nice it would be to just stay like this, with a grateful man peacefully at my belly. Jack would probably arouse me to orgasm all day if I asked him to. Then I thought about Zoë.

'What the hell are we doing?' I said. 'I'm making love

with my best friend's husband right in her bed. Something bad will happen.' But I did not speak these words with passion or fear. I spoke them soothingly, and Jack did not move.

I started to get up. Jack looked at me. He let me go.

'We've gone too far,' I said. 'This is insane. In another moment you'd be inside me like . . . like a man.'

I sat on the edge of the bed feeling shame and guilt and scanning the vast floor of the loft for my panties. I wanted them to be there; I wanted to leap up and put them on and end this horrible episode. I hoped I wouldn't see them. Jack wrapped his arms around my waist.

'Please wait,' he said. 'Don't go.'

'Jack –' The name stuck in me. 'I can't believe it's your name coming out of my mouth in this situation.' I twisted in his arms to look at him.

'Please.'

'I almost went over the edge just now,' I said. 'Don't make this difficult. If we go any further we can only regret this. I'm nervous just thinking about what we've done.'

He slid his hand down into my pussy, an effort I confess I allowed to happen without the least resistance. In spite of all my guilt, I had an overpowering sense of happiness because he wanted me. As if he read my mind, Jack said just then, 'I want you; even if you can't go through with the human bond we need, please stay here. Just stay a while longer, let me feel you near me. Please let me hold you a while longer.'

I leaned over and lifted one of my breasts into his mouth.

'What a strange man you are. You treat me this way and you treat your wife even better and yet you act like you're starved of love.'

'How do you know how I treat my wife?'

'Women know a lot of things.'

He looked into the distance like a clairvoyant staring into the past, present and future. His arm remained wrapped around me and his hand rested motionless in my lap, in my pussy, and I placed my hands on his to keep it there. He said, 'There are parts of the story of life that men have only watched from the sidelines for all of evolution. There are little events in our everyday lives that women recognise and that men can never see. There is an eternal feminine mystery to women. We men might look like we're starved of love. But even when we're loved, we feel empty because we know we can never have the answer to that eternal mystery.'

'I know that you love your wife. And yet, the way you hold your hands around me gives me such a good feeling. I want to be held by you. I need you to hold me. I feel guilty even though I know that I will never take you away from Zoë. I want you.'

I gave in to temptation. He seduced me.

Jack let his arms go and I stood up. For that instant he must have thought he'd lost me and resigned himself to the fact that he would never have me. I stood there before him, standing naked on that bare wooden floor and he looked up at me. I looked at him lying on the bed: he was both content at having pleased me and filled with sadness at the loss of me. I savoured for a delicious moment how cruel I would be to leave him now. But Jack was not the one I should have left. I had left my husband; I should have left David sooner. If my husband had been like Jack, I could not have left him. It was, now, I who felt filled with sadness at the years of my life I had lost, years that could have been like this, years that I could never reclaim.

I climbed back on to the bed and nudged Jack over on to his back.

I climbed astride him, poised to descend, feeling sweat trickling down the side of my face. I was fully aware of my pussy gaping open, wet and aroused, only inches from his gaze as he looked up at me.

'Are you the kind of man who likes to fuck a girl in different positions?' I said. I could feel him wanting me, I could feel his desire beat the air. I leaned over and kissed him; I felt my breasts sweep his chest as I did so. He put his strong arms around me and I felt again how smooth I must seem to him. The strength of his arms around me and the roughness of his shaved face and his response to my caress made me feel womanly. I felt sad at the power I held; the idea that this dew-dampened crevice he so obviously needed was something I could easily take away on the merest whim. But my emotion bound me to this man: if the truth be expressed, I couldn't open my legs wide enough; I wanted him so badly – would that I could wrap my legs around my head. I raised myself up on my knees and glided the head of his cock into me, lowering myself down, his shaft sinking into me. Oh, God! Such heavenly coupling. Your pussy, where your body and soul meet; fucking, where the bodies and souls of two people converge like beams of light on a single point.

Jack was the kind of guy who likes to fuck a girl in different positions. We tried many, on whatever furniture most suited us. He had me on my knees. He had me on my back. He took me frontways, he took me sideways. Finally he had me bend over the back of the couch so he could enter me from behind. Something came over him. I slapped the leather in ecstasy as he slid in and out of me at different rates. A magical, unmeasurable span of time. We came together. He stood me up and turned me around.

'Sorry,' he said. I stared into his beautiful, liquid-looking deep-brown eyes. 'I didn't want to come that time. You probably would've preferred missionary.'

'I came. It was nice,' I said. He was still hard. I don't know how to put this into words, but I will try: there is something nice about being a woman who has just come and looking into the eyes of the man. You feel like something more than a person; you feel like a woman. Jack slid his cock into me frontways and we held each other for a long time. Though he had just come, it was a while before he became soft. And we held each other in that embrace the whole while.

8

The dinner party at the Groves' loft was for the members of the limited partnership for the new Broadway play. The caterers, three young men, were setting up. Jack had done the accounting on structuring the original partnership when at the last second all the original partners withdrew. Jack liked the script and decided to form his own partnership, pulling in people he knew, like me and David. 'For the lack of a better term,' Jack had said, 'there's just something *groovy* about this play.' So, David invested – I didn't pay much attention.

Opening night was tonight. The play cost only $5 million to put up, cheap for Broadway, and it would open in New York first thing rather than go through tryouts elsewhere – a risk we had to take because we couldn't afford tryouts. I say 'we' even though my involvement is nothing more than my name on the partnership papers thanks to David's money. Financing a play is always a huge risk: like a runaway train, we had a destiny with a hairpin curve called opening night. We would have cocktails and a catered dinner at the loft and then go to the theatre to watch our investment go up in flames.

The young playwright, Albert Norton, had had mild success with something called *Turn Left at Poughkeepsie*. He had followed that with a disaster of a play in which every other word was a swear word. That one was so bad that after twenty minutes I started laughing non-stop, although it was a serious play and the woman behind me kept telling me to shush. David and I left after the first act of that one. Yes, there actually were fun moments in our marriage now and then. The new play, however, an erotic farce called *Oh! Calculus!* had a quirky appeal. David and I had invested what we considered a token amount: $1.25 million. Those were the days, when a million to invest was play money. Hah!

If I could sell off my share of the partnership and get it back, I would, but at this moment the partnership was, technically, worthless.

When Jack had called David's number at Bittleby & Cranly, David's secretary was evasive and brusque. So, Jack left a message inviting David to the pre-show dinner party. I couldn't face calling David. I watched as Jack called our home number and then hung up without saying anything.

'Somehow I doubt David got the message I left at his office,' Jack told me. He paused uncomfortably and then said my home phone had been disconnected. This heightened my fear that some sort of awful scene could develop with David if he showed up for the dinner party.

Jack handed me a gin and tonic.

I felt guilty, having made love to my best friend's husband on her bed the day before. In the twenty-four hours since, Jack had not let drop the least hint that anything had happened, which annoyed me terribly. Surely he should not be able to keep his cool after a lustful indulgence of such splendidness and gravity? What an insult that he managed to keep a straight face. What other lies was he so capable of coolly concealing?

I admit, however, that I maintained my composure equally well, although perhaps I felt relief from guilt because I knew Zoë always eventually knew everything.

My sense of personal hypocrisy was minimal, therefore, because I knew that all attempts to conceal the truth would ultimately prove to be fruitless. At some point, I was sure, there would be a conflagration of apocalyptic magnitude, consisting of accusations, recriminations, threats, tears and truth. The consequences would be faced.

Jack paced the loft in his tux. 'God, I can't wait till this is over. Win or lose, I just want it to end,' he said.

'Now, Jack,' said Zoë, 'I told you we should have gone to the previews.'

'Really,' Jack interrupted. 'This is worse than an IPO.'

'You can say that again. Everything they say about investing with your friends is true,' said Zoë. 'I know we all said we wouldn't hate each other if this play went down, but now I don't believe everyone was honest.'

'When did we all say we wouldn't hate each other?' said Jack.

'Well, we *implied* it,' said Zoë.

'Do you get the feeling Carlton Westergaarde invested more than he should?' said Jack.

'No!' said Zoë. 'Since, well, all that happened with his wife, this seems like the one thing that's cheered Carlton up. It's the Ketts I'm worried about.'

'The Ketts only put in $500,000.'

'But they expect to get ten times that amount back. Carlton Westergaarde is a pathological gentleman – no matter how much it hurts him to lose his $750,000 he'll never bat an eye. And he's been having fun.'

'I wish I could say I've been having fun.'

'Promise me you'll be a gentleman – Oh, Julia, what do you think of us, hearing us talk this way about people you hardly know?'

'I wouldn't say you're being *vicious* about your friends and investment partners.'

'Viciousness is relative,' said Zoë.

'Of course I'll be a gentleman. A chance to prove that I'm a gentleman and the opportunity to take capital losses for tax purposes are about all I can count on just now.' Jack put his arm around Zoë and smiled: 'Just you watch, Zoë. We might see $2.5 million of our money go up in smoke tonight and my lower lip won't even quiver.'

'You promise to maintain your comportment?'

'When have I ever not maintained my comportment?'

'Well, I can think of a certain time in a hot tub in a certain mansion in East Hampton –'

'Comportment only applies to situations in which one has clothes on. And I'm sure Julia is not interested in further details of what may or may not have happened between a certain couple in a hot tub in East Hampton.'

I thought of all the people in this city who were only a paycheque or two away from being broke. The rich, people like Zoë and Jack and me, were not so different. Even Jack, ever the cautious accountant, was capable of error in the heat of rash decision-making. The Groves had kicked in $2.5 million at a time when they were flush with mad money. Now, after an adverse market swing and a change in the business climate, Zoë couldn't afford a little $47,000 sculpture. They were not broke, of course, merely out of money, their net worth being tied up in illiquid investments prone to erratic price swings: property, art, thinly traded Pink Sheet stocks, and the dream of a Broadway play.

The three caterers were aflurry in the kitchen. Like

most caterers, they were struggling actors. I listened to their resonant voices and watched their fluid movements as they assembled trays of hors d'oeuvres. I couldn't help thinking that these young men, still trying to earn their Equity cards, were probably better than the cast that had been hired for the show we had invested in.

The building-entrance buzzer rang. Zoë pressed the button to let in whoever it was – the microphone downstairs was broken. Most of the crimes in the neighbourhood were committed by drug addicts, who were in too dire a need of a fix to actually ransack people's lofts. Burglars in this neighbourhood moved fast. They went for jewellery, cash and stereo components, although these were usually the least valuable things in lofts in this neighbourhood. As soon as they found something – usually the stereo – they carried it out and went looking for their next fix.

The door opened and, as expected, it was not housebreakers but party guests: Art and Jessica Kett. I had only met them once. Art was impeccably dressed – sort of. The suit he had on no longer fit him properly. It was a tailored suit, but he had put on a few pounds, just enough to ruin the line. And it was a winter suit! – a suave shade of charcoal, wool, with a white shirt that had navy pinstripes. Perfect for a cold, overcast day in December.

Jessica wore a sexy black Donna Karan skirt, tight-fitted, a little over her knee, and a pair of Manolo Blahnik black sling-back heels. On another woman of her age the skirt might be too young. But Jessica Kett was one of those petite women who have supernaturally good figures and extremely well-shaped legs, which showed off superbly as she settled into one end of the Groves' plush leather couch. And with those sling-back heels!

We only expected two more guests – three, counting David – since everyone else involved with the play was uptown, at the theatre.

One of the caterers made the rounds with a platter of hors d'oeuvres while another fretted in the kitchen; the third took over Jack and Zoë's antique Art Deco bar and fixed drinks. Jack requested a Ritz Fizz. And I was surprised to see the bartender, without hesitation, take out a chilled Marie-Antoinette glass and toss in a quarter ounce of blue Curaçao and a quarter ounce of Amaretto. Then he squeezed in the juice of a quarter lemon and topped up with champagne. He added an orange twist and handed over the drink. I had never even heard of a Ritz Fizz.

I sipped my gin and tonic. I had no interest in ever drinking anything else as long as I lived. All you have to do is find the one drink you like and stick with it, that was my philosophy.

The bartender turned towards Jessica to take her drink order, when her husband interrupted: 'I'll have a Loyal martini,' Art announced, standing in the middle of the group like Mark Antony about to deliver a speech. The bartender immediately reached for the vermouth. Art stopped him: 'Do you *know* what a Loyal martini is?'

The bartender was about to explain, when Art stopped him: 'First of all,' Art demanded, 'you need to shake a dash of vermouth over ice and strain. This coats the ice with the vermouth, a very important step. Then you must add the two and a half ounces of vodka. Have you got that?'

'Traditionally –'

'Shake the vodka over the ice. Not stirred! After you have strained *that* into a martini glass, then you get your opportunity to *stir* something: twenty drops of twenty-year-old balsamic *vinegar.* Gently! And the black olive must not be pitted. An *Italian* olive, not a Greek,' Art went on, sipping the martini in his hand. 'Do you think you can handle that?'

The bartender, in deference to his customer, had pretended that the recipe for a Loyal martini was new information and that he appreciated the valuable lesson being taught. In fact, Art was so busy expounding in a voice loud enough for an entire theatre to hear that he did not notice the bartender had completed the Loyal martini and set it in his hand. Indeed, by the time Art reached the end of what sounded like a rehearsed speech he was already sipping the very martini he prided himself on his unique ability to describe.

Art turned his attention to the group: 'I wish it was over,' he said, lowering himself into the Groves' huge plush leather couch. He sat at the end opposite his wife.

'What a coincidence,' said Zoë, finding a fresh gin and tonic fizzing in her hand in its own quiet way, rather like an explosive with a lit fuse. She sipped. 'I just wish . . . Well, I was about to say something absurd.'

'What?' said Art. 'I'd love to hear something absurd, Zoë.'

'I was about to say I wish it was a year later. But of course a year from now it will be a year later and we will have been through whatever will happen between now and then.'

'Right you are!' said Art.

'That doesn't strike me as wholly absurd,' said Jessica. She was a tight brunette, a real-estate broker. I had met her briefly at a staged reading and party a year and a half earlier when Jack and the playwright were courting investors. There was just something 'tight' about Jessica. She was short and had a nervous pent-up energy that made her appear at war within herself, a war that I would guess had raged within her for a very long time. She seemed about to seize the least snippet of conversation and use it as her cue to destroy the speaker with a terse, withering comment, and yet I had never heard her actually say anything terse or withering. She looked like she was about to pounce. A rage boiled under the skin of this woman, and I understood the type. Poor Art probably wouldn't be allowed to behave gentlemanly about losing a $500,000 investment in a Broadway play even if he knew what being a gentleman was, which he didn't. Jessica would sure as hell demand that he cry foul and threaten to sue for fraud and generally rant and rave like a son of a bitch, which, for Art, was truer to form than the equanimity that perilous investments such as Broadway plays require.

A silver tray arrived silently before Jessica, a lone Cosmopolitan standing in its centre, enticing. Jessica lifted the drink off the tray – her hands were petite and lacking in personality and jewellery – a flicker of delight flashed across her face and then, in the next flicker, her tense, internally conflicted demeanour re-established itself. Jessica had not told the busy bartender what she wanted. And I thought he had taken a terrible risk: people can be extremely critical of bartenders, downright rude, in fact, especially if the drinks are free, and I figured Jessica to be the type. However, the bartender had evidently read her mind. Although she had not made a request – or said so much as thank you to the bartender – Jessica Kett had ended up with the right drink and in her own unhappy way was enjoying it, which is to say she enjoyed it very much indeed.

'If we make money on this, we should count our blessings and quit while we are ahead,' said Art. 'I for one would prefer the less nerve-racking frenzy of the crude-oil-trading pit.'

Carlton Westergaarde and the playwright happened to arrive at the same moment. I had seen the playwright at the staged reading, but I hadn't realised then that this young man was cripplingly introverted, to the point of functioning more like a piece of furniture – a floor lamp, for example – than a person. His demeanour and almost complete lack of body language were wholly in contrast to the wicked farce that was about to open tonight – the witty lines, the histrionics, the doffing of clothes; what world went on inside this silent boy's head?

When I turned my attention back to Art, he was opining about woman – Art was one of those men who are chronic opiners.

'What women want,' Art was informing Jack in a voice loud enough to suspend all other conversation in the loft and draw all eyes to him, 'is to have the least amount of sex possible and get men to buy the greatest number of things for them.'

'Just things?' said Jack.

'The harder it is for a man to buy, the better. The thing a woman wants most of all is something slightly out of reach, so the man has to overextend himself to buy it.'

'Jessica, have you made Art buy anything just out of reach lately?' said Jack.

'I don't know.'

'It doesn't matter what the thing is – that's why diamond rings are so popular. All women would prefer an $800,000 diamond ring that will never go up in value – and can't be insured – to an $800,000 stock portfolio that could skyrocket in value.'

My eyes darted involuntarily to Jessica's hand: no diamond ring, no jewellery at all.

'Art, you're too severe,' said Carlton, settling into a chair with a Scotch and soda.

I looked around for the playwright. He had a glass of ginger ale, no ice, in his hand, and he hovered near the bar observing us without any expression on his face.

'Am I exaggerating more than slightly?' said Art. 'What sex do men have except what they buy? I don't mean just money. I could ask every man in this room, how often did you have to earn the sex you got compared to how often a woman bought you things and romanced you before you granted her permission to have her way with you?'

'I suppose there's an element of truth there –'

'Jack!' interrupted Zoë.

'But to illustrate how you're wrong, just the other morning –'

'Jack!'

'Well, Art,' said Jack. 'You're saying men turn sex into a commodity –'

'The other way around. Sex is far more valuable for men than it is for women, so women turn it into a commodity and trade it.'

'There's the male side of the transaction,' said Zoë. 'The logical extension of what you're saying is that you would prefer it if women were sluts.'

'I don't follow.'

'Supply and demand,' said Zoë. 'You're only complaining about what you see as the mercantile side of sex because you consider the price too high. If you had more supply, the price would drop.'

'Now you're trying to make a moral judgment,' said Art. 'I was merely stating an observation about women in our society.'

'You're the one making moral judgments,' said Jessica. 'You're the one who was all in a huff tonight about that lingerie place two blocks from here and how it shouldn't be allowed in a residential neighbourhood –'

'That's another matter entirely,' Art snapped. 'And I would hardly call a leather bra and a whip "lingerie".' He sipped his Loyal martini with self-important satisfaction. He was pleased with himself at getting everyone riled up and having made himself the centre of attention.

Getting snapped at by her husband caught Jessica by surprise and she looked hurt.

'You're making the moral judgment,' I said. 'You're saying that more sex is better than less sex.'

'I would think a moral judgment would go the other way,' said Art.

'In your scheme of things,' I went on, 'sex is bartered. When women get their demands met, they grant men what they want: sex. You blame women – whom you seem to see as some kind of sex cartel – for keeping sex too expensive. Even if you were right about women – as if such a group could possibly exist in the general terms you conceive it – it might also be true that sex *should* be expensive. Maybe it should be rationed and controlled.'

Art turned towards Jack, expecting to find an ally. 'Have you seen what's in the window at that store two blocks from here? Is that where strippers buy the things they strip off, or what? I mean, silk tassels for nipples right there in the window in a variety of styles and colours.'

'I'm sure many perfectly respectable women go to

that shop, or a thousand others like it in this city,' said Jessica, now quite bored with the whole conversation.

'Respectable women! Hah!' said Art, who punctuated the delivery of this opinion by downing the rest of his drink and eating the olive. He spat the pit into his martini glass and, without dividing his attention from the conversation, held out the glass at arm's length for the bartender to take, which the bartender did, putting in its place another Loyal martini, all with the swift, silent efficiency of a magician pulling a solid object out of a scarf.

'Art, why do you even care?' said Carlton.

I could not take my eyes off Jessica; she was a woman I didn't much like and yet, looking into her eyes, I felt sorry for her.

'I *don't* care!' insisted Art, sipping the new Loyal martini that had arrived into his hand as effortlessly and seemingly without origin as ideas arriving in his head. 'I think women should wear what they want – I'm all for Women's Lib – I just happen to think that the stuff in that store should not be on plain view to the public. It's wrong.'

'Art, you make it sound like if a woman wears a sexy garter belt it's immoral,' said Zoë.

'I'd never say *that's* immoral. Merely the display of it in the window. That's all. And as for the loose floozies who want to wear it, that's their business.'

'You make it sound like women who want to do a little something extra to be sexy are beneath contempt – at least beneath your contempt – and yet I'm sure any respectable woman who goes to a trimmist would wear such things. I should think that would make perfect sense to a sexist like you.'

'Zoë! Please!' said Jack. 'Our guests should feel welcome to express their opinions without being attacked.'

'Please, Jack, I'm enjoying this,' said Art. 'I don't need you to defend me.'

A change had come over Jessica. The poor woman had become meek, trying to shrink down and hide in the crack of the couch. No. She didn't want to shrink. She was boiling inside. That thing that always toiled and troubled beneath the surface was really roiling now.

'I feel your opinions are sexist,' said Jack. 'But I don't feel *I* have a right to call *you* a sexist.'

'You didn't. Your wife did. And I should think she should feel free to express her opinions in her own flat even if she is a reverse sexist.'

'I am *not* a reverse sexist –'

'No, you only support the whole Liberal feminist anti-man agenda, don't you?'

'Fuck it!' announced Jessica, who was now on her feet and shaking with rage. 'Fuck off, all of you!'

'Jessica –'

'Fuck off, Art!'

Not one of us dared breathe.

'If you must know,' Jessica began in a quiet, deep voice, a deepness that I had not imagined could have welled up from as petite a frame as hers, 'I have been seeing a trimmist. You obviously couldn't tell, Art. So on this big night I had a surprise for you later, maybe even in the limo on the way up to the theatre.'

'What the hell kind of –'

'Shut up,' Jessica continued, turning halfway towards her husband so that she still commanded the room. All was silent again. Jessica reached down for her hem and slowly raised it, very slowly. Before she got to the top of her thighs she revealed the tops of her stockings, held up by the trailing ribbons of a black garter belt. I wondered if she would expose herself; I wondered if she had no panties on at all and she was debating whether she was about to go too far. But a wonderful thing was about to be revealed. There she stood, her dress hiked well above her waist, exposing her belly button and her garter belt and the fact that nestled upon her pussy was a triangular-shaped concoction of the bright green and blue eyes of peacock feathers – a stringless G-string, the kind of thing strippers glued on, a deliciously organic blaze of opalescent green and blue.

'I wonder how she goes to the bathroom in that thing,' Zoë whispered to me.

'I want one,' I whispered back.

'I'm dying to know who her trimmist is,' said Zoë.

'I don't have to stand here and be humiliated like this,' Art said, leaping to his feet and throwing his drink crashing to the floor. He stormed out of the loft, not even bothering to shut the door after him.

We gaped stupidly at the open door and dirty hallway outside, the sullen fluorescent glow cast by the hall light fixtures reflecting off the peeling white paint and filling the empty door frame.

Jessica's voice broke the silence. 'I'm sorry for all the trouble I've caused tonight.'

I looked at her. Her dress was back in place and, except for her face looking unusually blank, she appeared as though nothing at all had just happened. Jessica comported herself well. She left the flat quickly, leaving the door open.

We stood looking at the empty doorframe with anticipation, as if its yawning openness could only mean that the ones who had left were somehow about to return.

They did not.

'Is it just me or is there a tension hanging in the air?' Zoë said at last. She got up and shut the door, not bothering to look in the hallway to see whether Jessica and her husband might be there. We felt safe now that the door was shut. The tension was gone; in fact, the event was just too silly to sustain tension a moment further.

'Who could believe such a thing?' said Carlton.

'You mean that somebody figured out how to make one of those things out of feathers?' said Jack.

'That too,' said Carlton. 'I was thinking who could imagine that polite chitchat could so quickly explode into something else altogether. I guess we'd better stick to talking about the weather.'

'Oh, why write?' the playwright muttered to himself. He turned his attention to the bar and poured himself more ginger ale.

'A little announcement,' Jack said, standing and tapping his glass for attention. 'If there is anyone else in this room who has an opinion about the coating of ice with vermouth, I'm afraid I must ask you to leave now. No? No one else? I must also at this time impose a rule: after this round, no more drinks requiring recipes are permitted. There has been entirely too much of that sort of thing here tonight, and I think we can all see where it leads.'

I turned to Zoë. 'You egged him on,' I whispered to her.

'I never *egg* anyone on,' she said with far too straight a face.

'Clearly you did. I thought Jack was going to clamp his hand right over your mouth.'

'So what if I egged on that silly old sexist hypocrite. Art knows he's helping finance a play with full-frontal nudity. In fact he's been conveniently stopping by the theatre for the nude scenes in the full-dress rehearsals.'

'But there's something fishy. You were egging him

on about something else entirely. It's as if you knew Jessica was going to stand up and show us all her pussy.'

'Oh, that. I knew something was up; earlier tonight I saw a feather flash.'

'A feather flash?'

'Then she defended our corner lingerie store ... I had seen a feather flash, you know? When she sat, I got a peek up her skirt. It was just too juicy to leave alone. Then Art chimes in with that knee-jerk anti-women stuff. I knew something was up; I smelled a conflict in the works.'

'What a devil of a bitch you are,' I said.

'I know,' Zoë said, smiling. She took a sip of her drink; I was glad she was my friend. I feared for my life.

The next day I had lunch with Carlton. He was, as always, thoughtful and observant but kept his emotions bottled up inside. I still felt wretched that he thought I'd given him the brush-off last week. I half wanted to lift my dress to show him that I really did have an appointment to get to that day and that, like Jessica Kett, I went to a trimmist. But that would be vulgar. I was of two minds. Part of me quite enjoyed seducing Jack, casting all morals and common sense aside in a lust-driven frenzy. Another part of me quite cared for Carlton – in an utterly different way – because he was bright and humorous and courtly in his manners and had a lot to offer the world and was haunted with an aura of loneliness and loss that brought out my every instinct to want to cure. I could not help seeing a part of myself in him. Why couldn't his wife see it? Why couldn't she cure him? Or was she rather like my David? What had Zoë meant last night when she said 'all that happened with his wife'?

Carlton stopped by the studio at the museum and I got permission from the director to show him around. When I led Carlton back to my work area I saw that someone had taken a phone message for me to call Jane Conch. I set it aside to call her later.

'I spent the morning reattaching a fleck of oil paint to a Manet,' I told Carlton. It was a minor nude study in oil. I proudly showed him my work.

'I can't see it,' he said.

'Then I must have put it back correctly. I told you I was a kind of cosmetic surgeon.'

We had lunch at a little place on Madison, not far from the museum, that served French and Italian. We sat at a quiet table in the back, all for the best, considering that we were both very married and we were taking a terrible risk of being seen.

The meal was nice, although overpriced. I told Carlton I couldn't drink wine because I was working. In deference to me he refused to drink wine too. Carlton had rabbit which, when it came, was visually extravagant, the way the chef had arranged the rabbit legs to point up, accompanied on the plate with a Parmesan custard topped with a truffle sauce. I didn't feel like being responsible for the death of any animal today, even a free-range rodent, so I had a simple gnocchi with wild mushrooms in a Gorgonzola sauce with a side of haricots verts. We chuckled over Jessica's dramatic performance of the night before.

'I thought the play was tremendously funny,' said Carlton. 'Just like a real comedy.'

'It *is* a real comedy,' I said.

'I know,' said Carlton. 'But it seems like something we put together in a garage.'

I'm sure Carlton felt relief, as I did, that the opening was well reviewed and that the play had a slight chance of breaking even. Advance ticket sales weakly trickled in.

I had never gotten to know Carlton well. He and his wife had always been at the periphery of any cocktail party I had attended, and so at the periphery of my attention at best. I had spoken with him and his wife Marion at Jack and Zoë's two or three years before. The name 'Marion' had resurfaced in my memory as clearly being her name, although now I could not be sure that I was correct. She hadn't been with him that last couple of times I'd seen Carlton at social events, and her absence last night clearly was significant. Zoë had mentioned Carlton's wife last night, and in all the hullabaloo of Jessica Kett exposing her peacock-feathered crotch to everybody – and everything that happened later – I had neglected to ask Zoë the most obvious question: where is Mrs Westergaarde?

When you don't know someone well, and when you haven't seen them for a while, you always think twice about mentioning their significant other until they raise the subject first. You never know if they've divorced, separated or whatever, and you don't want to raise an unwelcome topic. Carlton was extremely charming at lunch and, like my colleagues at the museum, was very cultured. He pronounced the words on the menu correctly. In fact, he seemed to know what they all meant. Although I know French, I was uncertain about what a few of the items on the menu were. It was the kind of menu that had black spiced roasted poussin with kokum jus, porgies wrapped in grape leaves, saffron risotto with pistachios, sweetbread ragout and the like.

There was something Carlton evoked in me, something I'd been thinking about since that confusing encounter with him on the museum steps: he made me young again. The marriage I'd been through made me feel old beyond my years, each day life passed with dreadful slowness; life was passing me by and it was as if each year took another decade's toll on me. Carlton took me back to the fork in the road I had stood at all those years ago: which way to go? The choice to go with David had seemed so natural and right that it hadn't seemed like a choice; there was no apparent alternative. With Carlton I felt there was a choice. I realised how much freedom I had had all those years ago and that at the time I didn't even know how free I was; and Carlton made me see that I still had choices. If I shut my eyes in Carlton's presence I could easily believe that I had just set foot on the Columbia campus my freshman year: no major declared, not one class taken yet, enough youth in myself to take for granted for years before I would ever realise how young I had been.

I debated whether I should mention his wife, ask about her. I was suspicious of Carlton. He had it all. Perhaps, I wondered, he had everything except a young mistress. I chastised myself for allowing this thought to cross my mind. I had brushed up against such situations with other men, in my work, at gallery openings – you name it, hungry men are everywhere. Are men naturally impatient? Are they simply unable to distinguish fantasy from reality? In every case, when a man is after only one thing, he takes that fatal misstep, always sooner rather than later, and reveals himself to be a lowlife, one-track-minded pig. It is flattering when a man drops subtle, ambiguous hints that he'd like to have an affair with you. The moment he strays from subtlety, it's over. The magic has passed. The playful give and take of flirting turns poisonous – the relationship is forever changed. For men, it is a business transaction. That's what it comes down to. I kept waiting for this lovely lunch to have its pretence of civility – our mutual interest in the finer things in life – ripped away. But it was not ripped away. As the pleasantries and Carlton's witty conversation continued I started to let down my guard. This could be the real thing. How could I be so cold as to think of testing him by asking about his wife to see whether he brushed her aside or spoke of her with loving admiration?

Our conversation paused and I turned my attention to the food on the plate for a few, just a few, moments. When I lookèd up Carlton had misting eyes, as if he was about to cry, and that pained look I'd seen before, on the steps of the museum on that beautiful day. It could have been my imagination, I thought, or maybe hay-fever season. When I looked up again he had hardly moved, except for a tear that was now trickling down his cheek, which he wiped away.

'Is something wrong?' I said.

'No. Nothing is wrong,' he said, with all the unde-served defeats in the world weighing on his shoulders. He was a crestfallen, sad man and I could not under-stand what I had said or done to cause this abrupt change in him. I could have slashed my wrists with my knife. What had I said!

'Something is wrong,' I said. 'What is it? Has some-thing happened? I said something: it wasn't intentional.'

'No. No,' he said, wiping away a multitude of tears from his eyes. 'It's not something you said.'

'I know it's something. Don't tell me it's nothing.'

'I'll stop. Sorry. It's just, once I start, it takes me a while to stop. I can't pretend it's nothing now, but I wish I could.'

'I feel horrible now, whatever it was.'

'It's not you,' he said. 'Please don't think you made me cry. The truth is you cheer me up.'

'You are in such pain. I can see it in your face.'

He dipped his handkerchief into his ice water and wiped his whole face as if he could wash away the thing that scarred his soul.

'I can never tell you what it is,' he said. 'I try so hard to keep it all inside so I'm the only one who knows. Sometimes I can't. Even I, who has played the cool doctor while my patients face terminal cancer, even I can't keep *everything* inside.' Carlton took a deep breath: 'Please never tell anyone this happened. You are the only other person who knows I have pain inside; please keep this secret.'

He got back to normal. He paid the bill and we left. He was completely normal as he walked me back to the museum. I was shaken. Thoughts tumbled through my mind: who had done evil to this man? What horrible fate befell him?

Words failed me as I looked into Carlton's eyes. I kissed him on the cheek and ran up the steps to the museum.

9

When we had got back from the party for the opening of the play Jack was a dear and helped Zoë and me off with our jackets; the weather was seasonably cool. The play started out funny in a routine way. Then there was a scene that was genuinely sidesplitting. And it just got funnier and funnier from there.

'It just might have legs,' I had overheard someone say in the lobby. The Ketts' two seats remained empty throughout, as did David's. Jack looked quite fine in his tux, not like a clothing-store mannequin or something: he looked like a man. Extremely so. We stood for a moment in the spacious loft and I'm sure Zoë and Jack felt as I did: what a pity this fine evening should end. All those costumes and the unreality of the play's multiple-doored set, all the opening-night playgoers dressed up in tuxes and celebrities in *haute couture* brought in by our press agent. It was due to us that there was any play at all, and yet even we must face the fact that every party must come to an end. If only all that elegance could extend into our own lives, and not just be confined to the show. In a way, the audience at the play performs too: they play the part of a well-dressed, elegant audience. But I have always felt like an actress when I'm in such an audience, maybe because I knew what a fraud of a life was waiting for me when I got home; that my husband's wealth bought us the façade we displayed to the world – at places like play openings, the opera, society benefits – and I knew the real life I led.

There the three of us stood, in the front space of the loft, three souls wanting to sustain the moment, like three stars spending eternity in a constellation. I felt for once that I wasn't a fraud, that somehow with Jack and Zoë I really was elegant.

'What say we have a little drink,' said Jack, moving towards the Art Deco burl-walnut bar.

The caterers had cleaned up and left hours ago. The kitchen was spotless. All a vivid memory now, its vividness fading.

'Gin and tonic,' said Zoë.

I asked for the same. Jack poured a Martell Extra for himself. We sat down in the living-room area. Jack put on an Aldo Ciccolini recording of Satie piano pieces and turned the volume down low.

Oddly, and it had not struck me as odd until after some minutes had passed, we were sitting in a triangle around the huge glass coffee table: Zoë was not snuggled up against her husband as I would have assumed. She sat in one of the plush leather armchairs that matched the oversized plush leather couch, and I sat a ways away in the other one. Jack sat in the middle of the couch looking very handsome, like an advertisement showing a fine man drinking fine brandy in style.

He had draped his jacket over the back of the couch and looked quite enticing in his suspenders and cummerbund.

And so the moment went on and I savoured it. We were not pretending; we were living. Zoë wore an incredibly sleek-looking black, long-sleeved Bruno Magli dress. I had on Zoë's platinum double-satin Ben de Lisi halter dress. I was remembering how I had made love to Jack and how seeing Zoë undressed stirred me. Zoë didn't know I had made love to her husband. At least I hoped he hadn't told her. I recalled watching the two of them making love on that otherworldly morning when they – or, rather, Jack – thought I was asleep. Zoë kicked off her heels and curled up her legs.

'It sure feels good to get those things off. Too high.' She massaged her feet.

'Come here. I'll do that for you,' said Jack. Zoë sat on the couch and placed her feet in her husband's lap. Jack worked his knuckles over the full soles of her feet.

'Ahhh, Jack, that's so good. How are your feet, Julia? Those heels were always real crushers on me.'

I took off my heels too.

'It was no cakewalk,' I said.

Jack pressed the soles and tops of Zoë's feet with his thumbs.

'Jack, do that to Julia. She needs it.'

I reclined on the other side of Jack. Leaving Zoë's feet in his lap, he took my feet into his hands and worked his magic. I thought my legs looked rather grand – even if I say so myself – coming out of my dress, bending at the knee and descending into Jack's powerful massaging hands. I laid back my head and shut my eyes, feeling the skilful forces of Jack's hands making the twenty-six bones and the spiderwebs of tendons and muscles of my feet feel recovered.

When Jack finished we all remained in relaxed silence; I'm sure Zoë felt as I did, basking in the relief of having had a transcendent massage after an evening of cruel shoes.

'Would it be strange?' Jack asked gently, out of the blue. It had been several minutes since anyone had spoken at all. I opened my eyes to look at Zoë. She was thinking. Jack made no motion; there was a pleased look on his face. I wondered if I had nodded off to sleep and merely imagined that he had spoken.

'No,' said Zoë at last. 'I think it would be rare. I think

it could be beautiful; and I think it would be unusual. But I do not think it would be strange.'

I lay there with my feet in her husband's lap and absorbed her words, which echoed around the room like the whispers of a wandering ghost.

Jack looked at me. He had too much class to betray his hope for which way I might answer.

'It would not be strange,' I said.

Jack took off his cufflinks.

It was strange as we climbed on to the king-size bed and Zoë and I undressed each other for Jack. Zoë's simple $800 dress was heartrendingly sexy as it billowed emptily to the floor and came to rest as flat as a shadow. When I pulled her black panties off her I was in for a shock. Her cunt was hardly the sweet, rosy-lipped little flower I had seen before. It was already mightily aroused; its hair mashed and wet; the lips lusting wetly for cock with an insistent force of will that commanded my profound respect. I wondered what my aroused pussy looked like. None of us spoke again the rest of the night. I wondered if Jack would know what to do with two women.

He knew.

After Zoë and I had stripped each other, we set upon Jack. His shaft was almost bursting through his tight black tuxedo trousers, waiting for us to finally bring it out into the open. What had seemed strange only moments before, when Zoë eased the straps over my shoulders and exposed my breasts, now seemed a natural matter of human cohesion. For who can deny that pleasure is the object, the duty and the goal of all rational creatures? And there are no more rational creatures on this earth than humankind.

Jack lay back on the bed and Zoë lifted his cock into

her mouth. Then she offered it to me; we shared it back and forth, first her mouth then mine, over and over, all in wordless pleasure – this would all have to be done as slowly as possible. At one point, when we both had our mouths pressed against the head of Jack's dick, I realised Zoë and I were kissing each other, with only the cock keeping our tongues from touching tips, woman-to-woman. Kissing another woman was not so frightening as I had once supposed. I found myself elevated to a whole new plane. All the fantasies of all those past years roiled within me. I understood the heart of my curiosity. As much as I had been attracted to women all this time, I was still never sure if it was real. As real as it had felt, I had always wondered if I would get to the point where I was about to actually kiss another woman and at that instant, at the moment of truth, I would be seized with disgust and run scream-ing out of the room. Apparently not. Zoë's lips and mine sealed together to form an envelope around Jack's cock-head, and this confluence of flesh, this envelope of life, was the transition between my heretofore purely het-erosexual existence and my first real taste of the other world, the world I had longed for since the origin of my own memory – the world of women.

I wondered if Zoë realised this at the exact moment I did. We forgot Jack for a moment and let his organ fall from our mouths. I looked into her eyes. I had never touched a woman before, not with this level of feeling, not lovingly, and the maelstrom of old curiosity and new-found truth scared me. When I reached towards her and touched her breasts, her nipples were erect. I wondered if I had done that. We hardly noticed Jack moving beneath us. We lay on our sides and explored each other. I felt my breasts against her breasts, my knees against her knees.

I brushed my fingers over Zoë's skin and felt her fingers brush over me. She excited me. I wondered if my touch excited her. I wondered if my touch excited her as much as a man's could, as much as Jack could.

Below us, Jack guided our knees open and licked our slits in turn. First my slit, then Zoë's, then mine. He enjoyed himself so much I momentarily wished I had two slits to offer him – though with Zoë and me having tacitly made an agreement to offer ourselves to him together, I was, with her help, indeed offering Jack two slits. As I looked down the canyon formed between Zoë's torso and mine, I saw that our pussies nearly touched. I saw Jack's mouth alighting like a butterfly alternating between two flowers.

I admired a man who would be so brave as to lick the brazen display of erotic arousal that glistened between Zoë's thighs. Then Jack settled his tongue into me and I rolled on to my back. I felt so happy looking down my belly and seeing his face up against my hair, licking away at my lips so lustily. It made feel so like a woman, so feminine, so powerful, to feel the desire he had for me, to close my thighs around his head and feel his finger inside me. Zoë, climbing above my head, bent over me and kissed my nipples and I reciprocated, kissing hers. I felt so proud to have Jack performing on me with such obvious irrepressible need. Zoë lay down beside me again and kissed me and massaged my breasts with her adoring hands. As I wandered lazily among the lust and passions swirling inside me, and hardly knowing whose hands and mouths were upon me, I knew now was my time. What was another woman like?

I gently reached my hand down along Zoë's writhing body and stroked her pussy. Jack's hand was there too; he had a finger in her cunt as well as in mine. Zoë placed her hand on mine and reassured me, pressing my hand into her pussy. You can never actually feel your own pussy, because your pussy feels your hand as much as your hand feels your pussy. But when you feel another woman's pussy, then you know what it is that a man feels, although he can never know what it is like to have a pussy being felt by his fingers. Zoë guided my fingers over her, flattening them into a broad zone of pressure. We were grateful for every timeless moment as it faded into the next timeless moment. I felt Jack pull his fingers out of me and Zoë simultaneously.

With the slightest nudge from Jack's hands I knew his intent, his barely perceptible nudge carried all the force of a drill sergeant's command. He had me turn on my side so that Zoë and I were like two spoons in a drawer, Zoë wrapping her arms around me from behind. Jack licked us again, consecutively, our slits now being conveniently lined up for this. Though I could not see, I could feel him enter Zoë; I heard her suck in a surprised, quick breath the moment her hungry cunt finally got filled up with her husband's cock. Then it was my turn. I can hardly describe what pleasure it was to be fucked by a man with his wife pressing herself to me and holding my breasts. Then her turn again, back and forth, from woman to woman, with passionate thrusts. Jack was in me. Then he withdrew. I missed him. I could feel him thrusting in his wife pressed up against me, and I imagined him inside me. Then he was in me again, like a long-lost lover returned, though it had been a mere minute since I had lost him. Then he was away again. I pleasured myself contemplating his absence. Then he returned.

Jack had Zoë get on her hands and knees. He entered her waiting lips. What glorious fucking it was to watch, to see that drippingly aroused pussy fucked with such a force of desire. Jack drew me near him, his arm wrapped around my waist. He kissed me. I could feel my pussy pressed against his thigh, my breasts set against his chest. Jack reached down and fingered me while he fucked his wife. I reached under her belly to find her pussy. Jack's other hand was already there and her hand was on his fingertips, guiding. I added my hand, making all three intent on benefiting Zoë.

Then it was time for a switch. Now I was on my hands and knees receiving the fucking of my life, with three hands on me. Zoë climbed under, raising her hand to give me the gentle – and at times the knowingly not gentle – caress that I realised only a woman could give. Jack held my breasts, pinching my nipples. I stared down into Zoë's pussy, finally lowering my face towards it, but I was too deliriously permeated with ecstasy to be of any use to her other than to nestle my cheek down there and feel her hairs against my skin.

Soon, too soon, I came. But Jack was far from finished. He could feel the walls of my quim shiver with contentment. I crawled up to the head of the bed and sat on a pillow, spent.

Zoë lay back in my open legs and Jack entered her, missionary style. I cupped her breasts and pinched her nipples till Jack brought her around to orgasm.

We were in luck. Jack hadn't come yet. He was saving himself. After a few minutes' pause I was ready to fuck again and Jack was still erect. Zoë and I took turns doing quick, straight-out fucking for the sake of coming. I had Jack do me missionary style for a while, then I got on top of Jack and fucked him quick from above, Zoë's hand finding its way down my front. Oh God, I wanted to fuck her. Still Jack held off coming. Jack set Zoë on the edge of the bed, her legs up in the air in a big V, and fucked her that way; I held her legs so she wouldn't fall. Her knees tucked more and more as she twisted and fucked till she was an egg shape, her cunt pointing up and making soft sucking sounds while she sighed and cooed to the thrusts of her man till she came. Then Jack did me in the missionary position again, and it was sheer heaven. For me it became a contest: could I get Jack to come in *me* instead of Zoë? I don't know if Zoë thought it was a contest, but she sure acted like it was.

Jack lay on his back and Zoë straddled him. I watched with growing envy as she positioned her cunt right over him and lowered herself till he was in her to the hilt. I could tell Jack enjoyed it; I wanted him to enjoy me. I bent over Zoë and tried to pull her off. She laughed and refused to budge. I tugged on her. She wrestled out of my grasp; she was slippery with sweat. Jack loved having Zoë twisting on his cock as two women struggled to have him. At last I dragged her off – I suppose she let me win – and lowered myself on to him. I bent over to see myself: there is nothing quite like seeing a cock disappear into you, to see your hairy lips swallow him whole, to take that shaft up inside you. I rocked my hips and leaned over to kiss him as I lowered and raised myself on his happy, happy cock.

Zoë pushed me off. We laughed; it was like two girls fighting over a toy. She slid herself back down over Jack and was determined to stay. I massaged her pussy because I wanted her to come too soon, but she enjoyed it too much. So, I propped Jack's head on a pillow and ran my slit up and down over his mouth. I imagined what it was like for him to feel my pubic hair scratching his lips and chin. Zoë came; Jack still held off having his glorious moment.

Zoë had to take a piss. Jack and I followed her into the bathroom to watch. We made her open up her legs so we could really see. It was the first time I'd ever seen a woman up close do it. Then they made me piss with my legs wide open. I mean, really, it was embarrassing. They held open my legs and parted my lips. Jack reached down and gently held ajar one side of my pussy, and Zoë held open the other. You could see everything. It was the first time I ever got a good look at myself pissing. Then Jack took a piss. I helped him; I held his cock and within a few seconds I was able to aim it correctly so I didn't make him hit the floor. I didn't even get a chance to wipe myself before Jack was already hard again and had me on my back on the bathroom carpet with my legs up over his shoulders. It was one of those inconvenient positions. Zoë had to insert his cock into me because he was balancing himself on top of me in a kind of press-up position. This position was a good one. As I came I realised Jack was coming too – something I considered a victory for me. I thought he was all done, but when he pulled out his cock there were a few more jolts of come ejaculating wildly out of him; a couple of spurts hit me right in the face.

I stood up. Jack's come rolled out of my cunt and dripped down the inside of my leg. He saw it and wiped it with his hand. He finger-painted my pussy with it, making my hair all matted and sticky; he smoothed my come-drenched pussy hair with a centre parting, as if he was using a hair gel, and it dried that way, leaving my lips plainly visible.

Jack had to rest fifteen minutes. Then he fucked Zoë on the bed. First some missionary, then the one-leg-up position or whatever it's called. Zoë lay back, limp like a rag doll, with her head turned to me and her eyes shut. Her face looked peaceful and full of pleasure. The thing about the one-leg-up position is it put Zoë's pussy in a kind of profile, so I could see Jack's cock delve down into her. She didn't look like a woman getting fucked. She didn't look like someone lying there choicelessly taking it. And as she flopped like a rag doll it was not as if she was a frail woman who hoped she might come. No. It was very different, as I could see clearly her open pussy voraciously gulping Jack's cock. Her gash was open and hungry and Jack worked furiously to feed her, while her peaceful face incongruously drifted off into another world. I always hate it when men say 'gash' about such a beautiful part of a woman's body. The word makes it sound like it's something wrong, a faulty construction, a wound, something not meant to be there. But here, now, Zoë's was not a neat, closed-up thing, something so petite as a 'slit' or a worshipped abstract 'pussy'; it was a ravenous sexual mouth in the heat of action – a gash.

I envied dear Zoë terribly. I too wanted to drift off with my eyes shut at one end and my gash being furiously sated at the other. As a wise man once wrote, 'Wherefore they are no more twain but one flesh, what therefore God hath joined together let not man put asunder.' I could not resist: I needed to be joined together with him like Zoë was. I pushed Zoë to dislodge her from the thrusting wellspring of pleasure between her legs. She pulled herself aside willingly, to my surprise. I took up her exact position, feeling the patch of warmth on the bed where she had just now lain fucking, my leg over Jack's shoulder where hers had just been. Now Jack was in my gash. I imagined myself to be Zoë and laid back my head dreamily. I looked up to admire what seemed to me to be my accomplishment, namely Jack pleasuring me in that place that I could not quite see. I envied Zoë all over again because she could watch my gash in side view get furiously fucked but I could never see myself in such a way. I wondered if Jack would come in me again even though by rights it was Zoë's turn. Jack's fucking of me proceeded apace and I wished I could watch him fuck Zoë again so I could see what his plunging into me must look like. Otherwise all I really knew was the mysterious rumble of joy hidden below me, as hidden from my view as seismic waves below the surface of the earth. How lucky men are that they can look down and see this – or choose not to – whereas for us there is only the feeling.

I was helpless: Zoë straddled me, which I hardly thought twice about until she placed her pussy upon my mouth. This was the first licking I had ever performed. I am not gay and, although I had long fantasised about exactly this, my last impulse before she pressed her pussy all over my lips was a rush of revulsion exploding through me. I was then seized by the sweet hunger for everything woman, a hunger I do not believe to this day I can ever fully satisfy. I owed this woman everything. I licked her pussy in gratitude. It tasted metallic and sweaty, but there was nothing about it that I could honestly say was revolting or even somehow inherently wrong in a moral sense.

I was quickly overcome with curiosity. Though I had touched myself – and had touched another woman for the first time tonight – clearly fingers are not the highly sensitive organs of touch that a tongue is. Now I freely explored the leafy shapes of Zoë's sex, tracing my tongue over the fullness and delicate softness of her pussy lips, tracing the outline of her clit hood.

Zoë and Jack got off me and they settled down into a screwed-down tight missionary position. I felt so happy for this couple. Too often in this world we are expected to share the joy of others and we do not. We say, when someone else gets promoted at their job or moves into a beautiful new house, 'I'm so happy for you.' But we do not feel real joy when we say it. The 'joy' we feel is hollow, too heavily overshadowed with our own sense of accumulating losses. Zoë kissed her husband madly and he kissed her. They were delirious with love and madly deep in sexual passion. Zoë's mouth slipped away from her husband's kiss and she turned her head to look at me, holding her husband even tighter. I looked into her face, spellbound as her piercing eyes drew me to her like two whirlpools, as they pleaded for compassion, as they told me I could never be in her soul with her ... those cheekbones of hers that I had always admired.

A change came over her expression, though she never took her eyes off me: Zoë was coming, and her husband was coming inside her. And in that look, which we held in our prolonged, locked gaze, she was sharing her coming with me, for which I will always be grateful. I regretted not sharing my version of that look with her when I had so greedily snatched an orgasm out of her husband only an hour earlier on her bathroom floor. She had taught me a lesson. What higher demonstration of friendship is there than to give what Zoë had just given me? A friend saving your life maybe, but who else on this planet did I know who would give and give as Zoë and Jack had given to me this night?

Jack and Zoë lay still. Occasionally Zoë's pelvis shuddered with post-orgasmic pleasure-twinges. Jack rolled off her towards me and lay breathing between the bodies of two naked women. I'm sure Jack and Zoë were as thoroughly spent as I was and felt as content as I did to just lie there naked, not thinking about much of anything in particular.

Jack got up and wandered away; Zoë lay on the bed

looking semiconscious, her grateful legs still open. Silently, I followed Jack into the kitchen area of the loft. He cut two limes in half and started squeezing them into three glasses. By the time we got the limes squeezed Zoë had joined us. She took a bottle of tonic water out of the fridge and started pouring it into the glasses, making a fizzy limeade that really hit the spot after such an unimaginable round of hard-pounding sex acts.

We reclined on the bed, spent, naked, thirsty. It had been a real love-and-do-what-you-will situation. There was a silent sense, at least within me, that for as long as no one spoke, Love was the international language, as if Zoë, Jack and I might not speak the same word-language at all. Love was not only the language of all countries and all peoples but the language of all people through all time. As long as none of us spoke, except in the language of Love, we were as permanent a feature of this Good Earth as the whole history of life that we reclined on the living precipice of.

We all slept together in that big old nineteenth-century bed, Jack in the middle.

In the morning we laughed about what we'd done and cuddled together. Jack took turns fucking us very tenderly and affectionately – not to come, really, but more as a way of saying 'good morning' – till we all three got so hungry we decided to stop fucking and have breakfast. It felt as intimate as if the three of us had coalesced into one being, one being who comprised three dualities and three personal identities.

10

I hate having a plan. But that's what I see women do at the club. It's disgusting. It's demeaning. It's the lowest level of operating, but I see it every night. You see these women calculating which man they are going to take home. It's a process of sizing up guys, which usually involves determining the least-ugly richest guy that you can sleep with that night. It's a certain kind of woman who does this. She is usually past thirty and starting to look it – this gives her an air of desperation. She'll wear a dress that's three to five years out of date and that makes her look dowdy. Or she'll try to be current and look like she's trying too hard to be current, trying too hard not to look like an alcoholic.

They've staked out the likely men by about 1 or 2 a.m. They keep tabs on them geographically and circulate from candidate to candidate, trying to get the optimum one and get the timing right – a man will not leave the club if he feels he still has a chance of sleeping with someone better. It's a kind of evening-long musical chairs, with 4 a.m. as the deadline – 'musical beds' might be the better term, or 'musical cocks'.

These are not sensitive women. They are schemers, and the men know it. They are not even subtle in their scheming, but the men play along with the game because they do want to fuck the women and they are attractive enough even at 35 or 40. By 4 a.m., when a man has known for hours that he had no hope of having the 22-year-old model wearing the mere film of an outfit and not a hint of a visible panty line – she left hours ago with a younger, prettier, richer man – he is ready for the leftovers, the twice-divorced, middle-aged, scheming women, who might now be too drunk to execute their own scheme properly.

I got so sick of watching this night after night that I finally asked one of these women, 'Have you got your plan in place?' She looked at me horrified, like I was crazy. She was about 15 pounds overweight, had had a boob job and wore a bright blue gauzy dress that was the wrong colour, and its waistline was too high for her body, making her look even thicker than she was. Feigning incomprehension, she rushed by me and across the thinning dance floor. A couple of her prospective men had slipped away, with other scheming women, and now she was down to two choices – she looked back and forth between the two with the mortified desperation of a woman who'd just had her purse snatched. She chose one of the guys and left with him.

As I said, I never plan. I went on a blow-job jag for a couple of weeks. I felt like I wanted to explore cocks and would give five or six blow-jobs a night in a dark corner downstairs in the Willard Room. I was exploring my unravelling naïveté, and I needed to go at my own rate. Eight blow-jobs a night was really my limit, and it pleased me to know that in a mere two weeks my mouth must have explored the contours of a hundred cocks. But one gets tired of that sort of thing. One wonders if it puts laugh lines prematurely around one's mouth.

Without any planning at all, not long after my first threesome with Jack and Zoë, I had sex with two men in one night, for me a first. I went into the bathroom around midnight. The women's line snaked out into the hallway. When this happens the bouncer who monitors the bathrooms, Gus, diverts women into the men's. He chaperones them in. The scene had always struck me as rather cute. The guys at the urinals certainly don't care – they're tipsy and they've got to go – and the women usually have this astonished look like they've finally been allowed into the secret men's club, an exclusive fraternity, with its secret handshake – so to speak – where men freely confide the truth, their gossip about women and sex, where corporate strategies are discussed, leads to important news stories are divulged and so on. In fact, none of this happens in the men's room – this sort of honest conversation only happens in the women's bathroom. Men pee in concentrated silence, avoid eye contact with each other and leave quickly.

So on this night Gus led me in with a couple of other girls. It was a mixed queue, with the girls having to wait for the stalls of course. When boys choose to behave chivalrously they let a girl go ahead of them if a stall opens up before a urinal. A young man at the head of the line did this to me, graciously waving his open hand towards a vacated stall.

'Can I come with you?' he said. 'I promise to behave myself.' He was an attractive enough guy.

'Yeah, come on,' I said.

I slipped down my panties and sat on the toilet. The guy leaned over me and kissed me, lacing his arms around my torso. He didn't try to grope for my pussy. We held one long kiss for the duration of my peeing. He asked me if he could wipe me. I said of course he could, and set my thighs ajar for him. He was polite about it, doing what he was supposed to – nothing more, nothing less.

'Are you going to watch me?' he asked when I stood and was adjusting my panties. He looked embarrassed.

'I'll look away if you need me to.'

'No. It's all right,' he said, unzipping. 'I kissed you. Are you going to kiss me?'

'I think we kissed each other,' I said. 'Let me hold you.' I pointed his penis towards the open toilet and kissed him to the sound of his falling stream.

I wiped the end of it with a square of toilet paper.

'That's not the usual way,' he said.

'I know. But it's so much neater than just shaking.'

'Want to come back to my place?' he said.

We stepped out of the hot, loud club and found ourselves in the velvet-roped boxing ring that protected the front door from the street. At this time of night, the doormen–bouncers actually work hard to maintain an even boy–girl ratio, although they will gladly let in gay men since that leaves the boy–girl ratio unaffected.

Outside the ropes, boys claimed they were on the guest list and whined and complained. It was unusual to see so many unclubby boys trying to get in at this late hour. The boys were too stupid to have noticed that an easy way for a boy to get into the club is to have two female dates with him. A guy claimed he had given up a weekend in the Hamptons and now very much resented being kept out of the club: 'Do you have any idea who I am? I could buy and sell you a hundred times over!'

'Well,' said the bouncer, clearly impressed, 'your net worth must be in the hundreds and hundreds of dollars.'

Boys who whine and complain and otherwise try to wheedle their way into a club are not permitted to enter. These are boys who invariably end up insulting someone in the club. They get punched. They sue the club. They never should have been there in the first place.

I realised, as the velvet rope was unhooked so me and my new man could be on our way, thus maintaining an even boy–girl ratio, that, besides keeping the number of lawsuits down, the bouncers, these large men in black pants and dark-blue shirts, and a hundred others like them standing within velvet ropes at clubs throughout the city, indirectly decide who sleeps with whom.

The night was pretty, the air warm, and the buildings of Manhattan stood somnolent and quiet, the Empire State Building in the distance bathed in floodlights, its illuminated peak hanging in the night as delicate as a paper lantern.

A cab took us to the Upper East Side. We got out in front of a townhouse.

Ted stuck his key in the front door and we went in.

'I'm not going to try to pretend to you I'm someone I'm not,' he said, punching in a number to deactivate the alarm. 'This is my parents' townhouse. They're in the south of France this time of year.'

We stood in a grand, high-ceilinged entrance hall at the foot of a marble staircase. The woodwork was the original, probably from the 1870s. A large Rothko hung in the hall.

Ted wanted us to sip champagne. We spent far too long looking for champagne glasses. We found highball glasses, old-fashioned glasses, sherry glasses, white wine glasses, red wine glasses and water goblets, but no champagne glasses. Ted became sad over this and announced that we could not drink champagne. He did not want to wake the servants. I followed him up the stairs.

I didn't ask Ted what his parents did or what he did. I realised he had not asked me my name and I had not told him. I realised that I may well have been richer than Ted's family, although David and I had been less ostentatious than this.

Ted opened a closet and took out a box containing a brand new Ritratti negligé.

'Do you want to take a bath or something and put this on?' he said noncommittally.

I took the lid off the box and unfurled the airy black wisp of fabric. The negligé was a delightful thing, with organdie stripes alternating with opaque silk panels. There was lace and long black ribbons.

'OK,' I said.

Ted led me to a walk-in closet that adjoined a palatial marble bathroom. The closet – a room really – had a vanity, a full-length mirror, a sofa and a multitude of doors, drawers and cabinets.

'Please make yourself at home,' Ted said, pulling out a chair for me. 'Feel free to take your time with your bath,' he said, closing the door behind him.

After my bath I put the negligé on. It was an over-the-head type rather than something that tied closed – the ribbons that streamed down the sides were for show; they didn't tie anything together. Two slits ran up the front to above my thighs. I loved this dear little thing – it was truly negligent. Walking down the hall, I noticed that my thighs peeked out through the slits and, even though the slits opened high, the cut of the cloth curtained my pussy from view, which was hidden beneath a ribbon of opaque black silk down my middle that was not much wider than a 1970s necktie. All in all, very clever and very sexy.

At the end of the hall a bedroom door stood half open and from it a soft golden light threw itself across the floor and halfway up the wood panelling of one wall.

I found Ted sitting at the head of a huge antique wooden canopied bed wearing a dark-red silk robe. He had taken a bath too, in another bathroom. His wet hair was neatly combed.

I crawled across the great expanse of the bed towards him.

'What kind of guy are you?'

'I am a poor, failed romantic.'

'I don't see any evidence of poverty –' His kiss sealed off my sentence before I could finish.

He poured me over on to my back and wove his arms around me. Instantly we were two long-separated lovers at last together again. Ted closed his eyes and kissed my neck, and kissed lower.

'I don't mean to be improper,' he said, kissing me, as a corner of my negligé fell away, as if caught in the *click* sound of his kiss. His eyes remained closed as he continued to interrupt what he was saying to plant yet another kiss. He did not know my breast had uncovered itself for him.

As I lay there I lifted my breast to his mouth, like I was feeding him, and one of my nipples became a part of his kissing. As my nipple grew hard inside his appreciative mouth I felt that he was feeding me.

'I suppose it's only human nature,' he said, brushing away the other side of my negligé and kissing my other breast. 'I don't mean to be vulgar or anything,' he said, looking up at me as if he was afraid I would slap him for misbehaving.

'Why would you call this vulgar?'

Firmly clutching one of my breasts, he kissed me on the lips again.

'You'll lift up your hem for me?'

'Hem? What hem? This negligé –' I looked down at the roils of thin black cloth that swirled over my legs, less substantial than a scarf yet firmly shielding my pussy from all the universe. And I looked at Ted with his neatly combed wet hair and his dark-red silk robe, a naked knee emerging from a fold and his calf looking lean and muscular.

'What if I don't lift my hem?' I said. 'Then you'll have to lift it yourself.'

He pulled aside a fold of my negligé but stopped before revealing what he so clearly wanted. His fingers shook nervously. I couldn't recall when I'd ever made a man visibly nervous.

'Just because –' he said.

'Yes . . .?'

'I don't want you to have the impression that I think you have an easy crevice just because . . .'

'Go on,' I said.

We spent silent moments looking down at the dilemma of my lap with the strip of black silk lying over it.

'Here, Ted. Kiss me.' I brought my lips close to his. He gave me a cute peck on the lips. 'Now look at me.' He looked into my eyes. 'Not into my eyes, Ted. Look at *me.*'

He looked back down my front to see that in the brief moment that he kissed me I had pulled aside the strip of black silk and revealed my pussy.

He looked at it in wide-eyed earnestness.

'You can touch it if you want,' I said. What a different moment this was than the one we had shared at the club.

Ted was respectful, admiring of the sight before him.

'I suppose that all in all it is a simple, natural thing,'

I said. I saw that it curved into a shadow between my thighs.

'Your pussy is a sweet beauty, it is exquisite, it is splendid, it arouses all my instincts, it is a mystery I have no power to resist.'

He placed his hand on it and gave me a tender caress. I felt the hairs crush under his gentle touch. I enjoyed being touched. And as I thought he was about to withdraw his hand I pressed it on me. I felt his touch cling to me. I enjoyed being appreciated on the surface; I looked forward to being appreciated inside. I suppose Ted believed my pussy was exquisite; how could I tell him that I found his touch exquisite? Soon we would settle that question.

'We're going to do pleasure,' he said. His face was inches above my pussy.

'I think we've already started.'

'Just because we're making out, it doesn't mean . . . You're not worried about whether I'm going to fuck you, are you?'

'I'm not worried about that, you failed romantic.'

'I didn't mean to imply that just because we've got this far that I would somehow *expect* . . .'

I drew up my knees and opened them. 'I appreciate your thoughtfulness,' I said, placing my hands on his cheeks and drawing his lips towards my open pussy.

He licked me enthusiastically and I exalted in the pleasure he caused. He reached up and held my breasts, and all the while I held his head in my hands, guiding him.

I tilted his face up.

'Don't you need more?' he said.

'You are very generous,' I said. Wordlessly I laid him down next to me and opened his robe. His cock was stiff. 'Why didn't you tell me you were ready?' I said. His cock was so beautiful I stuck it in my mouth, more to give it a deep long kiss than to give him head.

'I'm helpless under your spell,' he said.

I squatted over him, guiding his cock up into me. I ground my pussy against him for a dozen or more pleasureful strokes and leaned forwards to kiss him. He held me and kissed me and fucked me.

'I'm enjoying you immensely,' I said. I slipped my hips forwards, dropping his cock out of me. He looked sad. 'Cheer up. I just want you to fuck me from behind.'

He fucked me marvellously from behind, reaching around and holding my pussy.

'One more position,' I said, detaching myself from him with a forwards crawl on my hands and knees. I flopped on to my back and propped myself up on my elbows to look at him. He wanted me terribly. I opened up myself for him, and he joined me in embrace.

When he started to fumble down there I fitted him into me, and happily we kissed and missionaried. I wrapped my legs around him and thrust at him with my pussy.

I came.

He came too.

We lay together, wrapped up in each other.

'I feel like I'm so close to you,' he said.

'It's nice, isn't it?'

I enjoyed feeling him hold me close. I wanted to keep him. His soft cock tumbled out of me. Ted snuggled up next to me and held my pussy in his hand.

'I still feel close to you,' he said.

'It's still nice,' I said.

We drifted off to sleep like that, not even climbing under the covers.

When I awoke I was alone and naked on the huge

canopied bed. It must only have been an hour or two later.

Ted walked into the room, fully dressed in an Armani suit. I propped myself up and looked at him.

'You're awake,' he said.

'Are you going to work now?'

'Yes. But I want to stop by the temple and pray.'

I got up and parted the white organdie curtains to look out the window. It was pitch dark outside and the street was deserted.

'Were you just going to leave me here?'

Ted gave me a hug from behind as I looked out on the empty street. 'You looked so peaceful I didn't want to disturb you.' He held my breasts and kissed my ear.

'Aren't you afraid I'd steal something? You don't even know me.'

He held my pussy and kissed me on the cheek. 'But you're not a thief.'

'Yes. But you don't know that for sure. You don't even know my name.' I liked being in Ted's arms. I looked out the window – no taxis, no milkmen, no newspaper deliverers, no police, not even a siren in the distance – and I just felt the way Ted's arms wrapped around me, with one hand holding one of my breasts and his other arm wrapping downwards.

Ted kissed my cheek and rested his chin on my shoulder.

'I could be a thief,' I said.

'Of course you could. Of course.'

'Can I come down to the temple with you?'

'Of course you can. Put on your clothes and let's go.'

In the walk-in closet where I had undressed, my dress was gone. Instead, a brand new cream-coloured Romeo Gigli couture dress lay draped over a chair, exactly where I had laid my dress only a couple of hours earlier. I put it on and it fit me perfectly, as did the matching Gigli heels. I wondered if Ted had a thing for girls of my height and figure. I supposed he was a failed romantic after all, if he was a planner and I was mere quarry. It was a $10,000 dress and, since I wasn't sure where my clothes had got to, I had every right to keep it.

Opening the vanity drawer I found a range of make-up, new and unused. I put powder on my neck, put on light eye make-up, just a little mascara, and chose a lipstick.

I put on the heels and went downstairs to find Ted.

'Look at you!' he said. 'I'm so glad it fits.'

'What did you do with my dress?'

'Those simple, classic lines really complement your figure.'

'Where did you get this Gigli? How did you know it would fit me?'

'I've got a car waiting.'

The temple turned out to be a Buddhist temple at the bottom of Chinatown, not far from One Police Plaza, practically on the edge of the financial district.

We got there around quarter to five, as the sky hinted at the coming dawn. Some kind of vigil was taking place. We took off our shoes, placing them outside the doorway among the more than hundred pairs of the other worshippers.

The temple was crowded with worshippers sitting in meditation on the polished wooden floor, with only votive candles to light the scene.

At the head of the room, on a dais no higher than a cigar box, a monk sat, eyes closed in meditation – the main monk I supposed – while other monks, on either side, chanted. I had no idea what language the chant was in; it could have been Tibetan or Chinese or maybe even English. I sat down as gracefully as I could, arranging the folds of my dress. On so little sleep it was easy for me to feel transported as dreaming and waking blurred within me and without me. I stepped off the ledge of living consciousness and dipped my toe into the river flowing through the universe, on whose surface the world sat safe in a floating lotus blossom. I opened my eyes to find myself looking directly into the eyes of the main monk. Everyone else in the room sat still, eyes shut and deeply absorbed in their meditation. I gave the monk a smile and turned to crawl my way through the meditating crowd towards the door. Ted looked too eagerly consumed for me to bother him; I decided to slip away without disturbing his fervid search for inner peace.

The devotees were annoyed with me as I stepped silently among them towards the exit. A woman scowled at me. 'Sorry,' I whispered. *Shhh!* somebody hissed. I took one look back at the scene I had extricated myself from: it was as if I had never been there. All was well. The chanting burbled on like water in a brook, like ripples of gravity in the universe. Perhaps the monk and I had looked at each other; perhaps we had not. Perhaps we neither had nor had not. All was well. All was love.

In the vestibule there were twice as many shoes as just fifteen minutes before. A slender young man wearing a well-fitting suit, and whose face I couldn't see, kneeled in the vestibule, carefully examining shoes, turning them over, looking inside. In a moment I understood why: I could not find my shoes anywhere. He was obviously in the same predicament.

I just wanted to get back out into the air, to get outside, away from the waxy air inside the temple that was mortally thick with meditation and overearnestness.

The reason these people so desperately needed to meditate was that they tried too hard to do everything – they even tried too hard to meditate. I pawed through pair after pair of Prada, Gucci, Clergerie. I was not out of place in my Gigli couture dress.

'Oh, come on,' I finally said aloud. 'How many pairs of Gigli heels can there be here?'

'If you see any black-patent Paul Smiths, let me know.'

I held up a pair of Prada calf loafers.

'The hell with it,' he said, taking them from me. 'Let's just put on shoes that fit and get out of here.'

I thought it overly familiar of him to recruit me into his conspiracy. But he was right. I found a pair of Yoriko Powell summer sandals that complemented my dress and fit, and the two of us stepped out into the morning light. The Yoriko Powells were deliciously comfortable and strappily suave.

'How about some breakfast?' said the slender young man.

'I'm starving,' I said.

'Do you suppose the transmigration of our feet into different shoes at the temple is a metaphor for anything?' he asked. His question reassured me that he was a normal person, not some kind of shoe-fetish-pick-up-chicks-in-couture-dresses-at-the-Buddhist-temple-type weirdo.

'Sometimes losing your shoes is just losing your shoes,' I said.

'Hey, the International is about a block from here. They have a great breakfast.'

The waitress at the International took our order. She didn't use a pad. She poured us coffee and went.

'My name is Ken, by the way.'

'Julia.'

'Do you go to the temple often, Julia?'

'Why would I?'

'I know,' he sympathised. We sipped coffee.

'Oh, never mind,' I said.

'Sorry,' Ken said.

'I don't mean to seem cross.'

'Apart from how you got to the temple this morning, how did you decide to leave?'

'Ken, I don't mean to be aggressive, but how important is it that you be at work today?'

So, there I was in the back of the cab with Ken, who slid around the slippery back seat in his new Brooks Brothers suit as the driver sped up the East Side, weaving through morning traffic. We came to a stop before a drab 1960s apartment block on Third Avenue, one of the many featureless white-glazed brick cubes that flourished after the demise of the elevated railway. Ken took me up to his floor.

'I guess it's hard to know how to start when the girl has already surrendered,' I said, surveying Ken's modest living room. He had a buff-coloured carpet and his couch and chairs were upholstered in a cream-coloured material that looked like undyed cotton duck. He had a kitten, which rubbed against my leg.

'That's Jenny,' he said. 'Would you like a drink?' He stood at a bar built into the wall.

'If you have something ridiculous, like peppermint schnapps, that you could give me a shot of.'

'I regret to admit that I have an oversupply of such ridiculous drinks.'

'My God, you have Herbsaint.'

'You don't want it straight, do you?' he said, picking up the Herbsaint Liqueur d'Aris bottle.

'Oh, come on, it's 7 a.m.'

Ken measured sweet vermouth over crushed ice in a cocktail shaker, shook, and poured in Herbsaint and a couple of dashes of Peychaud's Aromatic Cocktail Bitters, shook again, and strained the mixture into two brandy snifters. We sat down on his couch, funky drinks in hand. From far below us came the sound of buses in rush hour as the traffic clogged up throughout the city like flowing rivulets of lava hardening to stone.

'Ken, do you suppose there is any other couple in this entire city doing anything remotely like this?'

'You mean skipping work to . . .' He played with my hair.

'I mean, look at us.'

'It's a big city.'

I turned to him. 'Ken, I don't want you to take advantage of me.'

He twirled strands of my hair around his fingers and kissed me high on my cheek. I held back my desire.

'Right now we belong together,' he said. 'That's why we found each other. I truly believe we will never understand each other. That doesn't mean we should never know each other. And it doesn't mean it's wrong for us to be together this morning. We don't have to know everything. Physicists don't know how matter works, but molecules exist and here we are. I want to be with you. I don't want to take advantage of you.'

'You know that whatever you want, I will give you.'

'Yes. I know that.'

'But doesn't that make me cheap? Why would you want to be with me?'

'Oh, Julia. I told you that you would never understand me . . . Think of all those people in the temple this morning. Why are they there? What do they think they will get?'

'You're right. They think they're going to *get* something.'

'Yes. They think they're going to get an inspiration, maybe enlightenment, maybe some other miraculous insight. Maybe they'll get it in an instant, maybe it will take a lifetime, maybe never. Why do they think this? Isn't life miraculous enough? Do they need some kind of magic trick because the mere fact of life itself isn't transcendentally amazing enough for them? Who cares what they think. I am very happy to be here with you, on this morning, Julia.'

'You know that this won't work.'

'If we got married and tried to invent a domestic life for us, it wouldn't work. But sitting on this couch and sipping Herbsaint with you works.'

'You won't –' Ken leaned close to me and kissed my neck. 'Very nice,' I said. He clasped my shoulders in his strong hands and drew me closer. We kissed each other a long and leisurely kiss. My heart galloped off with a racing beat, and his arms wrapped around me tighter. I was helpless in the fast embrace of this puzzling man: it was so right and so wrong at the same time.

'We're not going to have sex, are we?' I said. He examined me intently. I waited and waited, feeling my instincts take hold, thrumming inside me. Ken kissed me. Ken would find me, soon, I knew, quite moist.

'Julia, if all we were going to do was have sex . . .' He kissed me again, his hand sliding between my knees. My deepest passion flowered effulgently. I wanted Ken to possess the full structure of my physical being.

'Go on,' I said.

'What I meant to say was –'

'No. I mean, go on.' His hand ran higher between my thighs; our kisses continued; his fingers discovered I was pantyless and he massaged eagerly.

Suddenly, Ken stood and went over to his bar. The bottle of Herbsaint had been left open, its stopper resting next to it on the glossy black bar top.

'What if I don't feel like going on?' Ken said, pouring a straight shot of Herbsaint.

I liked this Ken. I was hot and wet and he knew it, and he knew the precise moment to step back, making me want him all the more. Two can play at that game.

'Hey,' I said, jumping up. 'How about a blow-job?'

'All right.'

I kneeled to undo his trousers. Surely no one else in the city was wearing couture at this hour of the morning, I thought, unless they were lying in the morgue as the result of an accident.

Clearly . . .

So I eased Ken's boxers over it.

'You liar,' I said. 'You're as stiff as a . . . stiff as a dead metaphor. You act all nonchalant, pouring yourself a drink, and really you're ready to explode for me.'

I put him in my mouth. His shaft was fully rigid – well, you know how you can feel the whole range of a cock's stiffness in your mouth. Ken was absolutely solid, which, as I had learned, meant it was good to massage its head with your lips and tongue. This was the time, I found, that guys like the rim of the helmet to part against your lips – and they always like the moment your lips sink *down* over them, and not so much when your lips run *up* the sides.

'Please fuck me swiftly,' I said, getting up rapidly off my knees – a bit too rapidly, because I felt momentarily faint.

Ken leaned me against his bar. Despite my insistent demand, his suddenness caught me off guard. I felt a shudder run through me as Ken planted my feet apart.

What force had I let loose? My asshole flexed involuntarily and felt hot and sweaty.

'I will be gentle,' he said, pushing my hem over my bare bottom.

'Swift and gentle –' I started to say. I was wet and ready for him, and he inserted himself immediately.

He took my breath away. I panted uncontrollably like we were in a footrace. Sometimes one likes it fast, sometimes slow, sometimes cycles of fast and slow. It is always best when a man is sensitive enough to feel what you need and service you thusly.

This was a time for rapidness. My butt slapped against his torso as he rocket-fucked me. Slap. Slap. *Slap*.

We came.

He stepped back, and I heard the suction sound as my quim reluctantly allowed him to go and his cock pulled free like a cork from a bottle.

I stood and smoothed down my Gigli dress – I'm sure that strands of my hair wisped here and there in the dishevelled way you see in a woman after she has fucked to coming and does not much care about her hairdo.

'Your cheeks look so rosy,' Ken said, and then he kissed me.

'Well . . .' I was still catching my breath.

'You look like you ran across Lincoln Center to get into the opera house before curtain.'

'Do you like this dress?'

I kissed him and held his cock, which was all slippery with come and quim juice.

He gave me a quick kiss on the temple. I rested my head on his shoulder. I was glad I'd had him.

'So this is your dick,' I said, stroking my fingers lightly up and down it and admiring its shape.

'Um-hmm,' he said, pulling me closer with his arm around my shoulder.

'I'm glad,' I said. 'He's quieter now...'

'He was bound to be.'

'The little guy looked angry there for a moment.'

'He's not angry now.'

'This silly instrument pleased me so much.'

We took a bath together, a good old-fashioned bubble bath, with deep hot water, the kind of relaxing bath that makes you forget time and all the frantic irrelevant urgency of the city beyond these walls, the kind of relaxing bath you always dream of sharing with an attractive young man with well-defined chest muscles who soaps up your breasts for you. Ken, I was sure, spent more time working out than he did meditating at the temple. I stood up so Ken could shampoo my pussy. He was attentive, making sure he washed the folds between my lips.

We soaked in the tub with our arms around each other, letting the time pass, and our thoughts drifted from the daft palette of sexual positions to the sublime unfathomable of what two people mean to each other's psychic interior. One of my hands rested comfortably on Ken's cock, my fingers forming a shield over his balls.

Ken grew stiff.

We got out of the tub and went naked to his bed to explore more of those daft sexual positions.

By lunchtime we were hungry enough to pause. We had shrimp toast, chicken almond ding and General Tso's chicken delivered. Ken put on a robe to pay the delivery boy.

I sat at the top of Ken's bed and ate straight out of

the cartons with chopsticks. Ken reclined, and used a plate.

'Do you often have Chinese food with a naked girl on your bed?' I asked Ken.

'Now, what could I *do* with a naked girl eating Chinese food on my bed?'

'You could always fuck her,' I said.

Ken kissed my knee and reached into my cove. I looked down between my thighs to watch his fingers caress me.

'Since when is it polite to tug at a girl's pussy lips when she's trying to eat her chicken almond ding?'

Ken's kitten started investigating the food. She was very curious about the General Tso's carton.

'No, Jenny! No!' Ken said.

Jenny gave him a frightened look and then hid her face under the takeout menu.

'If we have a quickie, we can get back to lunch before the food turns cold,' I said.

Ken bent his head into my lap and rode his tongue up my slit.

'Oh, Ken. If you keep doing that, I think I'm just going to come in about two minutes.'

It's hard for men to give good head because they just don't know what's going on down there. Ken was very good at delivering head: I kept him on me and would not let him up, rocking my hips to guide him towards my needs. Eventually I came twice, and then released him.

I had been missing this all these years.

He sat next to me at the top of the bed. I straddled his lap.

'Thank you, Ken.'

'Thank you,' he said.

'What are you thanking me for?'

'You let me give you head. Do you have any idea how that feels to a man? Think how I feel, knowing that you want me to kiss your pussy.'

I got up to take a piss.

'One moment,' Ken said, rolling over and catching me by the wrist as I stepped off the bed.

I turned and faced him.

'If only this day could stretch on and on,' he said, looking up at me from where he lay on the edge of his bed.

'It is sad, I suppose, the way we know it can only be this one day,' I said.

He reached out his hand and held my pussy simply and snugly. I widened my stance so he could hold all of it, and then closed my thighs upon his hand. I looked into his eyes; it felt nice to hold his hand snug.

'I bet a lot of girls have stood here like me, feeling you hold their pussy.'

'True,' he said.

I reached down and placed my hands around his, caressing his arm.

'I am sure you please every one of them as much as you pleased me. And I bet all of them have thought something like I'm thinking now.' I ruffled his hair. A girl likes to be liked, and I liked Ken holding on to me down there. 'We wonder, what do you see when you look at us?' I bent down to kiss him. 'You don't know what it feels like to be a girl in a moment like this, with a boy holding your pussy.' I kissed him again. 'It's so cute of you to want to hold me.' He *was* cute. I gave him a long passionate kiss. I looked into his eyes and gave him a smile. 'Now let me go take a pee and I'll be right back to be with you.' I stepped out of his reach, reclaiming my pussy for myself. 'Let me just use this for a minute and I'll bring it right back to you. Will you still be here? Good.' I patted him on the shoulder and went.

Ken and I lay next to each other, naked under the vast quilt that covered his bed. Ken's kitten walked over us.

'She weighs eight pounds,' said Ken. 'I wish I could tell her where to step, then she could give me a shiatsu massage.'

I felt the footsteps progress up my body. 'Why does your kitten walk over us like it's not our bodies but just a lumpy quilt?'

'Her brain is the size of a walnut,' said Ken. 'Remember when she hid her face under the takeout menu? She thought she was hiding from us.' The kitten paused at the top of my chest and looked into my eyes. She was kneading the quilt, first one paw and then the next, and purring. 'When she sees us like this, she thinks we're just heads, propped up on these pillows, spouting gibberish.'

'We are,' I said.

Ken said he really ought to go to work, and that I was welcome to stay in his place. I said no, I really should get home. But Ken made no move to go to work, and I did not go home. We spent the rest of the day sleeping naked in Ken's bed, folded up together. In the afternoon I awoke and found Ken semi-asleep with his erect cock poking against my belly. I thought this was a good time for a goodbye couple. Ken sat up on his knees and I lowered myself on to his lap, guiding him into me and having him suck my breasts. I lay back and gripped myself, dividing my fingers around Ken's shaft and slowing him down to a meditative coupling pace. Ken willingly offered himself into me, letting me take the lead. I wasn't in the mood to get thrusted. It was nice to lie back and feel Ken inside me holding steady. He did that for me while I leisurely massaged myself. I closed my eyes and very nearly forgot Ken while I made marvellous self-love. Then came the moment I had to pull away: there are times when you wish the man would temporarily cease to exist – and a proper man will fulfil your wish, as Ken did now. Without opening my eyes I pulled away from Ken and stretched out with crossed-ankled straight-legged pleasuring alone, raising my legs just above horizontal so that my stomach muscles quivered in an endurance contest between whether they would get exhausted and let go and how much pleasure I could stand to take.

At last I came, and I drifted into a nap, my right hand holding my pussy and my left holding my right breast. When Ken moved, I awoke.

'Thank you, Ken. Sometimes a girl wants to please herself and just wants the boy to be close with her.'

'I know,' he said. 'And I felt very happy to be close with you.'

I made a motion to raise myself but instead settled my hand on Ken's soft cock and lay back down and relaxed. How nice to just hold the man and daydream on a bed. I opened my legs for him. I'm never sure what men want to see women do with their pussies. Do they just want to see it like this? Do they want to see what really pleasures you or just what they imagine feels good to you? I casually, more unconsciously, nudged my pussy lips open and withdrew my hand – it was not so important.

'Ken, look at me . . .' So far as I knew he had not taken his eyes off me. 'Do you feel I have left nothing to the imagination?'

Ken leaned over and kissed me. I placed my hand behind his neck to hold his lips to mine longer. Then I allowed him to sit up.

'I am a girl with no secrets.'

I climbed off the bed to find my dress. Ken followed me. Before I put the Gigli back on, I kissed Ken one more time; our lips parted; he lifted a loose strand of hair from the side of my face and placed it behind my ear.

'You are a woman of infinite mystery. I will always regret that this day has been perfect. If we were incomplete, we could stay together in a search for harmony. But we are complete to each other. You are a woman of infinite secrets and you hold a profound appeal to the imagination. But the key to unlocking all of that is not with me. In truth, you have already found your soulmate. You already know the person you will spend the rest of your earthly existence with.'

'Not my husband.'

'I don't know who it is. You know, and yet you don't know. Your understanding of this destiny has yet to surface into your consciousness – beneath the surface, you already know who the person is.'

I went to work at the club that evening. I never saw Ken or Ted again.

11

I found myself standing outside a large shabby building off Cooper Square with a slip of paper in my hand on which Lata had written an address. This was the place.

The photographer, Janice, was Lata's friend. The magazine photography session would pay, in a few hours' work, what I would need for the first and last month's rent on the flat I had found, with money left over for food and new clothes. I went inside and pushed the button on a very old, very slow-moving lift.

Janice's studio was a large empty loft on the top floor; lights on stands and other photography paraphernalia were pushed up against the exposed red-brick walls. Janice sat next to me on a plush leather couch and showed me her portfolio. There were several pictures of Lata, many of them in black and white.

'These are art photographs,' Janice said. 'They were hung in my latest show in Soho; and right now they're at a gallery in Los Angeles. I've only used two models in the last five years for my serious work. Lata and someone else, but now I only work with Lata. My commercial work is completely separate from this.'

She was right in this. Janice showed me her commercial book – the kind of pictures she would be taking of me – and I would have sworn it was the work of another photographer entirely.

'Has Lata done hardcore photos with you?'

'Understand that I only use that terminology in the commercial sense,' Janice said. 'In serious work there is no such distinction; and I never betray the confidence of a model.'

Janice handed me another, quite large portfolio, a leather-bound wooden box, which I unlatched and looked through. The works consisted entirely of black-and-whites of Lata. 'These have been exhibited,' said Janice. 'But I have never permitted any of these to be published, not even to accompany writing about my work by serious critics. You can see these works in exhibits, and you can lease them. I have never sold any of these; I lease them for 99-year terms so I can keep strict control of the copyright and the actual print.'

These were pictures that took my breath away. Lata looked extraordinarily beautiful and plain at the same time. I wondered how Janice would react to my stating this observation aloud. I had a dreadful fear that Janice would be insulted by such a comment and slap the portfolio shut, denying me the chance to see the full series of photographs. There was every sort of picture of Lata, and every one of them was deeply personal. There were pictures of her naked in abandoned flats and in factories with long-since-defunct machinery, she lay on desert rocks worn smooth by centuries of wind and rain, there was a picture of her easing a silver ben-wa ball into her vagina, a picture of her wearing only a black scarf tied around her waist as she arranged lilies in a vase by the light of a window in an empty room, a picture of her holding a baby tiger in her bare arms. Finally I was brave and made my comment.

'You're right,' Janice said. 'Lata is one of the most beautiful women in the world. And yet there is some-thing utterly common about her face. I can't resolve this. It doesn't need to be resolved. I am irretriev-ably drawn to her. I would not even say that I'm wrestling with opposites. She is neither beautiful nor not beautiful. Of course, she was born in Trinidad, but I suppose there are millions of women in India who look just like her. No, that isn't it. She looks like all women – I see the defining beauty of womanhood in her – and yet, when she walks down the street I doubt if anyone thinks of her as beautiful.'

I flipped over the penultimate picture to reveal the last, a portrait that showed Lata's face emerging from a shadow like a three-quarter moon. She was so beautiful I felt an instantaneous disorientation, as if a trapdoor had been released under me and I was free-falling through space. I sat there like a brain-damaged auto-accident victim staring into that photograph of a face. I wondered how I would hide from Janice the tears that rolled uncontrollably down my cheeks. I wiped away my tears and looked at Janice, expecting a mild rebuke for my descent into emotion. I saw that Janice's eyes were filled with tears too.

'Do you think hardcore is a possibility for me?' I had asked Janice – this was a commercial shoot. In the end I said no, not even for the extra $400. We agreed on $1,700 for a 'boy–girl session'. Janice told her assistant that the session was booked for the next day and to find a male model who was available, which, as it happened, turned out to be the first one the assistant called.

'Don't think it'll be a couple of rolls of film and you're out of here,' cautioned Janice. 'The magazine might only buy a dozen, maybe eighteen, pictures. It's a lot harder to get eighteen saleable pictures than you might think. By the time we're halfway done tomorrow you'll be cursing me and claiming you're underpaid.'

I didn't doubt her for a minute. As I left Janice's clean

loft studio and stepped on to the rubbish-strewn cross street off Cooper Square I thought about times – dare I call them happier times – when I could go to Bergdorf's or Barneys in a funk and buy a $1,700 dress on his credit card to cheer myself up for a wrong the bastard had done me. To think that I never gave it a second thought that for most people $1,700 was real money. Hell, I had once spent $3,400 of David's money on a pair of evening shoes I'd had handmade to match a dress.

I arrived for the session exactly on time the next day, 9 a.m. Janice's assistant, Ruth, buzzed me in.

'What name are you working under?' she wanted to know.

'Julia,' I said.

'Really?' she said. Ruth led me into the studio; what had been an empty loft room the day before had sprouted in its midst an extra two walls and a carpet – half of a cosy bedroom surrounded with umbrellaed lights and myriad snaking cables. A camera stood in position on a tripod.

The male model had arrived earlier. He stood wearing a pair of sleek black briefs and a baseball cap backwards on his head; he was chewing gum, patiently allowing a make-up assistant to give his muscular body an impossibly perfect uniform skin tone. He had the square jaw – indeed, the whole look – that was very in.

Janice directed a flurry of activity, a Pentax slung over her shoulder. All of her assistants were female, an even mix of butches and femmes.

'Tristano, I'd like you to meet Julia,' Ruth said.

Tristano looked at me dully, rather like an ox yoked to a wooden cart. 'Hi,' he managed.

'Nice to meet you ... Tristano,' I said. He was so young and handsome and stupid. 'His name isn't really Tristano, is it?' I whispered to Ruth.

'Of course not. But please call him that.'

'Oh, Ruth,' I said, 'whatever happens today I don't want him inside me.'

'We'll see that doesn't happen. Tristano is good at responding to instructions.'

I was led to a dressing area and stripped down completely. Janice stopped by and asked me how I was doing and then she discussed with her assistants the look she wanted. Next, I had make-up applied. Three women introduced themselves to me and began work on me simultaneously; including full body make-up, it was two hours before I was ready.

The woman who did my hair, Diane, told me she also needed to look at my pussy. Diane liked what she saw. 'This is a really good trim job,' she said. 'I know what this probably cost you, but don't worry, I'm only going to do a light touch-up. OK?'

'OK,' I said. With an electric razor the size of a fingertip, she edged my pussy. 'How can you tell it's a good job?' I enquired.

'First of all, your trimmist took a hands-off approach. That takes a lot of guts these days. And the next thing, every woman curves differently. Your trimmist was obviously sensitive to your unique shape. Who did your work?'

'To tell you the truth I don't know his name.'

'Over on West 4th?'

'Yes.'

'That's who I would've guessed. Touching up his work, I feel like I'm restoring a great work of art by an old master.'

'I know how that is.'

'As much as I hate to admit it, he sets the standard. Hard to believe a *man* can set the standard in something like this.'

'What's his name?'

'No one knows.'

When they were done, I stepped into the 'bedroom' and looked at myself in a gold-framed floor-length mirror that was a prop in the shoot: I was not me. My hair was fluffed up into a natural dishevelled look that I never wore. My eyebrows were darkened and extended in a way that bordered on unforgivable. I now wore a dreadful set of false eyelashes, although I must admit I was pleased with their effect. I saw a beautiful woman standing in that mirror, but I felt like I was looking through a doorway at someone else.

The session only took six hours. We got off to a bad start when Tristano accidentally kissed me on the lips and my face had to be redone. Janice had decided not to do a striptease-type layout, which would have had us start fully dressed and remove each other's clothes frame by frame. I started with a simple white cotton tank top and traditional high-cut white cotton panties. Tristano had his sleek black-satin briefs.

Something about Tristano – do not doubt for a moment his looks; he really was gorgeous – had me on edge the whole time. There was an aura about him, and I'm sure this is not my imagination, that he was the kind of guy who wanted to fuck me and go. I am a girl who likes to fuck, I had found, but it had to be what I wanted, and I certainly didn't want Tristano.

On this morning I felt guilty about betraying my husband. Even though he had ruined my life, he was my husband. And for the same reason, I felt relieved of guilt. The pure joy with Jack and Zoë had turned into complicated, mixed feelings. I wanted to fuck my best friend's husband, of course. I wanted to fuck him with his wife, and I had a deep desire to fuck him alone. Ken and Ted had been pleasant enough diversions. Jack was not the kind of guy who wanted to fuck and go. I had seen that when I had watched him make love to his wife; and I had felt it when he was inside me. Jack was not only the kind of guy who wanted to stay tangled up with me on the bed all day, but I truly felt a bond with him. Tristano was the kind of guy who wanted to catch my snatch, the kind of guy who probably thought in those kinds of phrases. And here I was at the start of the session knowing I was about to slip off those cotton panties at some point and open myself to him, offering him a self that he would not be properly able to appreciate.

The session went along routinely, or what seemed to be routine. Janice and her crew acted in concert, like a well-trained team. They hardly spoke, in fact. Janice gave instructions to me and Tristano. Sometimes she needed a light adjusted. Tristano started out in semi recline on the silver satin sheets on the bed; I squatted on the floor and looked up into his eyes, my hand down the front of my panties. I put my finger on my clit as Janice suggested, even though my panties hid my hand from the camera.

'Some things might as well be real,' Janice said. Most of her instructions were suggestions rather than out-right orders. I took comfort in her suggestions and did not deny her any of them; they all felt right, and they took my mind off Tristano.

We worked through a series of poses in a slow-motion *pas de deux*. I looked like I'd slipped off the bed or was about to faint; Tristano looked like he was about to scoop me off the floor in his muscular arms. Almost every other time I moved, the hair assistant stepped in and brushed my hair into what I supposed would be picked up by the camera as 'natural' yet photogenically perfect. What a strange feeling for me to have spent my career doctoring art and now I was in the hands of artists, being doctored to make saleable medium-core magazine photos.

I lean on the bed, extending my neck as Janice requested, my tongue reaches up and touches the tip of Tristano's tongue. This is work.

Tristano sits on the edge of the bed, I stand next to him. I lift one side of my tank top to reveal a breast. This is the first appearance of one of my nipples. Tristano's hand is flattened near the centre of my panties. I know he can feel the rough texture of my hairs through the thin white cotton. His mouth is up against my other breast, the covered one. Janice asks my permission for her assistant to spray my exposed nipple with cold air. I am getting bored. I say yes. Janice says she hates to use ice. The cold air makes my nipple stiffen. I don't feel turned on at all; this is not at all like the wrenching desire with Jack and Zoë that stirred in me – desire that called me even now, like a voice in the distance. The session grinds on.

Tristano eases up my top, exposing my other breast. Tristano is following instructions from Janice well. I don't imagine he feels anything. Maybe that's what disturbs me, his robot-like lack of feeling except for his obvious desire to fuck me, collect his money, and go. A few shots of cold air on my newly exposed nipple, a little touch-up chill on my first breast. My top is slipped off over my head. Hair brushed again.

In a seeming gap in continuity, it is only after my top flutters to the floor that Tristano is asked to take one of my breasts in his mouth. Not so fast:

innumerable shots of his lips close to but not yet touching one of my nipples. His mouth closes over it. Hold. *Click, click, click.*

'Put your hands on his head like you're drawing him to you. Open your mouth halfway.' More hair brushing. 'Arm around her waist, Tristano.'

When he pulls his mouth away, a make-up assistant dabs the glisten of saliva off my breast and applies powder to smooth out my colour. The warmth causes my nipple to calm down. More cold air.

Another position. This one uncomfortable. Tristano still sits on the edge of the bed. I lean back on to him. He supports part of my weight, but I must support the rest. Janice says it shows off my leg and stomach muscles. Tristano slides his hand down my front as requested, his thumb hangs out over the waistband of my panties, his fingers encumber my pussy, a fingertip rests on my clit, which has yet to make its appearance before Janice's camera.

Now we come apart. I pull down the back part of my panties, showing my ass to the camera. Tristano pulls the panties up; they are high cut, so his action shows my cheeks to the camera in another way.

The panties are to come off. Janice takes particular care with this. Tristano is asked to pull them off countless ways: I lie on my back as he lifts them skywards along my upraised legs towards my ankles. He stops at my ankles. I pull my panties back into position. Another pose: I stand over Tristano, he pulls them off. At this point I suspect Janice is obsessive. No man has ever pulled panties off me so many times, not even my husband in all the years we've been married.

At last the panties are off for good. It is my turn to pull off Tristano's briefs. Janice has me go through a whole to-do of lifting up his waistband and peering down into his briefs. I do this in positions that show my pussy to the camera. Tristano is already hard. I have this vision of him fucking me; it is not pleasant. This is awkward: I push my face into Tristano's briefs while reaching with my hand and stretching open my pussy lips, an assistant guides my fingers so I get myself properly, photogenically open.

Tristano's briefs come off for good. I hold his hard cock between my breasts. It is attractive; Tristano is very attractive – I just can't get over the unpleasant thought of this stupid sex ox sticking his dick inside me.

I lean my head on his stomach, a proto blow-job pose. More hair brushing. I feel the hair assistant, Diane, arrange my hair artfully across Tristano's bare torso, as if it had just happened to fall there that way. My tongue is out, tip touching his shaft; an assistant adjusts my leg to give a better view of my pussy in this shot. The assistants know to do this without spoken instructions from Janice. Tristano starts to lose his erection. A nightmarish thought strikes me that I am going to be expected to maintain him up. Tristano has it easy, lying back while I hold his sagging cock in the thumb and forefinger of my right hand while holding myself open with my left. We take a break: four hours have gone by. A moment more and I think I would have had a muscle cramp.

I go to the bathroom and drink coffee. Ruth offers me a doughnut. 'Go ahead,' she says. 'You're make-up needs touching up anyway.'

The touch-up only takes fifteen minutes, and Tristano and I are back on the bed as we were.

'OK, we're in the home stretch,' Janice says, which I don't like the sound of.

The next series of poses is more natural, without the

weird twisting we'd done earlier, or at least *I'd* done. The poses are full-body poses, not the strange alignments of body parts that had called for keeping still while lights were adjusted and the like.

I'm standing on my knees on the bed. I've always been told I had a good figure and this is the kind of full-frontal exposure that shows it off. Tristano is behind me, his erection having reappeared in full bloom. I can feel his cock bent downwards by my ass crack. I'm pretty sure it's hanging below my pussy in full view of the camera. His hand is on my chest; I clasp it to me with my left hand. Tristano kisses my shoulder. My right arm bends up and over to press his head towards me.

'I need to brush your pussy hair, OK?' says Diane. The trimmist had cut the hair to expose my centreline. I guess it had grown back a bit. Diane parts my pussy hair with a little brush and spritzes on hair spray, to keep the line and my clitoris hood visible.

I took a liking to Diane, who went about her work conscientiously and professionally. She was an attractive femme with a silver labret pierce below her lower lip. That little silver ball under her lip started to turn me on. I wanted to tell her this. I survived the rest of the session by imagining Diane licking me and enjoying me. I supposed she had a lover. Why wouldn't she! Although the touch of her hands on my pussy made me feel that she actually cared about me, I reminded myself that she was probably just doing her job.

Strangely, for the rest of the session Tristano's hands almost never touched my pussy again. Though at the start of the session he'd reached down into my panties and cupped my full pussy in his hand, now that it was fully bare for all to see in its neatly trimmed, combed and hair-sprayed glory, he was not asked to actually hold it again, and he didn't try to.

'Shut your eyes. Gently,' suggested Janice. 'Pleasure ... Good.'

The next pose was the roughest one for me. Janice asked us to 'evolve' into our poses, photographing our transition poses as well as the final ones she instructed us to get into. I ended up on my hands and knees on the bed. I couldn't see what Tristano was doing back there and I didn't trust him. This is it, I thought, *this idiot is going to fuck me*. The head of his hard cock was pressed into the fold formed by my pussy and my leg. Since the camera was on my right side, in profile it probably looked like he was in me. I reached back there and held the head of his cock, pressing it against me, to reassure myself that it was outside my lips. My understanding of what it was about Jack grew clearer; I couldn't put it in words but I knew what I felt. Jack was someone I *wanted*, and oh how I wanted him. Every part of me wanted him; I could even imagine my pussy lips trying to stretch towards him, like lips puckering for a kiss, knowing he was near. Tristano was someone I obviously wanted to avoid, and I truly hoped I never saw him again.

'Touch the head to her inner lips,' Janice instructed Tristano, and then she added, 'Don't stick it in her or I'll cut it off, I swear.' I could feel the top of his cock slide and press gently against the inner lips. The end of it was kissing the opening of my cunt. I broke into a sweat; I was sure I was about to be raped.

'Place your dick on top of her,' Janice instructed. I felt the hot thing lie very still between my ass cheeks. I could feel how slippery my sweat had made my skin there; I was probably slippery everywhere. 'Close in on her, so you look like you're deep inside her. Good, good, very realistic. Beautiful.'

It was then that I felt it, the hot liquid spurts against the small of my back; Tristano was not pumping, but the heavy penis, pressed between his torso and my ass cheeks, flinched with a mind of its own, disgorging itself of its load.

'I couldn't help it,' Tristano said, pulling away from me. His cock was still spurting come.

'The sheets!' an assistant yelled. A woman dived towards him with a cloth to catch what she could. I laughed. Tristano kneeled by me like a ridiculous, aston-ished Adonis, his dick squirting out the last few shots of come into the silver satin sheets.

'It was too *hot*,' Tristano whined.

The assistant with the cloth was too late. She tried to wipe up what she could before it soaked in. Diane wiped the come off my back.

Janice and assistants were in urgent consultation. 'Just fold the sheets to hide the drop marks,' someone said. 'Will he get hard again?' someone said.

'Lie back, Tristano,' said Janice, issuing an unambig-uous order. He was still hard, but his erection was failing. 'Julia, how about you pick it up and hold it near your mouth? Don't be afraid; it can't do much for a while.'

More hair brushing from Diane as I tilted my face over the shaft I coddled in my hand. A make-up assist-ant had opened up a can of coconut milk and dappled a few drops of the thick white syrup on my lower lip. 'His head, his head,' said Janice. The assistant obediently dribbled more of the white goo on to the dimming bulb of Tristano's cock.

'Just in time,' said Janice.

But the photo shoot didn't end there. Janice needed to fill in scenes to maintain the sequence leading up to the climax. These scenes were not unreasonably unpleasant to pose. There was a kind of 69 pose, pressing Tristano's cock against my face in a way that revealed his balls by my lips and hid that fact that he was no longer erect. This pose was one of the few other times Tristano touched my pussy with his hands: he held my sex apart in his fingers and placed his tongue against my clitoris. He held his tongue there a long while as Janice clicked away at different angles and had him tilt his head slightly this way then that till she was satisfied with the angle.

The last pose we took – I had the impression Tristano's spill had ended the shoot prematurely – was easy enough. I lay on my back and opened up my legs for Tristano.

'Pull up your knees a bit,' Janice suggested. Even though I lay there with my pussy open and exposed, and even though my sense of dread had lifted, I did not feel inviting. And I suppose that, after having shot his load, Tristano wasn't in much of a mood to feel invited. I lay there, my thighs propped open for all the world, Tristano's face close enough to my quim that I could feel his breath, and I contemplated the absurdity of portraying desire, probably the most intimate and powerful expression of desire a woman can physically offer a man, and we felt no desire whatever for each other. I did not even worry that Tristano would try to slip his finger into me.

'Hang on to her ankle, Tristano. Tongue into her. That's right,' said Janice. I bent my knee over his shoulder and drew him closer into my pussy. I was in complete control.

* * *

Tristano received his cheque for $250 and left. He didn't even try to pick me up.

Janice had me do a quick series of solo poses with a telephone as a prop.

At the end of it I received my cheque for $1,700.

'Men don't get paid much,' Diane told me when she was redoing my hair before releasing me to the outside world. 'Most men would do this work for free; so, they tend to get paid a token sum. It's their own fault.'

12

I moved into my own flat late that afternoon, feeling a mixture of regret and the sense of relief at taking this step towards my freedom. Jack and Zoë pleaded with me not to go. I enjoyed sleeping with them in the big cast-iron bed, the three of us naked and sharing body heat during this spring's cool nights. When I slept between them I could awake and reach in one direction and run my hand over Jack's muscular chest and down to hold his cock. Turning the other way, I could wrap my arm around Zoë, who usually slept on her side. I enjoyed it when we paired off. I felt secure waking up to find my friend making love to her husband next to me. When Zoë was on top of Jack, looking up to see her turned me on so much I couldn't help climbing over Jack's face to receive a tonguing, which he always obliged me with. And often enough it was me fucking Jack, with Zoë sleeping peacefully alongside us or, rousing, kissing her husband and massaging her pussy to orgasm. I found I was quite fond of holding Zoë's pussy while she held mine, forming a circle of female communication as we brought each other to orgasm with our interwoven manual rhythms. One night we played a game with Jack in which he had to guess which pussy was which in the dark just by sense of touch. When he held Zoë's pussy he guessed it was mine. So, as punishment for guessing wrong we made him fuck us both. Well, we were sort of going to do that anyway.

More quickly than you'd expect, we had fallen into a

pattern of sex *à trois*. It was enjoyable, but it felt to me that the experience was somehow on loan. Zoë and I kept dildos on the bedside table and some nights Jack would dildo us in parallel. I must say, there is something about being dildoed by a man with a duplicate of yourself right next to you undergoing the same pleasurable treatment as you.

I knew I had to break it off. Never again had it been quite as spectacular as the first time, although a couple of times it had got close. If I wanted to keep my friendship with Jack and Zoë, I knew I had to end it while they still wanted more. Perhaps 'routine' is not the right word: there was something too close, and that felt increasingly ominous, like advancing storm clouds in the distance. Although everything between us was mutually enhancing, I had a growing sense that it could all turn quite nasty, unpredictably and suddenly.

I bid Jack and Zoë farewell. I told them my new neighbourhood wasn't safe; so, please hold my fur coat for a few days while I arrange to sell it.

I was moving towards a new phase of my life, one that they could not join me in. I was about to grow.

I felt like a magician I had seen as a child. He stood on the stage wriggling out of a straitjacket. First there was his agonised squirming, with a contorted look on his face that still makes me contort my face just thinking about it. Then there was the moment when the whole jacket went loose. Suddenly he was free. When I found my flat in the East Village, I knew I was about to slip my straitjacket.

My flat was bare when I moved in. I found housewares and pieces of furniture on the street that very afternoon and practically every day after that. My new place was in a rundown tenement on East 3rd Street, with dirty walls, peeling paint, cockroaches and a brittle sheet of linoleum covering the floorboards. I was very busy with my two jobs. I continued my dual existence, with the competing sides of the duality far apart. I worked in monastic silence by day, took a nap, and then worked in a club full of smoke and the sound of whatever deafening, ear-shredding shit the house DJ blew through his speakers. Tuesday through Thursday nights I only worked a four-hour shift. Friday and Saturday were full nights.

My work at the Where It All Happens Club led me deeper and deeper on a journey inside myself: it took me on the journey to the unexplored edges of my soul that I once thought fine art – for that matter, all the finer cultural things in life – would lead me to. The finer things in life had led me to a dead end.

No. I don't mean that. I had reached a detour in my life. The work of the great masters was still eternal, but I had reached a point where I had to grow. Fine art had taken me only so far and then left me at a deserted crossroads, the journey unfinished, the direction uncertain: the fault was not so much the paintings as it was the resonance of the work inside me and that mysterious contact with the soul of an artist and his time. The resonating instrument inside me needed something more if it was ever to play in tune, if it was ever to fully respond to life. I needed restoration; I needed to be known. And right now this had to happen in a club whose dance floor shook like an allegro earthquake and whose god was a semiliterate 22-year-old with a bone in his nose who looked down on his creation from behind his two turntables in his booth.

He called himself Flashmaster Jaz, and I had no respect for what he did. To me, his music had always been so much screeching, booming noise. Until he came up with something as good as Mozart's Clarinet Quintet, I felt, his contribution was just another part of the club like the decor or the lighting or the drinks.

But one night I sat with Jaz in his DJ booth and he revealed a whole new perspective to me. Jaz superimposed a social layer on the floor beneath him that I had never been able to perceive before. He orchestrated the motion of the dance floor as a whole, and he could move individual dancers like chess pieces. He really was the god of the dance floor. He would catch a dancer responding to a favourite flash of sound, snatch the LP back and repeat that, eliciting another response from the dancer. Armed with two turntables and this elemental relationship between dancer and DJ as a building block, multiplied across many dancers, each with his or her own tastes, Jaz shaped the danceflow of the whole room, and he could even cause couples to pull apart and pair off with new partners. He could form strangers into an open circle, he could get a straight man to dance with a gay. On this night I learned to read a dance floor. On another night, with another DJ with a different personality, the dance floor took on an entirely different shape.

I was someone new. Someone I never knew. Time passed ... long past midnight in the Where It All Happens Club the music was blaring, smoke hung in the air, I was selling cigarettes to half a dozen young up-market men and women sitting on couches around a low table, their knees above the rim of the glossy black surface like mountains surrounding a valley of overflowing ashtrays and a downtown of tall drinks. For some unknowable reason a great many bald black men populated the scene that night.

'Packet of Camels,' a voice said behind me.

'That's $5,' I said, turning. Yes, I reminded myself, you hold a position at the most important art-restoration studio in the world and you sell cigarettes to drunks like him. The guy put a Camel in his mouth.

'Have you got a light?'

I leaned towards him and lit his cigarette. His breath was so freighted with the stench of hard liquor I wondered if he would go up in a fireball at the approach of my lit match. When I puckered my lips to blow out the match he guided my match hand away from my mouth and kissed me. Our lips parted and we looked in each other's eyes. The lit match fell to the floor. I took off my cigarette tray and kissed him again. I was being swept away; I wasn't here to sell cigarettes.

He reached for one my breasts with his non-cigarette hand. I had something of a reputation at the club, sort of a Do-Touch Girl. Nevertheless, I slapped his face. The management didn't mind that I'm by and large not very good at selling cigarettes. But I insisted that what I did with anyone be by my rules, and I had just changed my mind about this guy.

The guy with the Camel laughed feebly in his humiliation. He was drunk enough that there was no sting in my slap. I still felt a sting on the palm of my hand. The slapped guy took his fist back to wallop me. Gus, a bouncer, caught it in one of his monstrous hands. It was comical the way that drunken slime tried to punch me yet couldn't figure out why his hand was caught in midair somewhere just behind his field of vision. He turned feebly to discover Gus and was whisked out of the club like a cat put out for the night. If he had woken up with a broken arm the next day, he wouldn't remember how it happened.

I reached for a guy standing next to me. He wasn't as good looking as the guy I had just slapped. In fact, he was not much to look at – nose too big for his face, a stooping posture. I took one of his hands in mine and placed it against my breast. I was, after all, turned on. I found myself leaning back, more and more, until, without knowing why or how, I was lying on the low table, all the while kissing the guy, who had brought himself down to a kneel, the drinks and ashtrays having been swiftly cleared off the table by the couples clustered on the surrounding couches. For better or worse, people have a way of acting on automatic pilot in a club. Another hand was on my other breast – it was another guy, kneeling to my other side in his jacket and tie. I saw knees and faces, the bare knees of girls peeking out from sexy black club skirts. The young men sipped their drinks. Their girlfriends were sitting next to them, watching and sipping the kind of martinis for squares that their grandparents drank in the 1950s. I looked up and saw a blonde, her long, thick hair hiding her eyes. Slowly, and very gently – I closed my eyes – my red satin blouse was unbuttoned. I was not wearing a bra.

The two guys, one on each side of me, each kissed and massaged a naked breast. I was enraptured – this was exactly the sort of embarrassing exhibitionism I wanted to be the centre of. I wondered what sort of nerve these boys would prove to have. I opened my eyes. The blonde with long, thick hair was with a guy. She was his girlfriend and they had stopped to watch. They were getting turned on watching me lie there getting my breasts massaged by strangers. The guy turned and kissed his girlfriend. I felt hands circling my breasts, and I watched this other guy as he reached down and lifted up his girlfriend's black miniskirt. His hand curved under her, massaging over the front of her black thong panties. They kissed, losing this world for one of their own making. As they became more aroused and oblivious, the guy curled his fingers under the ribbon of cloth of his girlfriend's thong and pulled it to one side so he could massage her pussy. I saw her pussy hair flick over his fingernails and between his fingers. He held her pussy in his hand. She had not opened her eyes. I envied her: she was one of those women with cheekbones that catch the light lustrously and whose cheeks are lost in a depression of shadow. She was a beautiful girl. Her boyfriend drew his hand up and I saw her slit fold over his finger. She clasped his fingers to her and opened her eyes to look straight into mine. Around me the girls still sat on the couches sipping their martinis next to their boyfriends – unthreatened, unturned-on, disinterested. They knew their boyfriends would hold their breasts later, just as the two boys were holding mine, and they knew their boyfriends would reach down into their pussies later, just as the beautiful girl's was being reached – her face emerged from her long blonde hair and her eyes turned hungry, and I knew we understood each other.

Watching the beautiful girl and the boy aroused me all the more intensely. I pulled up my satin hem and rubbed my panties. The guy with his hand on his girlfriend pulled down her thong. She kissed his ear and any part of his face and neck she could reach while he did so. This proved awkward as he got the thong down below her knees and worked it past her ankles and over her patent-leather-stiletto-shod feet – and the awkwardness was a turn-on for me, their awkwardness making the experience more real.

The thong lay on the floor forgotten, frivolous and twisted as a bow torn off a wrapped present. The guy worked his hand over his girlfriend's vee, which I couldn't see now, under her skirt. She reached down and guided his hand. The guy had a questioning look in his wide eyes, as if he was helpless in the beautiful girl's power. He searched her face for an answer. He had no understanding of what had seized her body and soul. All he knew was that he must satisfy her. I reached down the front of my panties. By now more people had closed around, watching. I felt comfortable, like I was in a small room, like my small flat. I closed my eyes: I was in a cosy, soft room whose walls were people. I could hear their clothes and feel the warmth of their bodies, and I felt the boys' hands on my bare breasts.

I couldn't stand the wait: I pulled up my knees and tore off my panties with one wrench. I didn't want to fuck – that would hide my cunt from view – I wanted everyone to see me come. I guided one of the boys' hands off my breast and over my pussy. I pushed his hand lightly, sometimes vigorously, and then guided his fingers over other parts of my body, having him brush my thigh or the inside of my knees. I pushed his hand back up to my breast and I massaged my pussy myself. The crowd started chanting a deep whisper, their dull rumble sounding like a heartbeat. I heard the life, I heard the rhythm: 'Come, Julia, come! Come, Julia, come!' I was enwombed within the body of people and their chant flowed in and out of my orgasmic soul like breath. My senses were hyperacute.

The beautiful girl came: I heard a quiet moan emanate from her and I sensed her body slowly sinking to the floor in melting orgasmic pleasure – her boyfriend sank to the floor with her, holding his hand still on her calming, now satisfied pussy. Her hair brushed my thigh. I came, my hand shuddering vigorously over my pussy and dropping a blanket of pleasure over me, over all of me, I did not know where.

I opened my eyes to see that another girl had her

hand down a guy's pants. Just then, come squirted up through her fingers and messed the guy's shirt. And there: a cock entered a shaft of light like an assassin's gun through a crowd in grainy news footage. He had been unnoticed. The come shot from him and I felt the warm drops hit my chest and legs and I saw drops rain down into the blonde hair of the beautiful girl resting quietly on the floor with her boyfriend, by my thigh.

I looked at the girlfriends smoking their cigarettes and sipping their martinis, placid, as they were before. They were pretty, they had money, their eyes were empty. I knew that whatever they saw that night, which they pretended had had no effect on them, had touched them deeper than they would ever admit, a depth they would not admit to even when they were passionately fucking their boyfriends later that night, and for many nights beyond, as the memory burned bright within their consciousnesses. And they would remember it on the tube Monday morning as they headed to Wall Street, to the banks and brokerages and law firms where they work. Their cool, implacable faces will never change, even as these ferocious images assault the insides of their skulls, trying to get out.

That night – more properly it was early morning – Lata walked home with me. She said she was living alone and didn't want to spend the night in her empty place again. I knew she could take home a man any night she wanted, just pick one out of the crowd. But that's not the same thing as not being alone. Although Lata was constantly approached by men, I could not recall her ever taking one home.

Lata hadn't seen my exhibitionism of less than an hour earlier. On days when she had her period she worked in the bar instead of splashing around naked in the fountain downstairs. She told me she liked working in the bar better, and wanted to work there full time.

'Your honest opinion now, do you think that makes me a slut?' I said, as we walked along the desolate street of what in Europe would be assumed to be buildings bombed out in World War II.

'What do *you* feel?' said Lata.

'No; tell me objectively,' I said.

'I don't see how objectivity applies. Whether or not you're a slut is a matter of perception. And it depends on who is doing the perceiving.'

'And what do *you* perceive?' I said.

'You did it, right?' said Lata.

'Yeah,' I said.

'You liked it.'

'Oh, God, it was exhilarating; that's why I'm worried.'

'But what harm did you do? None that I can see. I *envy* you. I *really* do,' said Lata.

'Why would you envy *me*? After all, you've . . .' I let my voice trail off because I thought 'fucked in front of a crowd' might sound rude.

'I know,' said Lata. 'Except I could never bring myself to masturbate in front of a bunch of strangers. It's just too personal. You must feel so free having done it.'

'You know, I have no regrets at all; how can I when I enjoyed it so much?' I said.

'I wish I saw you,' said Lata. She started to tickle me. Her fingers ran lightly all over me, under my arms, along my ribs, behind my knees.

'Stop! Stop!' I said, hooting with uncontrollable laughter that echoed off the sooty-bricked façades of the empty street.

'You really *are* ticklish,' she said, not letting up for a

moment. I thought I was going to piss, I was laughing so hard. I grabbed her around the waist in a clinch, her hands were everywhere. Tears were coming to my eyes. I tried to tickle her into submission, but all I could reach was her bum. I tried to catch her wrists but they kept escaping. When I tried to tickle under her arms, she tickled under mine worse. She might as well have been one of those Indian deities with eight or ten arms. Finally I held her to me in a tight embrace, her arms pinned. I could not recall when I had last laughed so wholeheartedly.

I looked into her deep brown eyes. We were both out of breath, breathing hard. Her face floated in a pool of black hair that poured away from her face and spilled over her shoulders, and a strand ran over one of her cheeks, sparkling shiny where it caught light and disappeared in darkness, in the shadow between her lips. 'You little torturer,' I said.

She turned serious.

'I'm sorry,' she said. 'When I was a child I did some cruel things that I regret to this day. Childish things, and yet I still regret them. I guess there will always be that cruel streak in me. Do you hate me?'

I held Lata tight in my arms, feeling her chest expand and contract with breath. The world was silent again. We were the only souls on this street. I could hear her breath interlaced with the sound of my own breath.

I looked into those deep eyes of hers. 'I wish I could freeze this moment in amber,' I said. 'I wish I could hold this moment and keep it for sixty million years. Why would you ever imagine I could hate you, when you have made me feel more alive than I ever remember being?'

* * *

All moments end.

There is only one moment: the ever-continuing present.

A moment is a point in time and, as such, has no duration and thus has neither a beginning nor an end.

We turned the corner on to my street – which to myself I silently referred to as Dresden Street – and found ourselves confronted with a pile of old wooden furniture that had been hauled out of an abandoned tenement and dumped on the sidewalk.

Lata and I marvelled at the heap, which was taller than us. One always pauses at such sights in the city, the way one might pause at an inappropriate sculpture in a public space. Until two days ago, I had never felt any need to inspect furniture strewn about the street to decide whether to take it home. Now I looked through every pile I saw.

'Maybe there's something good,' said Lata, removing a three-legged chair. 'Although not this.'

I needed furniture. I was open to any piece that might fit, and the pieces of furniture were of the appropriate aesthetic for a tiny East Village flat. Furniture in the East Village is, after all, a renewable communal resource: it is found on the street, it resides in a tenement for a few years, it ends up back on the street. It has been this way always.

Most of the furniture was broken. There was a rickety armoire that was light enough for us to carry to my building, and its doors were intact. But it would be too hard for us to carry up the stairs.

'Lata, do you need anything?'

'Naw, just hoping there's something better than what I have. Do you need any kitchen stuff?' There were pots and a frying pan and a spatula, a ladle, a spoon.

'Already got them,' I said.

There were smashed plates and an extremely dirty carpet.

'This love seat is complete,' said Lata. 'Do you need it?'

'It's cute,' I said. 'Is it heavy?' The little love seat was probably from the late 20s, a Frankensteinian bringing together of lion's feet clutching balls, ivy and other plant motifs, and a Greek fret design, all rendered in cheap wood, no doubt mass produced and sold nation-wide on the instalment plan prior to the Great Crash. It had been reupholstered, probably a couple of decades ago, and consequently was not irredeemably decrepit.

'It's light,' I said, picking up one side. 'If it isn't infested with fleas, we're in business.'

'What's this?' said Lata, pulling at what seemed to be a walking stick. 'It's like a golf club, only it's made of wood.'

'It *is* a golf club,' I said. 'It's an antique, probably worth $100 at least. You're good at this. Are there any more?'

We searched as best we could in the early morning darkness by the insufficient light of a lone street lamp. But there were no other hidden treasures.

We laid the golf club on the love seat and carried it towards my building, Lata carrying the front and me the back. I don't know anything about golf but I sup-posed we had found a sand wedge, for the head was cast iron and had teeth like a giant comb, which made me suspect it was for whacking balls out of sand traps. To think that respected grown-ups such as doctors devoted themselves to such an activity! I looked down at the golf iron nestled in its bier like we were carrying the old thing in a funeral procession.

'What was that?' Lata said.

We stopped.

All was silent. We looked at the surrounding darkness. All was still and dead.

'I feel like we're being followed,' Lata said.

We got the love seat up the stairs to my flat, setting it down at each landing and resting on it. We set it in the centre of my room facing my window. Lata, seeing no obvious place to display an antique object, propped the golf club on my window sill, and we sat down to catch our breath. We talked about whether we should attempt to go back and haul up the armoire. Looking around my little room, it was clear there was nowhere it could go. We were too tired anyway. What pitifully few clothes the average sweatshop worker must have had in the nineteenth century. A family once lived here, I was sure, not just a single person like me, and yet the one closet was as small as a phone booth.

The morning sun awoke me. I had fallen asleep on the little love seat and found Lata asleep, curled up with her head resting on my arm. I looked into her sleeping Indian face and wondered what thoughts she was dreaming just then, if any. I realised this was what Lata needed, this was why she didn't want to sleep alone tonight. I felt privileged that she had needed this from me and that I had given it to her – whatever it was, human warmth, a sense that she was wanted; maybe it wasn't even something that could be put in words. The repose in her expression made me feel calm and happy, and with that feeling I drifted off to sleep again. In two hours I would have to wake up and get ready for work at the museum.

13

After I got home from the museum I slept two hours. When I headed over to the club, light still tinted the sky.

Zoë and Jack wanted me to come over to their loft that night, and they were disappointed when I said I had to work. I had expected that it would be harder on Jack, who had got used to sleeping between me and Zoë – and took turns fucking us often. But after speaking with them I realised it was harder on Zoë.

I had called my furrier and I had an appointment to see him on Friday. I was putting my coat up for sale. Zoë wanted to buy it, but all her money was tied up.

Some nights my tips from the club were substantial. With my two jobs I had enough money to live, although I had to economise. I found a silver lining in this; it forced me to scour dusty used-clothing stores throughout the East Village, which otherwise I might never have set foot in. My days of buying $4,700 evening dresses on the top floor of Barneys were over, and I found that I did not miss it. Rather, I enjoyed stores such as Love Saves The Day, Absolutely Valueless, and Trash In Action. Some 'thrift' stores are, of course, quite pricey, which is why I had acquired a fondness for Trash In Action, which I would describe as cheaper than the Salvation Army and with taste. It was here that I found a glistening white dress from the 1940s for $32.

The sky still breathed gold as I walked over to the Where It All Happens Club in my white dress on what really was just any late-spring night. I do not like the modern look of cutaway pantyhose, so I had on my white stockings and garter belt – wedding lingerie. At the club I changed into my cigarette-girl uniform and strolled through the crowd to see if anyone was there yet. Nobody was. Down in the basement – the Willard Room – it was still minimum-wage stock-clerk boys and other New Jerseyesque denizens, like the boy who slumped immobile in a cushy black leather armchair with his fingers knotted around a bottle of beer. His eyes wandered bored over the crowd as he waited for something to 'happen' at the Where It All Happens Club. No one was down there either. I went over to the basement bar. Lata wasn't around. The New Jerseyans – and the people who merely looked like they came from New Jersey – arrived as early as nine o'clock, and provided the club with its revenue. The club is empty and the doorman lets anyone in. The *clubgoers* – the people who made this a scene, people whose portraits hung on the walls of hot photography exhibits in Soho – never showed up before midnight, never paid to get in, and never paid for their drinks. This early in the evening I got bored and ended up doing some work; it was early enough that strands of clean air ribboned their way through the smoke.

A boy wearing jeans and a flannel shirt tried to chat me up: some books are best judged by their covers. The silly boy bought me a drink. I toyed with the idea of giving him a blow-job to see if that would make him lose interest in me. But this sort of thing is simply *not done* at 10 p.m. – one needs the cover of lateness: sometime after midnight, when no one knows what time it is and no one else is awake in the city, we are the actors in a collective dream. So, the proximate boy with his bright little eyes and a face younger than his years, a face untouched by pain, buys me a 'drink'. The bartender gives me the 'gin and tonic' I ordered. This is how the scam works: The boy pays $9 for my drink, but the bartender gives me soda water with a slice of lime. If the mark doesn't order a drink for himself as well, I insist that he does. He gets a real drink. Other girls who work here have a quota of drinks they're supposed to sell. The quota doesn't apply to me, but if it did, I'd blow past it faster than any girl here except Lata. I make more money for the club doing this than I do selling cigarettes. These New Jersey boys think I'm so taken with them that I'm standing around chatting with them instead of doing my job as a cigarette girl. They think I'm risking getting yelled at by my boss. Some nights I get forty or fifty drinks bought for me, which is another reason why the bartender doesn't put alcohol in the ones he gives me. The boy spoke with the kind of over-self-confidence that young girls find attractive and that I consider a sign that a boy has no character, at least not beneath the surface. I acted slutty, like I was *definitely* interested, that I would sleep with a guy who bought me one drink and that I was impressed by whatever the hell job he had that he considered superior to cigarette girl. Then I slipped away, offered cigarettes to a guy, and got bought another drink farther down the bar – this drives guys wild because it makes me look quite slutty and they get jealous. It's like, *Hey, she's just a slut and I'm not good enough for her!?* Of course that makes him want me more. The more a guy doesn't know a girl and doesn't respect her and doesn't care about her, the more jealous he will get over her.

Between 11 p.m. and midnight is the shift change. The New Jerseyans filter out. Some are *tired* and are going home. Others stumble drunk into country and western bars, biker bars, lesbian bars and the like – another Big Adventure in the Big Apple for them. It is after 11 that the doorman at the Where It All Happens Club becomes choosey about who he lets in. Costume becomes important. A young milliner in a crazy hat of her own design, a shoo-in. A famous East Villager in a sparkling Elvis-style dinner jacket goes in – he is famous for being famous. An alcoholic blues singer who records on an independent record label, overweight, in an ill-fitting blue-serge suit, three days' beard growth, and already drunk – in. A transvestite dressed up as a fading Broadway legend who can no longer hit the high notes – the transvestite *can* hit them – in. A group of drunk boys from Long Island dressed in Bermuda shorts, sneakers, and wearing T-shirts emblazoned with the names of popular rock bands – not in: and after 45 minutes of overeager wishful thinking on the wrong side of the velvet ropes, the Long Island boys begin to feel sober and head towards a bar.

Now that I had become something of an attraction at the club, I didn't have to actually work. I didn't have to meet a quota selling cigarettes any more, and I was given a raise. My position now was more like a shill at a Broadway play, clapping and laughing so the paying customers think they are at an *event* on opening night. Lata had been a shill, throwing off her clothes and leaping into the fountain, the actual customers following suit, illusion becoming reality. The difference between me and a shill was that for me, everything was real. Whatever I did, it was because I needed to do it. At 11 I got up from the bar, not having touched the drink that yet another boy had bought for me.

'You didn't touch the drink I bought you!' he exclaimed in one of his more astute observations. He was so drunk that if he downed my drink he wouldn't be able to tell that it was non-alcoholic.

'And?' I said.

'And what?' he said.

'My point exactly,' I said, turning away with my cigarette tray and making my escape to the Willard Room.

As I scouted the Willard Room from a neutral corner I realised I was standing next to tonight's performance art. On a raised platform a pale-faced, bald, fat man reclined on a couch wearing a royal-blue silk robe and scanned the crowd blandly with blue eyes. I had heard he would be here. He wasn't a performance artist; he was an actor hired by the performance artist who had thought up whatever it was that was supposedly happening. I set my drink – a real drink – on the platform and looked over the crowd with what must have been as bland an expression as the pale, fat actor's. If this was going to be a sex night for me, I wasn't going to drink much: I didn't want my clit to get numb.

I overheard a couple: 'I didn't really want to stay over with him,' she said. She was petite, and quite cute, with a cowlick at the top of her forehead, which accented the blonde hair that fell straight downwards everywhere else on her head.

'But you stayed over anyway,' he said. He looked like Clark Kent, complete with the thick-framed glasses, except he was wearing jeans and a black leather jacket.

'Well, I don't know. I mainly didn't feel like driving all the way back to Garden City.'

'He had a separate room for you, I hope.'

'Of course he did. You know, I really don't like him. That's what was so odd about the whole thing. I mean, it's not just his squealy laugh.'

'That would just drive me mad.'

'He taps his fingers all the time and talks with his mouth full. And he keeps repeating the same jokes. Not that they're so funny to start with, but the second time he tells it you think, Now, should I laugh and pretend I've never heard this before? And then the next day he tells them *again*, and you sort of force a chuckle.'

'Madness. Sheer nightmare,' he said.

'Even though I didn't want to have sex ... We were watching a video of *The 39 Steps* and, well ...'

'You had sex with him? Why?'

'I know! I don't know. We're just kind of watching the movie and you know how Robert Donat and Madeleine Carroll are handcuffed together?'

'Yes, of course.'

'And there's this incredible scene in which Carroll takes off her wet stockings.'

'I see, I see.'

'So, we turn the movie off and he's showing me up this grand staircase to the second floor of his duplex to get his handcuffs – and we're sort of kissing halfway up the stairs, and pretty soon he's feeling me up. And God, I don't know – we never did make it to his bedroom to get the handcuffs. He gives me some OK head and he's in me, right there on the landing.'

'Well, it can happen to the best of us,' he said. 'I hope he used a condom.'

'Oh, he was prepared. Had one in his shirt pocket.'

'What a bastard. He planned the whole thing.'

'I know. There's something cute about a guy who plans to seduce you. It's kind of romantic and old-fashioned. He wasn't great, he wasn't terrible, but next time can I stay with you?'

'Yes. Of course.'

I had acquired an affection for these club conversations. Only in the East Village, I told myself. As midnight approached, the demographic transition in the club population neared completion – and the die-hard clubgoers were still a couple of hours away from making their appearance.

The music was blaring at the Where It All Happens Club and smoke hung in the air. I was making my last round through the club selling cigarettes. I looked at the fountain where I had first laid eyes on Lata. It was hard to believe that not so long ago I had not known that Lata existed, and now I missed her. I became aware of a presence next to me. I turned. It was Lata, dressed up in a short sexy leather skirt, vintage wedgies from the 1970s, and a black knitted-mesh top that veiled her bare breasts and exposed her midriff; her eyes were lined in kohl. She laughed at me. I felt like I had been rescued from a deep, dark well – pulled up into the sunshine. I wanted to hug her right there, but I couldn't because of my stupid cigarette-girl tray pointing out into space from my belly.

'Hey there, Cigarette Girl, got any Marlboros?' said Lata.

'It's $5 a pack,' I said.

'Could I bum one off you?'

'I really shouldn't,' I said.

'I'm just kidding; can't you see I've got my purse with me?'

'Oh, right,' I said. 'I was kidding too.'

'No you weren't. You were serious. I've got a lighter.' Lata took a cigarette out of her purse and lit it up. 'What a non-night.'

'It's boring.'

'I'm gonna finish this cigarette and go,' said Lata.

I looked at the crowd of black-clad dandies, oblique

figures milling around in the smoky basement. I turned to Lata to make an idle comment about how tedious it all was, but she was gone. There wasn't a face I knew anywhere in the room. I went up to the manager's office to slip out of my uniform and into my white dress.

Lata was right. All was dull throughout the club. By 2 a.m. I was clocked out and roaming around the club.

When it comes to sex, one makes little rules for oneself, especially if it's all just too easy: I'll fuck this guy, but only if I can fuck this other guy first; tonight I will only fuck a man if he's wearing a wedding ring; tonight I will only give blow-jobs to men with black hair; I will only fuck one man per night this whole week; and so on.

This last rule intrigued me. I had also never openly fucked at the Where It All Happens Club, not the way I had seen Lata do in the fountain or Vivienne upstairs – there was in my case always a measure of discretion. That is, until this night, with this white dress.

A young man slumped irrelevantly in a cushy black leather armchair in a dark corner of the Willard Room. He looked to be a stock clerk or some such job that doesn't matter. I had seen him before. He stirred to life. The music was better, and the boy stood. In just that action of standing up he transformed himself from a lazy low-wage-earning no one to a young man with the look of a lover. Just looking at him gave me an irrational sense of envy, as if I wished I could take his girlfriend's place. He was not well dressed. He wore a horizontal-striped shirt – white and earthy greens and browns – of no recognisable origin or fashion trend. He was taller than I had realised, over six feet, slender and muscular. In fact, he seemed to be alone at the club. He wasn't with anyone and he wasn't looking for anyone, a combination I find draws my attention. A young woman standing near him spoke to him, an exchange of lines of conversation that perhaps they themselves could not hear above the music. I don't know what he said, but her eyes lit up – she was interested. But he wasn't. He did a couple of dance moves, alone really, despite being next to the girl. He exuded confidence. He snapped his fingers over his head, shutting his eyes and swaying his hips. With those sketches of movement, in an instant, every woman in the place knew that this boy could have any of them – and he knew it.

Men, I saw, had not noticed the subtle changes that had come over the women they were chatting with. But from my vantage point, the chemistry of the room had transformed. The social–sexual shift across the floor was as dramatic a change as loose water molecules freezing into a crystal lattice. All over the basement, as if by mental telepathy, women had rapidly become aware of the wildfire erotic presence that had announced itself in the visual sign of a few hip swings, a sign that resonates within every strand of a woman's DNA, thin male hips with a compact butt to propel them that every one of us longed to contain between our thighs; it's enough to make your womb ring with a note like the echo of the bell lingering inside a cathedral.

The young man probably *was* a stock clerk in a chemist's, but all over the floor women who were artists, high-strung Wall Street traders winding down, corporate lawyers, avant-garde musicians, the freaky milliner – they all looked vaguely ill at ease. They oriented their bodies around their boyfriends so they could keep the young man in the corner of their eyes – the women scattered around the room were aligned like pins and needles within the force lines of a magnetic field of which this boy was the pole. A group of five too-trendy-for-words women dressed in black opened up a half circle towards him like a parabolic antenna scanning the starry sky for signs of intelligent life – their well-practised facial expressions of East Village mordant detachment dropping away, to be replaced by giggly girl teenager-in-love self-consciousness, and one of them dared to actually *look* at the boy.

I had come to the conclusion lately that I deserved what I wanted. I looked directly at the boy across the room. He wasn't looking at any woman. He was not hungry. He was not predatory: this was a boy who was used to having any woman he wanted. No rush. No hurry. There was merely the amount of time he would take to make up his mind. I had made up my mind, and I was the only woman here – I was sure – who knew how to make up his mind for him. I knew how his mind worked. He'd got us all hooked – he knew how to do that to a room full of women. But he had never come across the likes of me; he had no idea that the gamehunter was about to become the game. These other women didn't stand a chance; they were flirty girls who would gladly fuck him if they could slip away from their boyfriends and offer themselves to this stock-clerk Casanova. No doubt that was his plan. But in a roomful of women who wanted him, he would want me precisely because I had decided he didn't interest me. Sometimes the only way to get what you want is to not want what you want.

I allowed the boy to disappear from my radar screen. As for the woman he had spoken too, her pussy was no doubt already wet for him. That was too easy; he'd have her some other night. I fetched a fresh gin and tonic and wandered over to the fountain. All around the room, girls were behaving strangely, laughing just a bit too hard, smiling too broadly and uncomfortably, staring just a little too intently into the faces of their dates. I saw women patting their boyfriends' cheeks, slipping their arms around their boyfriends' waists, trying just a little too hard not to notice the young man who had unleashed a pheromone attack on the women and gay men from one end of the room to the other. The music coming out of the DJ booth went askew as Jaz fumbled to get a grip on the phenomenon that was disrupting his floor.

I paused at the fountain, cocking my hip just so, and thought about what it might be like to fuck in the water, Lata-style – not with anyone in particular, just the concept of the water, the music, the sound of the splashing fountain, beneath the statue of the angular-featured Fascist man, with his coil of copper tubing, in the dim light, the smell of the smoke. Not tonight. I did not feel like getting wet. I did not feel like anything at all. It was at that moment that I – I alone – seized his attention. My back was to him. When I caught a young woman staring at me and she looked away, I knew for sure from her expression that I had my man hooked. The expression she maintained while looking resolutely in another direction for no reason told me that I held the attention of my intended prey. And all the other women in the room knew it.

I don't know that the boy understood what had just happened to him, that I had won him, but soon I found his face hovering near mine. It was that fast. He looked at my profile as I stared straight ahead across the pool of the fountain, my arms folded, unaware of his insignificant existence. I sipped my gin and tonic, remaining oblivious to him long enough for him to feel awkward about having approached me.

'So?' I said, jerking my head towards him and crossly demanding an answer.

That sealed it. He knew he needed me. It was now down to the tightening vortex that, with both of us circling around each other, would take us closer to consummation.

We did not unlock eyes as I let him take the drink from my hand. He finished off half of it. Although it was a strong gin and tonic, he drank as quickly and unflinchingly as if it were water. He offered it back to me and, speaking only with his eyes, ordered me to finish it. I splashed it in his face – I was hot with anger: who does this boy think he is? Does he really think he can … Does he really think that I would … We held each other in a stare. Without a word he took the empty glass from my hand, slowly, as if it contained nitroglycerine, and set it on the edge of the pool. The moment his fingers untouched the set-down glass my body broke into a dance, a hip-swinging all-thighs-and-breasts dance that took hold of me like I was a marionette. The music took off – and it was so terrifyingly right.

I was possessed by the dance of life as I had never known before as we wended among the dancers. And my boy, my store-clerk Casanova, was hooked to me by that invisible force, the ineradicable force that hooks two sides of the double helix together to form a new spiral with boundless hope for the future; our motions complemented and clashed like a key travelling across the pins of a lock in search of a fit.

Afterwards we leaned against the wall in a dark corner but I did not let him have me. We kissed, and in the middle of our embrace his hand clutched one of my breasts. But when his hand wandered below, and it would have been so easy to let him have it up my dress, I pushed it away. I pushed it away again. 'No,' I said. We kissed. 'No. No. No,' I said, for I did want him.

We returned to dancing and this time it was hotter, more intense. Others were leaving. The dance floor thinned according to the usual schedule as lateness advanced. But I couldn't figure out what time it was or who I was or what I was.

He bent back in a limbo move. The lights were dimmer than they had been. The dancing took a new turn as I simply squatted on his stomach, leaned over and kissed him. Our breaths crashed against each other, heavy from our dancing, my heart was pounding and I then realised his hands were inside my dress, holding the sides of my legs nearly up to my hips. The dance, that primitive public expression, had now become the private expression as we made out in a dark corner of the floor.

I felt him find the waistband of my garter belt. I – or whoever it was I had become – did not discourage him. I felt him pull at my panties. As I helped him, getting to my feet, he slipped off the satin as delicate as a spiderweb; it went easily over my white stockings and white-lace garters and over my white high-heel wedding shoes. I made it as far as a couch on the side of the dance floor. The world faded as his tongue melted into my open pussy, my rough hairs scratching against his lips.

'May I kiss the bride?' We were not alone.

'No! Don't stop,' I pleaded to my store-clerk Casanova, who looked up to see who had joined us. A mouth was immediately upon my lips kissing me.

These were the kind of men I like. The mouth on my lower lips departed – I couldn't look because I was still kissing the new stranger. And as I was about to close my legs I felt gentle hands pushing them apart – a mouth was on me there again. The same one? A new one? My store-clerk lover of ten minutes sat beside me and massaged my breasts, unzipping the back of my dress and peeling open its low-cut front.

I discovered that he was stiff and we undid his trousers. I eased him on to the floor, pulling myself away from the other two fellows. I lowered myself on to my store-clerk Casanova, easing his cock up into me.

I had just started rolling my pelvis and feeling the exploration into me when a hand lifted my white dress. I was shocked, strangely, at the idea that anyone could so crassly violate my personal space. The new man was looking under my dress at my pussy at this intimate moment.

I grabbed the new man by the necktie and stared hard into his eyes. He was neither surprised nor apologetic. I wondered if he had any manners at all. I wasn't sure if he was the one who had kissed me on the mouth just now, or down there, or if he was a new man altogether. His calm expression was chilling. He had neither good looks nor bad. The concept of 'looks' did not apply to him. His averageness intrigued me. I saw him as a generic husband figure. I couldn't remember what it was like to have a husband. He was the husband next door in the blandest, most wage-earner sense. I wanted him. The utericious urge glowed in me: I drew his face closer to mine and kissed him. While we kissed I undid his trousers. He did not resist or help.

'Let's see if you've got anything,' I said, breaking the kiss. He was erect. He stepped astride my floor boy and placed his cock in my mouth. This was the first time I had ever had two men simultaneously. Feeling their slidings in and out of me turned me on. I shut my eyes and savoured my complete pleasure: they both wanted me. I enjoyed the balancing act of keeping the pleasure alive as much as I could without letting them come. I enjoyed being wanted. I felt like an infinite womb from my mouth down to the lips of my quim, my interior a Klein bottle of pleasure. Every girl, I think, should know the luxury of two men desiring her at the same time at least once in her life, to be filled by two men at once.

What was it about that evening? Was it the sexy white 1940s evening dress? Then I felt a hand slide up my thighs, over my belly, and delve down over my pussy, which I was easing up and down over the shaft that was already in me. What kind of person takes it upon himself to massage a woman's pussy without so much as introducing himself to her? While she is busy making love to two other people no less? I was strongly mulling over what it would be like to fuck different men in rapid succession. I was about to do exactly that, perhaps three, maybe more. I opened my eyes and looked at my mystery date, all the while keeping the man in my mouth and the boy in my pussy on the twilight edge of their advancement towards their final, all too brief, joy.

The mystery man was only marginally attractive, not helped by a broken nose. But I took a liking to him when he kissed me on the temple and behind my ear, my mouth being occupied. The way he kissed me betrayed a sensitivity within him that one would not readily have guessed from his boxer's face.

I pulled his hand away from my pussy and undid his pants. His cock was stiff, not too long, not too thick. I wanted it in me. He gathered the folds of my white dress, and he and my fellatio friend pulled it over my head, which necessitated temporary interruption of the sucking. Dressless, I found myself fucking quite openly in the room and utterly naked except for my white high-heel shoes and my white stockings and garter belt. People milled around and watched, but nobody paid much attention. The New Jerseyans would have happily stared – the lure of seeing a sight such as this is why they show up – but they had all long ago gone home.

The two men lifted me off my floor fuckateur, his thick hard cock flopping out of me and slapping against his belly. There was nothing overtly commanding in the way they did this, and the boy who had just lost me, and momentarily found himself sprawled on the floor with his pussy-wetted unsatisfied cock exposed, did not complain. The men had lifted me off as a matter of suggestion, rather the way a man leads a lady from the edge of the room to the dance floor with a guiding hand. And so they led me, a hotly aroused near naked woman, over to where the props for the evening's performance art still stood.

The fat bald man was no longer on his couch on the platform; so, it would seem the performance art had finished for the evening. How ironic that a performance artist had paid an actor to slump dully on a couch – to act – for hours while my store-clerk Casanova had done the same thing for real, slumping in a chair with a bottle of beer. But my store-clerk Casanova transformed from his insouciant boredom into an erotic irresistance for me to handle at my discretion. He was the fire, and I was the fire-eater. My silent men were correct, the couch was much more comfortable than the floor. The man I had sucked, my husband of the moment, then nudged my legs aside as I lay on my back, and he entered me gently. I propped myself up to watch the head of his cock disappear into me. This is a sight I enjoy greatly, the sight of a man disappearing mysteriously into me. It is a sight I wish to see many times, with as many men as possible.

I leaned back and the cocks of the two other men, the boxer-faced one and my store-clerk Casanova, floated near my face. It was amazing, that feeling of being in strong arms. The two men held me so that I could take turns sucking them, back and forth, first one, then the next, then the first again. I was keeping them hard for when I needed them. I must say that I rather enjoy cocks. They are really rather harmless and cute when a man just stands there and lets you hold it.

My man down there came and kissed me gratefully on my lips and breasts and belly and finally my pussy before he melted away into the thinning, darkly lit club crowd. Next my store-clerk Casanova, who had lain on the floor and let me fuck him so patiently, returned to his former place inside me to finish. My boxer man propped me in his lap. We kissed each other profoundly and he massaged my breasts while my store-clerk Casanova fucked me to his heart's content, and mine, and to his completion.

Then it was my boxer friend's turn. I was about to welcome my third man in fewer than fifteen minutes.

I lay back as he kissed my toes, and when he looked up at me I knew he saw my open pussy. His foot-caressing brought me much pleasure. I was annoyed when the man spoke.

'Do you feel OK?' He was patting the outside of my knee, as if to close my legs. What was the matter with him? 'Is this better for you?' he said, putting my toes back in his mouth and trying to close my thighs and make me more ladylike.

'A girl likes to be open sometimes,' I said.

'Sorry,' he said. I lay back and thought how I had transcended myself. I felt no embarrassment at all: I was wholly me and, naked, I was as thoroughly me and as happy to be me as if I had clothes on. If the world was not so sick, none of us would care.

The man climbed over me and kissed me.

I forgave him; he was only trying to be considerate. I

am a girl with a nympho problem and he was taking advantage of me and he knew it. I appreciate that he must have known that only an unfillable unhappiness could have taken me there – and I *was* joyful then – and that I deserved his compassion, which he gave, perhaps even with genuine affection.

He kissed me and produced a condom, which I helped him put on. He turned me face down and set himself between my legs. He spent some seconds – it seemed like far longer – prying my cheeks apart and examining my asshole. I was not going to let him do *that*, but before I said something he entered my more-than-ready cunt.

The fucking was slow and magnificent. He was not the physical specimen that my early-20s store-bought Casanova – as I now thought of him – was. He was older and in less-good shape – maybe he was a boxer who had gone to pot – but at a pleasant seven inches his cock was neither astonishingly long nor too short. His body moulded to mine and was responsive to the peaks and valleys of my pleasure as we progressed on our journey together. In truth, it was more discreet that way, and this man cared about that. Anyone watching us wasn't seeing much of me, just my naked side, which they could have seen just as well at a party I once went to in an open-sided couture dress. Perhaps clubgoers watched his bare bottom swooping up and down. And maybe that was better than watching the fat bald performance-art actor do nothing for all those hours earlier in the evening.

I felt his cock run in and out of me and his balls slap the tops of my thighs. His cock was a good length and face-down was a good position, one that allowed me to massage myself as an added enhancement. But I felt the loneliness too. The man was physically skilled, but

I was just using him. I'm sure he enjoyed me. But he could not know that I was wrapped in my private thoughts and pleasures and that, as much as he thrust in and out of me, he would never really be inside me. He could not know that physically I was enjoying it more than he ever could, that, as a woman, not only could I feel more physical pleasure than him but I could love more than he could too. This is the secret of being a woman. Men suspect it. They are jealous and so they want to control us. But they cannot stop us from being who we are any more than King Canute could tell the ocean to stop throwing its waves up his shore.

I had already come a few times here and there, and here we came together. He thanked me.

'Yes, thank you,' I said, turning on to my side and watching him trying to pull the come-engorged condom off himself without making a mess. My store-clerk fuck boy emerged from the crowd holding my dress, accompanied by my fellatio husband. The three of them helped me on with my dress. My last enterer, his seven-inch cock drooping tired and heavy, insisted on holding my pussy even as my dress settled over the rest of me. He just couldn't let go, I guess. I appreciated the gesture. I eased him into a prone position on the couch; one of his arms was pressed beneath me, his hand securely gloving my pussy. His other arm wrapped over, his middle finger coming to rest on the rim of my asshole. I fell asleep.

When I awoke he was gone. I was not sure if it was ten minutes later or an hour or many hours. With the sleep deprivation I had been experiencing, one day blended into another and my natural sense of what time of day it was, and my sense of how much time had passed, were calibrated more to the surreality of dream time than the regimented objectivity of clocks. It was time to go home and rest.

14

Ten minutes after I got into the museum that morning, the phone rang. It was Jane Conch.

'It's bad,' she said. 'I could go into it over the phone, but I'd prefer that you be here. Where have you been? I've been trying to find you.'

'I guess we'd better make an appointment.'

'Yes,' said my lawyer.

'Any time is good.'

'How quickly can you get here?'

I went to the director of the department and explained that something had come up. 'Not to worry,' I told him, 'but I do have to go down to Midtown and meet with ... my attorney.'

'I know,' he said. 'I mean, I *understand*.'

The cab zoomed down the thirty blocks to Rockefeller Center in ten minutes, unusually good time for Fifth Avenue morning traffic, and cut west on 49th.

I went up to Jane's floor in the glass-and-steel tower on 6th, hovering over the RCA Building. Her expression was taut, tough, when she came out to the reception area: she was all business as she marched me down the lawyerly moulding-trimmed hallway to her office. Jane Conch was angry. And clearly she was angry at me.

'Have you been to your flat lately?' she said, sitting down behind her oversized desk and slapping a file folder open in front of her.

'No.'

'I didn't think so. I don't know how to tell you this, but there is no flat.'

'Oh my God! What happened? Was there a fire? Did David sell it off without telling me?'

'Worse. The DEA seized it.'

'The DEA?'

'The Drug Enforcement Administration. Your husband was using the place to deal heroin.'

'Surely he wasn't a professional dealer? A purchaser, yes. A user. But not ... Has he been arrested?'

'I should qualify what I said,' Ms Conch went on. 'Your husband wasn't caught in the raid, but people were dealing and the feds found enough narcotics on the premises to put your husband away for life.'

'You make it sound like they have just *taken away* the flat.'

'That's what they did, a RICO seizure.'

'A RICO seizure?'

'The DEA says your flat was being used by two or more people in a conspiracy to deal narcotics. So, they seized it, lock, stock, and barrel.'

'But *I* am not a drug dealer. They can't take *my* flat: I'm innocent.'

'The law doesn't work that way. If it comes to RICO, you have no rights.'

'I mean there has to be a trial, a conviction of a crime, due process.'

'Under RICO, a straight-out seizure *is* due process.'

'But that place is worth six million dollars, and half of it is *mine*. Half of it is *my* flat. It's got my furniture, my books, my clothes. You've got to get it back. I'm an innocent victim. I ran out in the middle of the night. I didn't know anything about this.'

'Are you sure about that?'

'Are they coming after me?'

'They'll want to question you. But as long as you're married to David they can't make you testify against him.'

'Where's David?'

'Julia, there isn't any way to sugarcoat this –'

'Is he –' Jane moved the Kleenex box closer to me.

'No one knows where he is.'

'What about –'

'Bittleby & Cranly fired him two months ago.'

'But that would mean . . .'

'I don't know where he went during the daytime, but he had already been sacked by the time you left him. It was very hard for me to determine this. By the way, Gavril, that chauffeur, is being sought for grand theft auto and heroin dealing. He stole that Rolls from the firm. Didn't you hear about this?'

'No.'

'God, the tabloids are having a field day. How can a $200,000 Rolls vanish into thin air? You and your husband's names are showing up in print daily.'

'Sorry. I never read –' I stopped mid-sentence with the realisation that my old-money colleagues at the museum never read or talked about the tabloids. For generations they and every other member of their wealthy, esteemed families had grown up as tabloid fodder, their every foible, their fender-benders, their marital spats, their dates, their bad poetry, their suicides, their yapping dogs, their flat purchases, their split pants, their getting mugged, their new hair styles, their weight gain, their weight loss, their new book contracts, their paternity suits, their bankruptcies, their snubbings, their getting snubbed, their going braless in angora sweaters – real or imagined, it all went into that undignified blend of fact and fiction, heresy and hearsay splayed in the black-and-white-and-read-all-over mediacracy know as the New York City tabloids, none of which ever found their way into the restoration department of the museum.

'You're in seclusion, by the way,' Jane went on. 'You are not to speak to anyone except me about anything. Frankly, I'm amazed that a gang of photographers isn't following you around wherever you go. Now, do you have *any idea* where David is?'

'No, not a clue.'

'Whatever liquid assets he may have had are all gone now. When the DEA went to seize your assets there was nothing. They won't comment on an ongoing investigation, but I have been told off the record by a source that the DEA's hunch is that David's still here. Right here in Manhattan. The feds have him on their list at the airport. The only question is whether he had time to get out of the country and is living it up in Brazil or someplace.'

Jane nudged the Kleenex closer to me, although I was nowhere near crying.

'Jane, I took his passport.'

Jane smiled like a million bucks.

'You did! You never told me that. When?'

'I took it the day I went back to get my Thierry Mugler suit. That was the day I first came here.'

'Why would you do a thing like that?' said Jane, still smiling.

'Spite! After all, I knew I would never be able to replace all my make-up.'

'Well, Julia, you see how healthy a little spite can be?'

'Where could he be?'

'You're guess is probably better than anyone else's.

Could he be hiding out with a friend? He's gone underground, as they say. He needs to speak with an attorney.'

Jane consulted a calendar.

'What are you doing?'

'So you took his passport that day you first met me?'

'Yes.'

'He couldn't've applied for a new passport.'

'How do you know?' I said.

'Because I now know that the feds were already closing in on him by then,' she said. 'Do you have any personal bank accounts? Brokerage accounts? Anything?'

'All joint accounts,' I said.

Jane gave me a look. It passed. 'All gone,' she said.

'So he doesn't have any money either?' I said.

'Maybe it's all offshore –' Jane cut herself off here. All was quiet. Jane lowered her voice: 'Julia, you haven't got a penny to your name that I know of.'

I was too shocked to cry. I had thought of my escape from David as merely a sojourn, that I would reassemble the shattered pieces of myself and become a whole person again, that the divorce case would plod forwards, and that I would come away with a reasonable out-of-court settlement and continue on in my life. Now, upon this news, I found myself resigned to hearing a truth that didn't surprise me at all.

My past life rippled before me like my reflection on the surface of a pond: these past weeks, as I threaded my way through the crowd at the club in my silly cigarette-girl costume selling overpriced cigarettes to the art-eccentrics, the glorious drag queens, smug overpaid junior execs in their twenties, I was always confident that I had *chosen* to be there. Sitting in Jane

Conch's office, I mulled over my options – and whether there were any.

'There could be a tax problem as well,' said Jane. 'Are you sure you can't think of the name of the accounting firm that did your returns?'

'I always assumed David did them himself. I never thought about it. He was a financial guy. I left it all in his hands.'

'Julia, to be frank, this is the most difficult case I have ever seen. I say that because I don't see a lot of hope. There are steps I can take on your behalf, but it doesn't look good. I know an excellent investigator, and I know the best forensic accountant in public practice.'

She had a pinched look of concern on her face that made me wonder if she *had* sugarcoated the truth; I wondered whether in actuality my case was completely hopeless. I had no money to pay this attorney. Investigators? Forensic accountants? They cost hundreds of dollars per hour. I fully expected that, when I walked out Jane's door that morning, she would be done with me.

'If it turns out David under-reported, the IRS will expect you to pay the back taxes and penalties if they can't find him. They could levy at any moment. The tax you owe and the penalties could be in the millions.'

'Then they can fight over my flat with the DEA.'

I stepped into the lift mentally weighing how much self-pity I should indulge in. None, because I was strong? Complete – the non-functioning basket-case approach – because I was a woman who had nothing? Oh, but what good would that do? I still had my fur coat to sell. I ruminated as the lift descended. I decided it was best to cheer up and bravely play the hand life had dealt me.

Two floors below, who should step into the lift but Jessica Kett, with a big diamond ring on her marriage finger. It was of simply vulgar proportions – as she must have known – in fact, it was night jewellery. She was dressed in a schoolmarmish grey suit. Considering she was a major real-estate broker, it was not surprising to run into her in this skyscraper in midtown Manhattan.

'Jessica Kett, how are you?' I said, amazed at the impossibly musical cheerfulness swirling out of my voice.

'Julia!' she said.

'How's that play doing?'

'I think it broke even this week. Haven't you talked to Jack Grove lately?'

'I've been so busy.'

'Yes . . .' she said, and I realised that she had read about me and David in the papers. 'I bet you have been busy. Well, you tell Jack I want to know the advance ticket sales figures. I've left messages and he doesn't call.'

Her blunt suit was a size too small, but it was cut perfectly for her and showed her formidable petite figure. I could not get the image of her peacock-feathered pussy out of my mind, with its glistening metallic blues and greens and the black tendrils of feather along the edges tossing like seaweed in a current. Her frumpy grey suit was unexpectedly sexy on her – it might have made any other woman's figure look like a stack of boxes in a storage room – and I could not help wondering whether a trimmist had worked with her to make her pussy even more spectacular than the feathered thing I'd seen. But surely one does not wear such phantasmagoria under one's skirt in a business meeting even if one *is* the type to wear night jewellery in broad daylight.

'Oh, Jessica, that's just an ...'

'If you were thinking of using the words "obscenely huge" to describe the ring Art just gave me, I would not take it amiss.'

'Good for you,' I said.

'Well, you know Art. He's committed to his theories about men and women and the free market and politics and everything else. And he's absolutely right: women run the world,' she said, hoisting her hand and looking at her wristwatch with a flourish that showed off her ring. She gave me a sly look: 'I've developed this obnoxious habit of often needing to know what time it is.' The lift door opened. 'This is my floor,' she said. 'Good to see you again.'

'Good to see you,' I said.

'Oh! Look at the time!' she said, again with the flourish of her wrist and a blinding flash of D-flawless light. She smiled – I do not believe I had ever even thought her capable of smiling – and she waved goodbye, a graceful, balletic motion of her hand and wrist, and although her ring glittered furiously in the light, I was sure she had momentarily forgotten her outrageous symbol of material wealth and was sincerely wishing me take-care-and-hope-to-see-you-again-soon.

I stepped out of Jane Conch's glass-and-steel tower and walked along the base of the dreary black and grey boxes of 6th Avenue. It was late morning and everyone cheerfully headed this way and that in a Brownian motion of pedestrians up and down and across 6th Avenue, this in a city known for its grim, tense faces. When would I ever grow? My spirit malnourished, I tried to smile and cheer myself up – no elation ignited my imagination, my equilibrium. I met with a revolt of conflicted will inside me, icy, dreary, hot with anger. Lifting my gaze skywards, what balking bleakness 6th Avenue was, what hideous, haughty glass-box buildings these were, each taller and more emotionally draining than the next, empty-looking, uninspired.

I turned towards 5th Avenue when I got to the famed Fifty-Seventh and felt what it meant not to be a fantastic wife. I, unmoored, strolled Fifty-Seventh aimlessly. I drifted as purposelessly as a dandelion seed carried on a current of air and came to rest at the intersection of Bulgari, Bergdorf's, Tiffany's and the Manufacturer's Hanover Trust Co. The fantastic, chatting, smiling fleet of wigged wives was already out and about ploughing Fifty-Seventh, trawling for dresses and jewellery. The shopping women passing me were laughing too much and carrying too many pretty shopping bags with colourful boxes inside and tufts of tissue paper poking up, and their make-up was so thick you could not see through to their real skin – they were a waxworks on the move. Is this what I was to have become? A blessing in disguise, maybe, had put me out on the street in this way.

Zoë did not know the true extent of my losses. She must have wondered at me and my failure to take all measures necessary for self-preservation – I was not superstitious enough, not greedy enough, too trusting, of course, of the man I loved. At least Zoë had never berated me for how I had handled my financial security my own way. I couldn't face the museum now. Hail a cab? Carry on with the pretence of having money. I got into a cab with a dented front fender – never an encouraging sign.

Immersed in thoughts of poverty, I began to feel I had always been poor. As these thoughts took hold of me, and my perspective shifted, I thought of what an unjustifiable luxury it was to take a cab, thinking to myself, So this is what it's like to be able to afford to ride in cabs, and went Downtown.

I knew that I had to be my own person at all costs – my choices had already cost me everything. I had always wanted to stand on my own two feet, and now I would. My last hope was to sell off my fur coat and keep Jane Conch and her investigators on my case. On Friday I had an appointment to discuss my coat with my furrier. Selling it could raise about $150,000, which I knew all too well would probably run out before Jane could find David, who was either a penniless addict on the run or living it up in a tropical tax haven.

15

The old cab halted lumpily on the cobblestone street
before the Groves' loft, brakes shrieking. Police cars
outside, their lights flashing bright and excited: this
was a common sight in New York and so it did not send
me into a panic or even arouse my interest as it might
a more naïve person living in a quieter city. Ah, to live
in such protected naïveté, to be shocked and stunned at
crimes committed against ordinary citizens. I hoped
someday I could be that secure, to expect the world to
run rationally, according to normal expectations. But
for now I was a resident of the Lower East Side of
Manhattan. I paid the cabbie and went into the
building.

On the fifth floor my heart sank. Something was
going on in Jack and Zoë's flat, the police had cordoned
off the hall. Vivienne and Arthur Li stood in their front
door talking with police.

'What happened?' I said.

'They've been robbed,' said Vivienne.

Zoë was in tears. She saw me. The police were
dusting for fingerprints. Dusting for fingerprints at a
break-in scene was very unusual in New York. I heard
voices on radios as cops milled around; men in trench
coats took notes about the scene.

'Oh, God,' said Zoë, running to me and throwing her
arms around me. 'We've been cleaned out; they stole
everything.'

The police let me through their cordon. I looked at

the blank, art-gallery white walls in the Groves' flat: the Pop Art had vanished.

'They got the lot,' said Jack, 'sometime after we went out this morning. Don't know how far they think they can go. They are original works in well-known series. Who do they think they can fence these to?'

'Oh, they all look the same,' wailed Zoë. 'Who's going to know one pink Marilyn Monroe from another?'

'Obviously they will not show up at Christie's,' said Jack.

'They got your fur coat too,' said Zoë. 'Gone, gone, all forever gone.'

'The art is insured,' said Jack.

'Oh that's just wonderful, fucking wonderful,' said Zoë. 'Julia's fur wasn't insured. Our umbrella policy isn't going to cover it. I knew we should've put it back in cold storage.'

'Oh, God, this is going to be in the tabloids,' said Jack.

Down at the precinct we all answered questions. Because the theft was in the millions, the police launched a major investigation. The Groves would not be able to stay the night at their loft, not until the detectives were through examining the crime scene. The FBI had been called in. The police spoke evasively and were eager to separate me from the Groves. Why would the FBI be called in on a straightforward domestic burglary?

'Do you think it was drug addicts?' said Zoë.

'Could be,' said a detective. 'Except drug addicts don't usually bring a moving truck.'

We explained to the police that I had been a houseguest but had recently moved out. Oh, really? they said. They wanted to talk to me in a separate room.

'You're treating her like a suspect,' said Zoë. 'Do you

have any idea who she is? Do you realise that she handles millions of dollars' worth of art every day? You need to hunt down those caterers.'

Zoë's comment about my handling of art caused the poker-faced detective's eyes to widen. I wished Zoë hadn't said that.

I had already seen my world dissolve into nothing that day and, as I was ushered down the hall to a grey, windowless interrogation room, I had a nagging feeling that things were about to get worse. I demanded the right to call Jane Conch. The police wouldn't let me, and they wouldn't let me see Zoë and Jack again.

I was questioned till dawn about David and Gavril and what I knew about the Groves having been robbed. But I didn't know anything about any of that, which made the police angry and impatient. They rotated interrogators, who shouted and swore and smoked cigarettes. Time stretched and condensed in the windowless room as I felt my very me squeezed and sucked in the accordion bellows of their questions. They asked me questions – the same questions over and over again – for twenty hours. 'Tell us exactly what happened when you got back from the party the night the play opened,' they said.

Oh, God! How could I tell them? This just made me all the more guilty in their eyes.

'We were tired. We went to sleep.'

'Your play opens on Broadway and you just go to bed?'

'Yes.'

'So this guy Warhol's a big deal or something!'

'Yes,' I said, so tired I could not see straight. 'Warhol is a big deal.' What did the police expect to find out by asking me this?

'Where's the shit at, Julia? Where's your husband?'

They wanted to know every detail about what I did last night.

'Who did you see last night?'

'I was *here* last night.'

'Cut the crap, Julia. We know all about you.'

Because I was not under arrest, my Miranda rights hadn't been read to me and my lawyer was not allowed to be present during questioning. Finally Jane Conch got me out. It was almost noon.

'Taxi! Taxi!' commanded a resonant voice as we stepped out into the late-afternoon sun and stood at the top of the precinct stairs. Strobes went off before me in a hideous popping quilt of light like the dendritic flashes that course through one's retina immediately before one is about to faint, and the glare of television lights pressed upon my skin. Zoë and Jack were right there by my side, along with Jane Conch.

Jane scanned the street for her driver. 'Where the fuck is that car?' she muttered.

Zoë pushed ahead of me through the crowd of reporters towards the sound of the familiar deep tones. Jack was imprisoned within a picket fence of microphones.

'Carlton!'

'Zoë!'

Zoë laughed at him. He opened the door of the waiting taxi.

'Carlton, dear, what the hell is that getup you've got on?'

For a moment he looked genuinely hurt.

'Oh this?' he said. 'These are my golf clothes. I came straight from the course as soon as I heard the news.'

'Never mind that,' said Jane, shoving me and Carlton into the cab. Carlton ended up in the middle. 'Uptown!' Jane shouted at the driver.

'Where Uptown?' said the driver.

'Never mind where, just get moving. And step on it!'

With a squeal and a lurch we were off. I realised we'd left Zoë standing on the sidewalk.

'I don't know that *I* would tell a New York cabbie to step on it,' said Carlton.

'Who the hell are you? You know my client?'

'Dr Carlton Westergaarde. Who the hell are you?'

'You're not a heroin dealer or art thief, are you?'

'Gastroenterologist.'

'Jane Conch.' She held out her hand and shook Carlton's vigorously. 'How do you know Julia?'

'I've known Carlton for years,' I interjected.

Jane looked through the rear window. 'Shit,' she said.

I looked: a gang of paparazzi was in pursuit on motorcycles.

'Don't look!' said Jane, pulling my face around.

We rode in silence. 'Boy has this been a long day,' I said, finally.

'You and I have to talk,' said Jane. 'But right now, we've got to hide you.'

The summer sunset over Carlton's house in Connecticut tied up the sky in yellow ribbons. Carlton had spirited me away to his place, a big old house surrounded by hedges and lawns and tall trees, eluding the press. I had to get out of the city. I had to survive. The contrast I felt in Carlton's quaint town, compared with what I had fled, was a glorious shock to my system: the peace sent a wave of repose through me. I wanted to run free as the wind, tossing back my hair and laughing idiotically. When shall I ever be who I must have been meant to have been? I stood on Carlton's back porch, resting my hands on the old wooden railing and looked at his grassy back yard sloping gently away to a stand of trees. An evening breeze cooled my face and in its leisurely wafting took away time and the terror.

Inside, in his kitchen, Carlton was cooking dinner; the oven had been preheating. I offered to help.

'You could chop this and put it in this mortar,' he said, indicating sprigs of fresh parsley, chives, rosemary, thyme and sage. 'Then really mash it with this lump of butter.'

While I did that, Carlton took a pot of water out of his fridge. There were two Cornish hens in it: 'I always suggest brining Cornish hens for two hours minimum. It really gives them a fresh flavour. I don't expect you to do the messy part.'

He patted the birds dry and inserted my butter mixture under the skin of their breasts.

Out of the fridge he took the bowl of stuffing I had watched him make earlier. 'This stuffing with currants, pistachios and apricots is one of my favourites,' he said. After stuffing them, Carlton trussed the birds quickly and expertly, and rubbed them with salt and pepper.

'The oven's ready,' he said. He rubbed the birds with oil and then with dried sage. He put them in a roasting pan and then into his oven. 'In about ten minutes I'll glaze them.'

He turned up the heat under a pot. 'How does wild rice with cranberries and toasted almonds sound?' he said.

'You cook more than I do.'

'I think simply sautéing the cocozelle in sesame oil.'

Carlton gave me two new beeswax candles and sent me to find two pewter candleholders and a box of matches in an antique wooden cupboard in his dining room. I pushed the candles into the holders and set them on Carlton's old wooden table. I lit the candles, and Carlton turned out the dining-room lights. We carried the serving dishes out of the kitchen and set them on the table. Carlton turned out the lights in the kitchen and shut the door. Wisps of steam rising from each dish caught in the rays of candlelight, the melodious scent of a well-cooked simple meal.

'It's an eighteenth-century house,' Carlton said. 'I like to do away with all the technology I can, sometimes, to get back to the original era of this house, even if it's only for a meal. Those candleholders are actually pre-Revolutionary. Everything you can see from where you're sitting is either an antique from the era or a replica.'

'What beautiful silence this is,' I said. I thought of the worlds in the eighteenth-century American paintings that I knew so well. I noticed that Carlton was not wearing his watch.

'We're far enough in from the road that we won't hear traffic.'

'If you told me that I am in my right century and that the twenty-first was just something horrible I dreamed, I would believe you.'

Although I had hardly slept for two or three days – the days had blurred into one – my fatigue fell away from me. I felt happy having dinner with Carlton. We talked about ordinary things. He told me about the local history, the Post Road, the Indians.

After dinner we sat in wooden recliners in Carlton's back yard. Above us, the sheer blue of the fading sunset sky. We had talked enough. Carlton's words over dinner settled in me.

I leaned back in my chair and looked up at the trees. There was nary a human sound from here to the ends of the earth, just a carpet of cricket chirps and the tap, I thought, of a woodpecker. There were no sirens, no shrieking taxi brakes, no straining bus engines ... I could hear my hair against my cheek when I moved. And when I lay motionless I could hear the faint whisper of the trees when the wind licked their leaves. I looked at their branches reaching into the darkening evening sky, an upthrust constellation of sticks, growing for decades unmolested by war or financial panic or any other human concern, heavy with leaves, the stars swimming among their green edges a trillion miles away. This was a peaceful evening indeed.

'Today is the day that I know I have lost everything,' I told Carlton. 'I feel happy now. I know I will always look back on this and remember how truly happy I feel in this moment.'

I fell asleep.

16

I awoke to find myself in an antique wooden bed in a cosy corner bedroom. Sunlight poured into a window by the head of my bed, and to the side there was another window through which I could see the back yard below, with its stand of trees at the end. The windows were open, and I could smell clean Connecticut air drifting through the room. I had no idea how I had got here. It was daylight outside, but I did not know if it was morning or afternoon – and from my surroundings I could not even tell what century it was. I felt safe. The world was quiet, and I thought how fine it would be to just stay right here. I was wearing a simple cotton nightgown, very old-fashioned looking, and I wondered if Carlton had dressed me in it last night. I heard the door swing open.

'You're awake,' said Carlton.

'Good morning,' I said. 'Or good afternoon.'

'Good morning,' said Carlton, setting down a silver tray on an old wooden table by my bed.

I could smell freshly brewed Earl Grey tea.

'How did you know I would be waking up just now?' I said.

'I didn't know,' said Carlton. 'Except somehow I felt I should brew some tea for you and bring it. And here we are.'

'Carlton, how did I get into this nightgown?'

'I carried you up here last night. But you were awake when I gave you this nightgown. You don't remember?'

'I don't remember anything. I'm just happy to be here.'

He half turned to go. 'Do you need me to leave you with your peace and quiet?'

'I need you to stay here with me.'

He pulled a chair away from an old wooden writing desk and set it near me. 'I can make you a full breakfast,' he said, taking a seat. 'Anything you want.'

'You do a lot of cooking.'

'I do.'

I knew I had to ask him . . .

'This tea is perfect. I am perfectly happy.' I sipped the tea and felt very much at peace. All the world had to do was leave me alone and I was restored. It was that simple. 'The calm before the storm,' I said.

'Let's hope it's the calm after the storm,' Carlton said. 'You've been through quite a storm.'

'I don't see how it could get any worse,' I said, taking another sip of the still, perfect tea. I felt relieved – and this is perverse – that there was no way for my situation to get worse. Hitting bottom wasn't so bad if it meant sipping Earl Grey tea in a cosy bed on a sunny morning.

'Who's looking for me?' I said.

'Don't worry, they can't find you,' Carlton said.

'If anyone wants something from me, there's nothing left. Not even a pronoun.'

'Julia,' intoned Carlton in that voice that I had grown quite fond of, 'there is everything left.'

I knew there was no escape, not really. The police were after me – albeit wrongly – and the press, shrill and irrelevant as always, was pleased to wallow in the destruction it reported.

'I, who have lost everything, am the one under suspicion by the police.'

'Julia, you are innocent.'

'But how can I prove I'm innocent if I haven't done anything? What did I ever do to deserve all this?'

'You have never done anything to bring this on yourself.'

'I walked out on my husband, and I have suffered endless misfortune from that moment on. If I had just stayed with him like a good girl – like I promised I would when we married – none of this would have happened.'

'Julia, I am sure everyone around you wants to see your life turn right again. *I* do. Whether you stay with your husband – or if you must separate – there is an answer, a right answer. All will be right again.'

I thought of all the crazy sex I'd had, trying to lose myself, trying to gain myself. I wanted to confess all to Carlton, dear Carlton – and I wanted to be forgiven, and accepted.

'Carlton, I'm not the saint you think I am. There are things about me that I ... I suppose if you knew the real me, you would hate me. There are things about me that might even hurt you. I don't want to hurt you. Especially not you.'

'Do you suppose there is anything you could tell me that would hurt me?'

'I – I don't know.'

'Of course there is,' he said.

'I believe that I could hurt you; and I would feel immensely sad to know that I ever did.'

'Julia, you can only hurt the people who truly love you. That's the way life is. There is no limit to the pain you can cause, because no matter how much it hurts them, they still love you. Try not to hurt the people who love you. But if you do, remember that they still love you.'

'I can't stand the thought of causing anyone pain. I have suffered. No one else should.'

'Julia' – he took my hand – 'everyone needs to be loved. The pain might be the strongest feeling, but that is the least important part of it. You might try to run away from love, but you would only be running away from life. You are loved, Julia, and there's nothing you can do to change that.'

'Intellectually, I know what you mean,' I said. 'Love is the sort of thing people can feel for you and you don't feel loved at all.'

'I hope you work things out with your husband. I hope he's all right and that the two of you will return to each other and be happy for the rest of your lives.'

'Carlton...' My voice sounded a hundred times louder to me than it was. I knew what I was going to ask him and I was filled with foreboding and regret. 'What happened to Marion?'

'My life will never be complete,' said Carlton. He took an audible breath and held it while his eyes fixed on a nonexistent point in space. Then he returned to me, as if from a distant journey, and spoke: 'Marion was shot dead by a mugger in Downtown Manhattan. We had left the Groves' loft and walked to the corner to hail a taxi. The young man demanded our money, and we gave it to him immediately. He turned to walk away, he took two steps, and then he glanced back at us over his shoulder and shot, and then ran. Please – I will finish the story. Marion fell to the pavement. She could not speak. We looked into each other's eyes, and in that moment she died.'

'I'm –' my voice vanished into a quavering whisper as I trailed off to say '– so sorry to hear that.'

'They never caught a suspect. For the past two years I assumed that I could never be happy again. But from time to time I am happy. But I also know that if I live to be a hundred I will not have lived a complete life. I know that even if I fall in love again and remarry and become the happiest man in the world, a part of me will always be missing.'

'Why didn't Jack and Zoë tell me?'

'I understand them. I know they feel guilt. Obviously it wasn't their fault: they know it wasn't their fault, but they haven't learned how to deal with what happened. I should sit down and talk with them – I wasn't able to before.'

I spent a lovely day with Carlton. We decided to go for a walk. I was afraid someone would see me. Carlton gave me a wide-brimmed straw hat to wear that I pulled down to my eyebrows. He gave me a long cotton dress that had belonged to Marion. He said he did not remember seeing her wear this one – perhaps she had not, in fact. 'Otherwise,' Carlton said, 'I would probably burst into tears if I saw you in something I remembered as hers.'

When I put it on I found it still had its price tag.

Carlton filled a picnic basket, and we set off late that morning.

It was a sunny, warm day. We walked to a brook in the woods and followed it to a farm, where the air was filled with the smell of new-mown hay. Carlton gave me his hand to help me balance as I followed him over an uneven row of stepping-stones across the brook.

We cut through an abandoned, overgrown apple orchard. Apples still grew, untended, and some had fallen to the ground – it had been years since I'd encountered that pastoral smell of fermenting wind-falls. In the middle of the abandoned orchard was a well-looked-after apiary.

We settled on a slab of rock to have our picnic.

'Just a simple cold lunch,' said Carlton.

He took out two paper plates and plastic forks and knives held in a bunch by a rubber band. Then Carlton unwrapped honeydew melon slices and put two on my plate.

'Do you like iced tea?'

'Mmm.'

Next he took the foil off a plastic container of cold fried chicken.

'I don't think you could have come up with anything more simple or more perfect,' I said.

He opened a bag of Lay's potato chips and a tub of store-bought dip.

'You are a brilliant chef!'

'I thought about bringing moulded Scottish salmon with layers of cream cheese, Carolina trout roe, American sturgeon and Russian Oscietre.'

'Of course you could have done that,' I said, watching as he opened a tub of cut, raw cauliflower. I pushed a floret into the surface of the dip. 'But it takes guts to zig when a more conventional person would zag. Sometimes it takes someone with sophisticated taste to realise that cold fried chicken is just the thing to hit the spot.'

For dessert Carlton had brought tins of chocolate pudding. We pulled off their aluminium lids and went at the stuff with plastic spoons. I hadn't had a tin of pudding since sixth grade.

Carlton decided to lead me back along another route, along rusty train tracks. It was sunny and warm and I was as good as lost. No one in the world except Carlton knew where I was – *I* didn't know where I was. I picked up a stick and dragged it along the rocks of the railroad bed. The rusty old tracks disappeared into overgrown trees ahead. I daydreamed, wondering how many years ago the tracks had been abandoned. I felt like I could keep walking along this way forever. Terror seized me: I was alone! I turned: Carlton was right there by my side.

'For a moment I thought I'd lost you,' I said, embarrassed at my silliness.

'You won't lose me that easily.'

'I'm glad.'

We stopped at a tapestry of robustly growing wild blackberry vines that ran up and all over an old, broken fence. Carlton took paper sacks out of his picnic basket and we filled them with two or three pounds of ripe blackberries for a pie.

'I don't play golf all the time,' he said. 'And the truth is, the doctors I golf with aren't really my type.'

'Can I help you make the pie?'

Back at his house Carlton said I could roll out the dough and place it in the pie tin.

'I haven't done anything like that since I was a little girl.'

'Let's not wait to chill the dough,' he said, working shortening into the flour with his fingers.

'You're making the dough from scratch?'

'It's only four ingredients, Julia. I think I can handle it. On second thoughts, let's chill it a little,' Carlton said.

While the dough chilled – and I'm not sure why he chilled it – we hulled four cups of the blackberries.

Carlton started the oven preheating. He ate a blackberry and said, 'There's always guesswork, but let's go with a whole cup of sugar.' He sprinkled in a couple of teaspoons of tapioca as well. He set the mixture aside and gave me the ball of dough out of the refrigerator.

I tore the ball in two and set to work on my bottom crust.

'Remember, roll from the centre out. You don't want to stretch the dough,' Carlton said.

With the pie baking, we sat down in Carlton's living room, which was lined with books. A television stood in the corner. I looked at its army-green dead eye.

'What time does the news come on?' I said.

'Julia, you won't want to watch it.'

'They'll have something about me, won't they?'

'I guess you don't watch television very often.'

I looked at the turned-off set and then back at my host.

He continued. 'You are at the centre of the biggest scandal to hit New York since ... It's a big one. It's a miracle the tabloids didn't track you down at the museum.'

'They probably never imagined that the wife of a wealthy stockbroker has a quiet, anonymous job.'

'Of all the people you could hide out with, I'm glad you chose me.'

'No, Carlton. I am the one who is glad. All I did today is have a picnic and pick berries with you. And bake a pie. I might be poor, and I might end up in jail, but I will always remember this as one of the happiest days I ever lived.'

'Julia ... the idea that I could ... for the past two years I have felt like I could never make anyone happy.'

'Don't say never, Carlton. You made me happy. I feel like a human being again.' He sat there quietly, my words, I hoped, healing the rents within him. I wanted Carlton to be happy.

'You used to go on that walk with Marion,' I said.

'Strangely, no. She was a city girl. She'd much rather go hear the Vienna Philharmonic at Carnegie Hall than hike in the woods. Marion always liked the peace out here, but I didn't start exploring until after I lost her. My grief took me on a lot of long walks, trying to make sense of this world. You're the first person I've shown my wild blackberries to.'

The television dutifully waited for us to ask it to disrupt our peace. I wondered if the police had made any breakthroughs in the Groves' robbery.

'The news doesn't have stories about my scandal every day, does it?'

'Every day.'

'You watch the news every day?'

'When I have time.'

'What do you suppose they're saying about this mess today?'

'I don't know. But I do know that the whole city is looking for David, a $200,000 Rolls-Royce – and the same clip of you and David attending a cancer fund-raiser gets shown over and over. No doubt they're now using tape of you on those precinct steps yesterday.'

'If I'm being talked about, I want to know what it is.' I stood up and turned on Carlton's television; it must have been twenty years old – it didn't have a remote control.

When the television warmed up the first words I could make out were as an arrow to my heart: 'A shocking new twist in the scandal that has rocked Wall Street and the upper crust of New York . . .' I watched breathless as Tristano's face filled the screen and in his ignorant broken grammar he went on to describe the shoot at Janice's studio, freely larding his tale with lies that were self-aggrandising for him and wildly slanderous of me.

'Are you sure you don't want to stay with me?' Carlton pleaded.

I had to get back to the city. I had to plead with Janice not to destroy the only thing left in my life: what would happen to Carlton if he saw me in those pictures, if he thought that what Tristano was telling the reporters on the news was true?

17

I took the straw hat Carlton had lent me for our walk, put on a pair of Marion's sunglasses, and rode the train to New York that afternoon.

I should have known that my moment of peace would be just that, a moment – you can hide, but you cannot run: no matter how far I tried to run I could not escape the forces tearing away at my life like piranhas biting flesh off a corpse.

Carlton begged me not to go, and he was enough of a gentleman not to point out what we both knew: I was taking a foolish risk. It pained me that I could not tell Carlton why. We had watched the news broadcast in which 'Tristano' – his real name was Walter Caswell – had said he had been in a photo shoot with me.

Tristano said that he had been in a hardcore shoot with me for hours in Janice's studio. The TV station inserted bleeps here and there as Tristano talked: 'Hey, I'm not calling her a slut – she's a real nice chick – but we was *beeeep* all day long. And after the shoot we went out an' got high an' we was at it all night at her place. I never seen nuthin' like it.'

The news reporter kept referring to this as his exclusive story, as did reporters on other channels reporting the same story and who had also conducted interviews with Mr Caswell. The reporter stressed that Janice could not be reached for comment and that Tristano had no proof of his allegations. The gallery that represented

Janice's serious work said they knew nothing of what Tristano was talking about. The gallery would not permit Janice's work to be shown on television.

The reporter had – irrelevantly – reached Jane Conch, who refused to comment. As we stepped out of Carlton's house we heard his phone ring. I was sure it was Jane. I told Carlton to please, please just take me to the station so I wouldn't miss my train.

I stared out the window all the way back to New York. The news had shown censored footage of Tristano in a gay male porn video. Tristano insisted he was straight – married, in fact – and that he only acted in gay porn to make a living.

Hugh Flint, the famous and wealthy pornography magnate, said he knew Janice and had offered her $1 million for the pictures – if they existed – which he would publish in his magazine.

I didn't know what Carlton thought of the news, whether he thought it was true or as absurd as the police theory that I had organised the heist of the Groves' art. I had thought about flipping off the TV and laughingly saying, 'What'll they think up next! It must be a slow news day' – but I knew those pictures could surface at any moment.

'Do you have to go back?' he said as I went out to the hallway and picked up Marion's straw hat from where it lay on a side table. Carlton knew, even as he asked, that it was futile to try to stop me.

'I can't tell you why.'

'Julia, please. You're shaking.'

'I must go.'

'You're hands are ice cold. Julia –'

'I must go.'

'Can you really fix anything? Can you really change anything?'

'I don't know, but there is someone I must speak to.' My whole body was shaking and I felt sick.

Carlton was wounded.

'I'll drive you into the city,' he said.

'Please understand that I can't explain anything to you now – never – not even to you. I wonder what you're thinking after that news story. It's not like what they said on the news.'

'I understand.'

'I know you don't understand. What I'm doing right now can only appear to be senseless and stupid.'

'Julia, that's what I understand. I know you have strong reasons or you wouldn't do this – and I accept that you have private reasons why you can't tell me what is going on.'

'I need to go to the city alone. The train will take me there.'

'You know that I would do anything to help you. And you know that my home is always open to you as a refuge.'

'I know, Carlton. I only want to be here now, *with you*. Except I can't.'

'I will drive you to the station.'

I hugged him as tight as I could in hopes that my fear would go away. 'Please promise that you'll let me come back.' I wanted to stay in his arms for five minutes, for five years, whatever it took till my body stopped shaking and the blood frozen in my veins thawed.

'Whatever thoughts are going on in that head of yours, whatever it is you think you need to rush back to the city for, you are always welcome back here.'

* * *

As soon as the train pulled into Grand Central I flew down the stairs and caught an IRT Downtown to the Bleecker Street station.

When I got up the stairs to Bleecker I immediately realised that I was about walk into a murder of press cawing about the entrance to Janice's building and waiting to descend on me as I approached.

But Cooper Square was deserted. I went straight to Janice's loft, on the top floor.

On Janice's floor the hall light flicked on and off, making a *tink-tink* sound as it did.

There was no answer to Janice's buzzer. The sound died away. I imagined the huge empty space and the wretched buzz vibrating off the empty wooden floor and stony brick walls until the empty air itself absorbed the vibrations. Not one sound in response.

I pounded on the door: 'Janice, it's me, Julia! Please let me in. Please!'

I slumped to the floor and let my head droop down upon my knees. It was too late. Those pictures were probably rolling on a press in the Midwest this very moment and Janice had a million dollars. Conservative, old-fashioned Carlton would never want a shameless whore like me to cross his threshold again, not even if I was so filled with shame that I had no room left in my body to draw breath. To think that I threw it all away because I needed a quick $1,700; that anyone who had fallen as far as me had been so close to holding the key to happiness, only to drop it down a sewer grate.

I heard the dead bolt on that thick steel door draw back. Janice looked down at me through the space of her open door.

'Janice,' I said.

'Come in, Julia.' Her lips hardly moved when she

uttered the words and her voice was so hollow I wondered if I had only imagined she had spoken.

Janice wore no make-up, and her face was drained of
colour and emotion; her will to live had fled, as I saw
in her every movement and even the way she breathed
as she led me into her loft. All the lights were out, and
the natural light of late afternoon filtered in – but lent
no vitality to – the interior of the old loft space. Janice
walked like an old woman with osteoporosis.

'How did you get through the press? Did they finally
go away?'

'Janice . . .'

'I know why you're here.'

'Janice, I have a chance to live a life again.'

She gave me a world-weary, defeated look. Then,
'Some tea? Some coffee?' she said.

From the tone of her voice I knew it was too late.

'If there is *anything* I can do . . .'

'I want to show you something,' she said. She led me
to a bright corner of her loft where she had hung a
framed black-and-white portrait of a young woman – a
portrait of me.

We stood before it in contemplative silence.

I was bare breasted in the portrait. As I stood looking
into the black-and-white field, my thought tremoloed
back and forth between me looking at a portrait of
myself and the feeling of looking at someone else, a
stranger, from an unknown country, from an unknown
time. Looking at that stranger, I saw a woman who
radiated feminine grace and beauty and strength. She
did not look like she had been caught in an instant, the
mere sliver of time it took the shutter to open and drink
in enough of her light to capture an image. Rather,
there was an eagerness, an open-endedness to the time
in the photo, as if she would turn to me and speak.

Janice had taken this picture without my knowing it, and it had been taken before the make-up was applied to me for the shoot that day.

In the portrait she – me – looks not directly into the camera; a brush stroke of light runs from her shoulder down her arm. There is a naturalness in how she carries herself. She is a woman who is deeply respected – not an aloof, off-putting, formal dignity; she embodies the kind of respect that is inherent in woman after 100,000 generations. Perhaps Gauguin had caught this gene-deep heritage on canvas once or twice in his portraits of Tahitian women, when he served not as an artist or an interpreter of the world but as a medium to set down in oil-on-canvas a feminine quality that he could not have consciously captured or understood if he tried, a quality in woman as old as consciousness in our species.

'How could I ever betray *her*?' said Janice. 'What good would a million dollars do me if I had to live with myself knowing what I had done to her?'

'Thank you, Janice.'

'There is no thanking to be done ... All the other negatives have been destroyed ... May I exhibit this in my show?'

'Yes.'

But there was more. Janice had lost all will to live. 'Janice, what happened to you?'

'Julia, something terrible has happened. You must help me. Lata is missing. It hasn't been twenty-four hours yet, so the police won't take my report and look for her. But I know something terrible must have happened. I've known Lata for six years. When she said she would come by last night and didn't, I knew something was wrong. I went to her flat and there was no answer. I tried the club, her favourite coffee shop, I asked at her favourite vintage clothing store. I went to her ex-boyfriend.'

'Lata is a free spirit. Maybe she found a new boy-friend or something.'

'I truly hope so, but I know it is not so. She didn't do one-night stands; if she had a boyfriend, she would have told me. She told me everything. She didn't do drugs. She told me she was coming over to model some clothes for me that were funky but chic and she wanted me to take her picture. We did this a lot, Julia, and she would not have missed coming here for anything.'

I got no answer went I knocked on Lata's flat door. I stopped by my flat to change into black club garb and shoes for walking. I went to the club to search for her.

A customer at the club told me he knew Lata and that she would be at a party tonight; in fact, he was on his way there. I went with him; he was a perfect stranger, and he did not betray any recognition that I was part of a major ongoing scandal in this city. We walked past my street, Dresden Street, and I saw anew how desperate and desolate this area is; I had lived in these square miles of squalor long enough that the dirt, danger and ever-hovering evil had become just another part of my everyday life, invisible to me. Not now.

Urgency seized me. I needed to bring Lata out of this world, this dark-eyed beauty who trusted me and who had needed me that night she slept in my arms. She needed me now. I didn't know what to do. I would ask Carlton's help. 'Please help me rescue this girl,' I would say. 'Let's get her out of this nasty, brutish city and help her find the normal happiness she and anyone deserves, a normal job, a normal night's sleep.' I felt the moments slipping away with every step I took.

The party was in a couple's flat, which had once been a store. The couple's living-room window was a shop window. Their party in the shop window – surely they closed their curtains sometimes? – had a performance-art feel that made the party inauthentic as a party and appear, rather, as a clumsy portrayal, lacking in crucial details and given to unexplained abrupt transitions. The vision of them through the glass played out with the silence that grips a fishbowl, peculiar in that surely there was music inside whose beat should be pulsing through to us on the outside. The partygoers were as translucent and self-absorbed as seahorses in an aquarium. I wished Carlton was with me to protect me, but I couldn't risk his finding out that I had worked at the club.

We got buzzed in. The narrow hallway smelled of piss, ammonia, smoke and mouldy beer, and was filled with the sound of muffled music and excited voices. There was a film of laughter, occasionally pierced by women's shrieks, that billowed upon a tumbling sea of male voices. At these happy sounds, before their flat door opened – for the sounds reverberating through the hall were happy – I knew I did not belong. If Lata was here, I would know she was OK. That's all that mattered, and I would take her back with me.

Everyone was happy at the crowded party. A woman carrying a martini in each hand jostled me as I entered. She laughed drunkenly and then offered me one. 'Sorry,' she said. 'I don't need two.' She was thin – her hipless, bosomless figure was tubelike – and she wore a long, tight black velvet dress. I took the offered martini and then wished I hadn't. Her long red hair was clamped in an antique barrette from the 1920s. She was tall and tottered clumsily away from me into the crowd that filled the tiny hole of a flat, a flash of her red barretted hair disappearing between the closing black-clad shoulders of the crowd.

Everyone was chatting. People chatted with people they knew. I tried to figure out who these people were. Sitting over by a fireplace, the small utilitarian kind where coal – not wood – was burned by the shopkeeper as the only source of heat for the room in the late nineteenth century, a boyfriend hovered over his girl-friend, smothering her with kisses on random parts of her face and her long light-brown hair, which fell over her face. When she brushed away her hair she revealed a blank, innocent-looking face. She looked no more than thirteen years old, but when I got closer and heard her voice it was clear she was a mature woman, in spirit and actual years if not looks, more mature than her boyfriend, who made her weary with his love and kisses and needs.

My date fell into a conversation with someone he knew, not introducing me to him. I had the distinct sense that I was merely being shown off. 'Did Lata say she would be here?' I said.

My date shrugged.

I really wasn't interested in my sudden martini. I made my way through the crowd to find Lata, and a flat surface – I abandoned my drink. With each step I took through the happy heads guffawing their youth away I felt more fatigued and out of place, as though I neared the end of a long, exhausting odyssey. The very thought of consuming one drink and expending energy in the sort of tipsy inanity that surrounded me made me all the tireder. The crowd was distinctly young, almost everyone under 25. I slinked my way through the crowd to the only other room in the flat, a tiny bedroom in the back.

The couple that lived here, a couple of room-mates, were members of a band. In the bedroom, electric guitars hung from the simple picture moulding that rimmed the walls near the ceiling. An electric keyboard rested on a stand at the foot of the bed. Instrument travelling cases were piled up against one wall and people sat on them. The tile of a defunct, sealed-up fireplace was painted white along with the rest of the wall, the most recent of several decades' worth of coats of paint that now looked to be as thick as cake frosting.

A woman complained that she couldn't get photography jobs – the photo editors at magazines wouldn't even look at her book. 'It's all who you know,' she told the women clustered up to her. 'They all just hire their friends.' I thought of Janice turning down a million dollars – and who would never have let my portrait see the light of day if I had asked her to keep it secret.

Leaning against the wall a middle-aged man, surely 20 years my senior, with greying and thinning hair announced to the circle around him that he could put out a cigarette on his tongue. A cigarette was produced immediately and the man confidently accepted it, with his smile lasting too long. He took a swig of his beer and paused uncomfortably, like a shoplifter who had just been caught stealing something he had enough money on him to buy. He turned towards the wall for a moment and turned back, with his lips holding the cigarette backwards, burning end in his mouth. He delicately pinched the cigarette at the filter end and lifted it out: it was extinguished, and quite soggy. The man smiled proudly, a forced smile, nervous and stitched with insecurity.

'Oh fuck that shit,' a young man with deep-set brown eyes announced. 'Let's see you fucking do this –'

whereupon the young man pushed up the sleeve of his studded leather jacket and stubbed his cigarette out on his bare forearm. Without even looking at the middle-aged man to see what kind of effect this stunt had had, the young man downed the rest of his drink and threw his glass full force into the defunct fireplace and marched out of the room, his heavy leather boots grinding shards of glass into the wooden floor and shredding the varnished surface.

I'd seen it all before; it was all so tiresome.

I decided to leave. Lata wouldn't have come here. If she came, she'd have left immediately. I had been here too long. For these young people, this sort of thing was new. I felt if I stayed a moment longer I'd turn into that lost middle-aged man with his lame cigarette trick that he probably made up on the spot to impress one of the girls that surrounded him, any girl. My date was in the kitchen area rolling a joint. He saw me and nodded enthusiastically to indicate the joint he was making. I dismissed him with a wave and headed for the door.

Out in the hall I saw the slim, tubular, red-haired girl sitting on the stairs kissing a boy. I expected his hand to be up her dress or her giving him a hand-job. But they were just kissing. She looked at me and smiled – there was an intimacy in her smile, as if we knew each other well – and then she and the boy kissed again, chastely, even healthily, like an old-fashioned third date. I realised that she wasn't drunk, she had just been unsteady on her high heels.

I wandered the streets in vain hope that I would bump into Lata. Somewhere. Unexpected. Where else to search in this vast metropolis? Where to even start? I wandered back to the club, my sliver of hope guiding me through the dark barrenness of my neighbourhood.

I went to the club and waited at the bar, hoping she might show.

She didn't come. I went out. A few trendy people curled up on the sidewalk to puke and sleep next to their vomit in undignified and untrendy slumber; his fancy brushed-cotton shirt torn and smudged with side-walk dirt, she sits on the curb bent foetal, letting the vomit fall to the gutter between her feet, one of her high heels is broken and her hot, sexy stockings have more runs and sags than those on the plump legs of an old immigrant washerwoman on her knees scrubbing the mosaic floor of the Williamsburg Savings Bank. I would walk every street until I found Lata.

I left the club disgusted and sad. I had decided to walk a spiral pattern, starting at the front door of the club and expanding block by block, covering every street and alley until I found her. I walked along feeling sick and cursing happy people under my breath. What do they know? I thought of Carlton and his grief walks in leafy Connecticut. I wandered along the Bowery, lonely and empty and overwhelmed by the stone of it all.

When would I find her? I could see the streets, but what of the endless shut doors? The myriad dark win-dows whose rooms she could be within? How can I describe the pit I dangled over, my sense that I was flying apart, that crawling years of slowly dying in a bottle on the bashed-up dustbin-mounted streets was an option?

The wind blows on Lafayette, smelling of cheap wine, urine, motor oil and rotting garbage.

I wandered the night. It was no hour. I was dressed in black. I was invisible to the world and myself, dressed in black in the night with only my thoughts and my need to find Lata. And there were my no thoughts, unbeheld thoughts drifting in and out of me. I was an abandoned building, with my thoughts empty black windows, like the empty sockets of a skull. I belong to the vast no-belongingness. There comes a point when the crushing joyless mantle of existence, cold under the film of life, the receiving earth of the dead years, makes you realise you have done nothing; you mean nothing; whether you live or die means nothing; you walk for miles on the dark bluestone streets of this city and you cannot escape, you cannot find truth; you search, you search, in gutters, in the darkened windows of antique stores, in the shapeless breathing heaps of clothing propped here and there against a wall that are human beings slicing away at their own brains with an alcohol knife to escape what is the awful doingness of it all; you walk and the yellow light of an all-night coffee shop casts its yellow, hopeful glow through the greasy window on to the sidewalk and you hope to see a familiar face in the window. It was Janice with a cup of coffee. I went in.

'Lata used to come here,' she said.

I bought a cup of coffee and sat with her.

'I have been walking every street,' I said, clutching the blue paper cup with a Greek frieze printed on it.

'I reported her missing,' said Janice. 'I wish I had just lied before about how long she was missing and got them searching immediately instead of wasting twenty-four hours.'

'I have been covering the streets in a spiral pattern, working out from the club,' I said.

'Lata is a private person. I don't know how to contact her family. I don't even know if any of them are here or if they're all in Trinidad. You are the only other person I know who knows her.'

Janice said my system for walking every street made

sense and said she would go up to 14th Street and work her way back down to the East Village. 'I don't know where to go. I don't know what to do. I have checked the waterfront. I can't sit in my studio and do nothing,' she said.

We finished our coffee and went in opposite directions.

The sun was already emerging from its purple blankets of night. I looped back to Lata's flat and tried her door. No answer. I made my way back to the club, following a route she had probably walked a thousand times. I just need to find her and everything will be OK, I thought.

The club's tiny blue-neon tube above its door had turned colourless and void in the brightness of the morning sky. I felt joyful and depressed. Joyful because what I once thought was impossibly hard – the complete and amoral giving in to my deepest desires – wasn't very difficult after all. I was filled with joy for having done it. I was happy at the freedom feeling of having given in fully to my desires. I was depressed because it was over and, the truth, all I had was an empty flat and suspicion gnawing at me that maybe I was unwanted after all, that I am a girl who is only ever wanted in a moment and then never afterwards. Maybe I was only wanted in an emotion-charged moment like fucking, and then ceased to be a person in the eyes of my enterer. Maybe that's what my marriage had been all along. And maybe that was the true unfilled need I had: that the truth of my emptiness was that something was missing, something essential. Fine art, marriage, expensive dresses, high-powered dinner parties, gluttonous sex, all of that was nothing more than a distraction from facing the essential, unfillable void within me.

I was oppressed with thoughts that my appearance

on this planet was to be brief and trivial. Whose life had I touched? The sun was going to go on shining today as it had for five billion years. The first rays of light threaded through the streets and upon the dingy old buildings lining these blocks of Downtown, gilding cornices, changing them from the backdrop of old photographs and dreams to the solid structures that they are in our time, and maybe, in the grand scheme of things, there was nothing about me that was any more important than the role of the lowliest speck of soot in any square millimetre on any of them. I was just a drop that fell from the lip of the meat spigot, for that was all of life there was. I walked towards Zoë's loft. I must have walked ten miles that night. I needed rest, and then I would search for Lata all over again.

I walked along the grim barren streets and thought about how I had chosen them as a temporary home, another world to step into for a brief essential moment, to be left. As the sky grew lighter and the buildings took on form and mass and too solid a reality, I decided that with the onset of a new day I must put the best face on it. I was tired, I was sad, I felt flashes of hopefulness.

I had chosen well; I liked these streets. As disheartening as they were to the trapped, I did not see myself as being trapped, at least not by anything physical. I reflected in the tranquillity of this morning that I had not *felt* rich when I was rich; now that I was poor, I did not feel poor either.

A hundred years ago these streets were astir with life, crowded with shirt-factory workers, horsecars, moustachioed men in bow-ties and suspenders. Within a few hours on a warm day such as this, every window on these streets would be loaded up with pillows and mattresses set out to air.

What I had this morning was this overwhelming feeling: I felt like *me*. And it didn't matter whether I was miserable or happy. The most important feeling in the world for me was something that would not change: every girl should know in her soul what it feels like to be herself. I had never been anyone before. What if...? What if...? If only...? I knew I was poor, but I still felt free. Perhaps my newfound poverty would have weighed more heavily on me if my life as a Wall Street wife had not been so hemmed in.

These were my fatigue-driven musings as I walked along the cool bluestone-slab sidewalks of this old part of town, when suddenly I froze in my tracks at an indescribably disgusting sight beneath my feet: a row of dustbins, putrid bags of rubbish, boxes, a piece of decrepit carpet. The carpet moved. It had a face. It was David's face. For an instant I stared at his decapitated head among the rubbish. I stood there speechless as this face I know turned in a patch of sunlight, my shadow cast long in the pink rays of dawn. He was alive! Lying among the rubbish.

His face had aged ten years, and dirt filled lines across it. He had grown a ragged beard, which was matted at the end with what I would swear were crusts of vomit.

He stared at me. He blinked slowly, painfully. I couldn't tell if his watery eyes recognised me. He crawled towards me, dazed. My natural instinct was to help him. I resisted: can it really be him? No! My David, who lost millions of dollars and ruined my life? The man who wielded such psychological power over me that my mind was my worst prison? Could he have sunk so low? He paused on a grease-stained piece of corrugated cardboard and, looking weak, propped his torso up, as if his legs were deadweight.

'Don't run away from me. Don't move,' he said.

'I'm not moving,' I said. It was him all right: he was wearing the ragged remains of one of his $600 Burberry raincoats. He reached a hand towards me. I saw that it was streaked with blood – the phrase 'caught red-handed' flashed through my mind like a tabloid head-line. I wondered if he had been beaten up or stabbed, but there was no pool of blood on the ground, no bruises or cuts on his dirty face. His bloody fingers shook unsteadily. He reached forwards, to touch me, to see if I was real or a hallucination. His fingers, lit up in the dawn rays like a dead blossom about to fall from a bush, hung weakly in the air between us.

He tried to stand, supporting himself on a garbage can. It looked like someone had taken a paintbrush and swished a stroke of blood over his dirty, greasy raincoat. It was a strong red-brown, perhaps a day old. The intense fumes of fermented piss wafted up from him and the place where he had lain.

'Don't run away from me. Don't move,' said David, now standing unsteadily. 'Oh shit, everything's spin-ning. Don't let me go.'

'It's going to be all right, David. Wait here while I call an ambulance.'

'No. It's just morning. Don't leave me here.'

He dropped to his knees.

'You need an ambulance. I'm going to call an ambulance.'

'Don't be stupid. Don't do that to me. You don't know what you're doing. Holy shit. You're not you,' he said.

'It's me,' I said. 'I want to help you.'

'My eyeballs are going to pop out. They feel like big fish eyes and they're going to explode . . .'

'I've got to get you to a hospital.'

'Oh, it doesn't bother me too much,' he said. 'With

drugs, you know, it's ... they make you feel like you're having fun even if you're not.' Even in this state I saw the spark of his old ability to charm, to win my sympathy, to con.

'David, you're not making sense.' More stirrings of carpets and cardboard. Another face. Then another. It was a nest of addicts, camouflaged in garbage, and I had stirred them up, like opening a cupboard door and setting cockroaches scrambling. A sheet of cardboard lifted and a man stood up. Then another emerged. David stood up, steady now. 'Julia, come here.' He was strong now, his voice commanding, his face set with the calm determination I had once known, and the cold lucidity I had formerly known him to possess had re-established itself firmly. I ran to find a pay phone.

The first pay phone I found had been vandalised and had no dial tone. Two police cars whisked past. I ran into the middle of the street to flag them down, but they were gone.

'Zoë, David scared the shit out of me this morning.' I was still out of breath.

'You saw David!'

I pushed past Zoë and dialled 911.

Zoë pounded on the bathroom door and told Jack to get out of the shower.

The 911 dispatcher told me the police were on their way to drive me around to find David.

I couldn't remember Jane Conch's number and looked for Zoë's phone book.

'Zoë ...'

'Yes, Julia,' said Zoë.

'Do you think I fuck too much?' I said.

'What?' said Zoë.

She was in her bathrobe, pouring us coffee.

'Do you think someone who was sick can recover and live a normal life?' I said.

We spoke in hushed voices so that Jack would not overhear us in the bathroom.

The coffee was good. French roast, a little cream in it, nothing fancy.

Inexplicably, I was cheered up. Cured even. I felt so good being back with another person, people I know, instead of alone on a city street. I felt hopeful. To think that David is alive. He couldn't get far in his condition. Lata would be found too. She was out there, as David had been, as I had been.

'Jane Conch's card has her pager number on it,' Zoë said, sifting through a stack of business cards.

'Do you think I fuck too much and that's why I haven't got it together?'

'It has nothing to do with that. You're just going through a bad case of what we all go through at one time or another,' said Zoë. She sat down with me at the table. 'Just call it a slight case of – oh, what's the word? *La foutromanie.*'

'Yeah?' I said.

'Yeah. The way I see it, you can never fuck enough; it's just that you hardly ever get to fuck the right people at the right time. But I don't think that's what you're going through now,' said Zoë. We sipped the French roast in silence. 'God I envy you. I could *never* do that. I *want* to. But I'd never get Jack to share me with another man. Do you suppose Jack is hypocritical?'

'You mean about sharing his wife with other men?'

'Well, I shared him with you. Do you think he'd ever return the favour?'

'I don't know,' I said. 'It's impossible to know what men think.'

Zoë found Jane's card and handed it to me. I dialled

her office number and left a message. Then I dialled her pager.

The bathroom door opened and Jack emerged.

'You saw David?'

He sat down and we sipped our French roast in silence. Jack looked hurt that we had ceased talking.

'We were just having girltalk,' said Zoë. 'Nothing personal, but it's not for men's ears.'

I was tense waiting for the police to arrive, for Jane to answer her pager. We sipped our coffee. I liked Jack. I reminisced about the sex the three of us used to have and felt nostalgic. Through the process of being recollected over coffee, the memories had become more dear to me. I wondered if my memory of the enjoyment had over time superseded what we had actually enjoyed, the way fond memories become more valuable than the event being remembered. I looked at Jack and could not help smiling. I was glad to know that he had made love to me. But having had the experience, and experiencing a pleasant memory, I wished it had never happened and I wished I could forget it ever happened.

As we waited for the police to arrive I watched Zoë and Jack in their kitchen fixing breakfast for three. I was struck by how much of a husband and wife they were, so much more so than David and I ever were. There was no trace, now, that I had ever entered their bed. I had performed a role in their marriage, a role that had ended. We had returned to being friends, a friendship that had always been stronger than any of us had ever realised and that would endure as just that, the strongest of friendships.

I stared at the phone on the Groves' kitchen counter and wondered if I could call Carlton, if I could ever live again.

The police arrived before Jane answered her pager.

Only four and a half minutes had passed. The eggs Zoë had broken into her frying pan weren't ready. I rode with the cops, and I knew Jane would be upset with me for not waiting for guidance from my attorney. As we cruised around I saw the boy I had met last night who lied and said he knew where to find Lata.

'Stop him,' I told the cops. 'He has dope on him.'

The police leaped out of their squad car and searched him. He had a little bag of marijuana on him and a larger bag of cocaine. The cops radioed for backup and in less than two minutes three more cars had pulled up, parking all over the street at dramatic angles.

'Who the fuck do you think you are?' the boy screamed at me as the police held him over the hood of the car spread-legged and handcuffed. 'I never did anything to you!' He started crying.

He was right. And I had no clear reason for plunging that boy into the long legal ordeal he had just entered. It's for his own good, I decided. I got into another car and we resumed our search for David.

The police car pulled to a stop at the end of Crosby Street. There were police cars and vans and lots of yellow 'POLICE LINE DO NOT CROSS' tape hanging from blue NYPD sawhorses.

'Homicide scene,' one cop told me. 'A whore's body was dumped in a trash can. She probably got robbed for drug money.' Crosby is dark and narrow and crowded with dustbins. It is more of a back alley than a street, peculiar in that New York does not have alleys, not more than a handful such as Crosby.

I couldn't see what the cops were doing at the crime scene. I had walked down this alley last night and all had been quiet.

18

It had been Lata's body that a city sanitation worker had found in the dustbin on Crosby Street. She had been shot four times with a .45, probably minutes after she had spoken to Janice and left her flat. The tabloids went to press before the police had identified Lata. The papers published the usual two column inches describing the finding of a prostitute's body and the lack of leads. There were no follow-up stories.

The memorial service was held Uptown at the Unitarian Church, at Lexington and 80th. Lata's immediate family was quite small, just her parents and younger sister. But there were fifty other, more-distant relatives attending. The church was filled with people who had never known her but couldn't bear to see a young girl who had lived and died a stranger to them die alone and forgotten in a city that was too big to care. People did care. I asked an old black woman how she had known about the service since it wasn't announced anywhere. She said people she knew told her. Most everyone there had heard about it through word of mouth.

I rode down in the lift from the Groves' loft that night with Carlton Westergaarde. He would drive me over to my flat to get some things and take me back to Connecticut. The lift stopped and all the lights went out. We stood in the dark, in the cage of the ancient lift, listening to the century-old silence emanating from the cool bricks of the building.

'It's a power failure,' said Carlton. 'I wonder if it's just this building or the whole city.'

There was not a sound anywhere, not even a creak in the arthritic old lift machinery. The black emptiness looked infinite, as if I stood on the edge of a cliff, on the edge of infinite nothingness.

'It's like there's nothing in the whole world except our voices,' said Carlton.

'No,' I said, my voice startling me, although I had not spoken loudly, 'we're here.' I put my arms around him.

'You're not afraid of the dark, are you?'

'No.' I felt his warmth, his arms around me, I listened to his heart beat. 'I *hate* the dark. My life was meant to be about light. That's what paintings are. That's what I repair. In paintings, even the shadows are light. I left my husband in the dark ... Light, light and truth. My husband was not honest with me. I loved him, and still he did not tell me the truth. No one I have ever loved has told me the truth. No one has ever loved me.'

'Julia, I know we are not just voices in the dark. I was wrong. How wrong I was. What a sad creature you are. I wish I could cure you. I know you have been loved, I know you are loved now, and you will be loved in the future. Somewhere a fuse has blown or a transformer, and we are trapped in the dark for a moment. I'm glad you hate the dark. I hate it too. As much as I hate it, there isn't any other person on this planet I would want to be trapped in the dark with but you.'

He held me tight and I knew he truly cared about me.

'Carlton, it does not seem so dark now.'

Within minutes the ancient hydraulic lift floated its way down to the ground floor. As old as it was, this technology has some advantages over modern systems, which would have ensured that we stayed trapped.

Carlton parked his car and escorted me to my place. He was protective because this is a dangerous neighbourhood. Carlton's town in Connecticut had had zero homicides for decades, and I had over fifty a year in just a couple of dozen city blocks around my place, and summer had barely started. Carlton was right. I was too sad about Lata to think about my personal safety. We paused outside my building. I pulled my light shawl tighter around my shoulders – it had got chilly suddenly.

'I'm here with you,' Carlton said, looking up at the ancient wooden door of my building. The paint on the door was so thick it peeled off like squares of chocolate, revealing the conscientious woodwork left underneath by craftsmen of over a century ago.

The light in the hall was out and we groped our way up the iron-and-tile stairway. For as long as I had lived in this neighbourhood I had joked to myself about how everyone was overconcerned about the danger – and at the same time always steeled myself for the worst: if the light is out in the hall, don't assume it is because the super is a lazy, drunken, bribe-taking shithead. Assume it is because someone set it up that way for a quick shakedown for drug money.

I needed Carlton to escort me even though there was nothing he could do if we were attacked.

When I put my key in the door, I found it unlocked.

'That's strange,' I said. 'I must have been so upset I went out without locking.'

'Let's be careful,' Carlton said.

'Welcome to my humble abode,' I said, flipping on the light. 'It's not much, shabby actually, but it was my new life.' I shut the front door and locked it.

'Don't call this shabby. It's very cosy.' Carlton made a small circuit of my eight-by-nine-foot room. 'This room looks more like home than my home,' he said.

'You have a beautiful home.'

'But even with your found furniture, I get the feeling this is *your* place. Does it look like anything was stolen?'

'There's nothing to steal here.' I looked around the room. 'Nothing has been touched.' I took off my shawl and tossed it on the love seat.

'The original woodwork is intact,' I said, pointing to the oak detailing of the front-door frame. 'The bathtub by the front door is original.' My building was one of those old tenements that had its bathtub in the kitchen right where the front door opened. The building was old enough that it had originally been constructed without any plumbing.

Carlton saw the antique golf club Lata had found. It stood on the window sill, leaning against the frame of the window exactly where Lata had left it. Carlton picked it up and looked at it. 'This is a valuable antique. With this wooden shaft and this style of head this must be from the 1890s. Do you realise what good balance this has? Wow, I'd like to try this sometime. It's a sand wedge.'

'Would you like a drink?' I said. 'Actually, all I have is tea.'

'I'd love tea.' Carlton reverently stood the sand wedge on the window sill where he'd found it.

'Have a seat. Earl Grey? Jasmine? Mint?'

'Mint tea would really hit the spot. You know, this room is a perfect expression of your personality,' he said. He ducked his head into my WC, which belonged in a museum for its quaint, very old porcelain fixtures and tiles. 'Actually, I have to spend a penny.'

'Be my guest.' I filled up the kettle and put it on. My

feet were killing me, so I kicked off my shoes and opened my closet for my slippers. My heart stopped beating: I was face to face with David. 'How long –'

'Shhh. Don't say another fucking word. Just listen to me.' He was cleaned up and had shaved. He wore a clean homeless-shelter-giveout-looking shirt, plaid flannel with mismatched buttons ineptly sewn on, and a clean but threadbare light cotton jacket.

'You've got to go!' I said, barely able to keep my voice at a whisper. 'How the hell did you get in here?'

'Listen to me. You get rid of that fruity gigolo you've been traipsing around with and you and me are going to have a nice quiet talk.'

'I will not get rid of him. You have to leave. Who do you think you are?' I stepped backwards; David kept pressing me forwards.

'I'm your husband, sweetie. Remember? You think you can tell your husband to *go*? There isn't a law in the world that says I have to.'

Just then the toilet flushed and I felt relief at my imminent rescue. I heard the WC's doorknob turning in Carlton's hand. Soon this awfulness would be over.

'You pretend everything's nice, see?' David flashed open his jacket to reveal a huge gun. My knees went weak – how Lata must have felt – a flash of heat went over me, cold sweat coated me; my throat balled up in a knot of speechless horror. 'You get rid of him and nobody has to get hurt.'

Carlton opened the WC door and was surprised to see David. Carlton stood there smiling sociably – a beautiful man I realised – and when I failed to make an introduction he took the initiative.

'Hello,' said Carlton. He knew he'd seen David before.

'I'm David, Julia's husband.' David reached out his right hand and shook with Carlton.

'Yes. Of course. It's great to see you again.' There was a silence as David did not answer. Finally Carlton spoke up: 'This is a bit awkward.'

'It would only be awkward if you had slept with my wife, which I'm sure you have not done.'

'Yes,' said Carlton, panic briefly taking hold of his face as he struggled to figure out what was going on.

'You remember Carlton Westergaarde,' I said. 'He's a friend of the Groves. He's one of the investors in that play.'

David stared at Carlton, not recognising him.

The kettle screamed.

'Tea's ready, everyone,' I said with a spasm of cheeriness that came out at too high a pitch. Carlton smiled genuinely, as if relieved that the ambient sense of threat he had detected in the room had all been some silly misunderstanding, a misreading entirely. I shut off the gas and pulled down three mugs. 'What sort of tea, David?'

'I thought you said your friend was just going.' David tapped his coat casually, a gesture Carlton saw but that had no meaning for him.

'Oh don't be silly,' I said. 'We were just about to have tea.'

'I don't need to have tea,' said Carlton. 'Maybe I ought to leave you two alone. You know, third wheel and all that.'

'You see, Julia –'

'David, I would not be much of a host if I invited someone for tea and then scooted him out.'

'It's really no problem, Julia,' said Carlton with all the terminal agreeability that my husband had never had and never would. My mind raced as I tried to think of how to keep Carlton in my flat to protect me from I did not know what; how to warn Carlton!

Perhaps this wasn't real, I told myself. Sure, David had flashed a gun. But maybe it wasn't loaded. Maybe he only wanted to scare me, get whatever he wanted, drug money. This sort of thing doesn't happen to people like me; I'm a fine-art conservator; I have a master's degree. Wasn't it true that most muggers used unloaded guns? This was just some crazyshit stunt of David's.

No. The sickening sense dawned on me that no, it was all true, all too real. I thought of poor Lata, found dead in a dustbin in a rubbish-strewn alley. I could be next, and I had dragged unsuspecting Carlton down with me. I tried to think of how I could pour the kettle over David or splash hot tea in his eyes, but he kept his distance, always standing. I put a mint tea bag into each of three mugs. David would get tea in his face if I could swing it, and I'd have a fraction of a second to get that gun away from him. But I couldn't count on Carlton in my plans; he would have no clue what was going on at the most crucial moment.

'Please, gentlemen, have a seat.'

'I prefer to stand,' said David.

I put the three mugs of tea on a tray and walked step by measured step towards my vegetable-crate coffee table. I was so nervous I could barely traverse the few feet from my stove to the centre of my tiny room, where my table stood; I thought the tea would splash all over the floor any moment, my arms were shaking so. I sat down and placed mugs on coasters. Arranging mugs on coasters: this simple, common task may end up being the last thing I do in this life, I thought. How absurd civility is; coasters for my vegetable-crate table and then murdered by my husband.

'Carlton,' I said, nodding at a chair. 'David, be a dear and have a seat. I haven't *slept* with Carlton. If you must know, he was escorting me home because this is a *very dangerous* neighbourhood. You should be thankful that he is concerned about my well-being.'

An evil smile came over David and he sat at one end of my pitiful little love seat. Finding that love seat on the street with Lata was a carefree happy moment, which I had not realised at the time. And now, as I was possibly about to die within a few minutes, I knew how precious even the most ordinary moment is, and how plentiful they are in life if we are awake enough to recognise them. This wisdom – not even a profound wisdom – was a simple piece of wisdom to live my life by; my chance to do this, to live life, rested with David, who was not capable of ever knowing any wisdom at all.

'Mmm,' said Carlton. 'Hits the spot.'

David looked at Carlton innocently sipping his tea; he was a cat toying with a mouse. David and I shared the awful secret that at any moment he could decide to kill us; David was smugly secure in this knowledge, that he was invincible, that he was the only one here with a concealed large-calibre handgun. David lit up a cigarette. He offered me the pack. I shook my head.

'Carlton Westergaarde?'

'No thank you.'

'Don't smoke?'

'Smoking is bad for your health.'

'Is that right?' said David, taking a long drag and blowing it in Carlton's direction. 'Thank you, Carlton.'

'What for?'

'You've forgotten already? That *is* suspicious.'

'I'm unclear about what you're referring to.'

'Thank you for escorting my wife home, because this is a *very dangerous* neighbourhood.'

'You're welcome.'

'David, there's no need to be rude.'

'*Rude*? I'm genuinely *thankful* that he is concerned about my wife's well-being.'

'I told you I never slept with him. You have no right to do this.'

'Well,' said Carlton, setting down his mug of tea and standing. 'This *is* awkward, and it's getting late.'

'No!' I said. 'It's not late. It's hardly late at all.'

'Julia, there's obviously a lot you need to discuss with your husband –'

'I need you here,' I said, like a drowning woman tearing at the waters for breath. 'Please. Sit.'

Reluctantly, Carlton sat. As far as he knew, he had been dragged into the middle of a husband-and-wife spat in the recrimination-laden throes of marriage break-up.

David took a sip of tea, a twinkle in his eye, the knowingness of holding the trump card. The game was sheer pleasure for him. He tapped his cigarette ash on to the floor.

'So, Carlton, married?'

Carlton gave David a steady stare. I kept waiting for a moment when David's hand brought his cigarette to his mouth to buy me an instant's more time to splash hot tea in his face.

'My wife passed away,' he said.

'Sorry to hear that,' said David. 'What of?'

'I beg your pardon?'

'What did she die of?'

Carlton froze in pain.

'Cat got your tongue? What did your goddam wife die of, Carlton? Something medical? Something Dr Carlton Westergaarde couldn't cure?'

My tea splashed in a manic arc across David. As soon

as I'd let fly with my cup I knew I'd got it wrong. I leaped for his abdomen, whether to grab his gun or stay his hand I knew not which in my panicked plunge.

David was on his feet in an instant, gun drawn. I landed on the floor.

'Get up!' is all I heard next. I looked up to find the barrel of the huge .45 gaping down at me. I felt dizzy, as if I stood on the fifteenth-floor ledge of a building. 'Get up! You've had it!' I now knew for sure that we were about to die. I felt what Lata must have felt; I prayed that she had died instantly. I prayed that I would too.

I looked over to Carlton in the vain hope that somehow he could rescue me. He stood, shaking, his hands raised over his head, his face as red as a sunburn. I thought he might vomit. His legs were jiggling. David was rock steady, holding the huge gun on me.

'That chickenshit little stunt of yours is going to cost you. Sorry, Carlton, I didn't want to bring you into this. But this crazy bitch, in all her wisdom, has decided we're all going to go together.'

Carlton stood shaking and weak, like a homeless alcoholic in winter.

'You, get down on your hands and knees,' said David, waving the gun at him. Carlton got down on the floor as instructed. 'You're going to watch. Make one move and it's all over for both of you.'

'There!' David yelled at me.

'What?' I said.

'There!'

'What? Where?'

He yanked my arm, twisting it painfully, and pushed me over to the love seat.

'You do what I say! Hear?' He slammed me face first over the back of the love seat and struck me hard on the shoulder blade with the butt of his gun. A numbing pain impaled me. I later learned that my shoulder blade had been cracked and a bruise, the silhouette of the heavy gun butt, marked the spot on my skin.

'Your doctor friend is gonna watch.' David shoved up my dress and tore at my panties. They didn't tear away; instead the band cut into me. David yanked and yanked, but they wouldn't break. He pulled them down my legs, spilling me forwards to get them off my feet. He kicked my feet apart and pushed up my dress. I wished he'd just shoot me so I wouldn't have to know what would happen next. I caught a glimpse of Carlton watching me. 'That's right, you watch him while he watches you.'

David laid the tip of the gun barrel against my bare back and traced it over my skin.

'A bullet going in here would come out ... how big do you think, Doc? Softball sized? Basketball? Or maybe gunshot wounds aren't your speciality.'

There was a knock at the door.

'Come in!' I said. David yanked me up.

'What're you trying to do?' he said.

'Hello? Julia?'

It was Zoë.

I had this horrible sense: there was no rescue, only more death. David was going to kill us all.

'Go away!' I shouted.

'Julia? Are you all right?' It was Jack too.

'I know you're in there,' said Zoë.

I looked at David. What did he want me to do?

'It's not polite to leave your friends out in the hall,' said David. 'Better let them in on our fun.'

David stood me up and patted my hair back in place. He kicked my panties under the love seat. I almost couldn't stand from the piercing pain in my back.

'Up,' he instructed Carlton. 'Sit there and drink your tea. Act happy.' David shoved his gun into his waistband and joined me at the front door. I could feel his hot breath on my ear.

'Hi there,' he said over my shoulder when I opened the door.

'David!' said Zoë, astonished.

'We're reconciling,' said David cheerfully. He put his arm around me and gave me a squeeze; pain tore through my back in the place he'd hit me.

'You should go,' I said. 'David and I have a few more things we need to discuss.'

'Perish the thought!' said David. 'I wouldn't dream of sending our friends away on a happy night such as this. Besides, Carlton Westergaarde is here.' David swung the door wide open and Zoë and Jack came in. 'Careful,' said David. 'Spilled some tea just there, on that part of the couch. Julia, dear, brew up some more tea for us. Jack, great to see you again.'

'It's been a while,' said Jack.

'That it has,' said David. 'Please sit.'

Jack took one end of the love seat. David took his seat on the other end, and Zoë squeezed between them.

I made my slow death march to the kettle and refilled it. In this small room David could easily kill us all, probably with one shot each. Everyone in the room was in close range.

'Say, Carlton,' said Zoë. 'What do you think of Julia's place?'

'Well,' began Carlton, standing and admiring the room. He smiled. 'Julia was telling me how shabby she thought the place was and I was telling her how cosy I found it.' At this, Carlton picked my sand wedge off the window sill and swung it full force into David's forehead, ripping a huge gash through his cranium, through which blood spurted out in thick ropes. The whole world slowed down so that I could take in every movement: Zoë twisting and screaming and Jack with his mouth wide open as the two of them sat jammed into a 1920s love seat with the ferociously bleeding corpse of my husband.

The scene took on an astonishing clarity, as if I could walk through time and space observing events at my leisure. I ran to Carlton as he, absurdly, set the golf club back in its place on the window sill. The windowpanes were spattered with fine droplets of blood and thicker drops that streaked down in bright-red parallel lines. Carlton was overwhelmingly calm as the screams surrounded us for what seemed like eternity. I stepped around David's vast bloodpuddle, taking care not to slip in the red ooze that coated the floor. As if Carlton and I were champion dancers executing a delicate and graceful *pas de deux*, he reached his hand down and took hold of mine, tilting that brave and gallant face towards me as if nothing else in the world existed.

'We must make love beside my husband's death so we know that we are alive.' I offered my pussy, the one that my husband had wanted to mangle, to the man I would gladly spend the rest of my life with. Carlton understood me perfectly – I need not have stated what we must do – and, in a moment, he was inside me perfectly, as if we had been lovers since the dawn of time. I wrapped my legs around him as tight as I could. I never wanted to let him go.

We came. It was a ceremonial come, one that must be shared by soulmates to certify the eternity of life and goodness when evil and death have been defeated. We lay on the floor kissing, Carlton Westergaarde's penis resting contentedly in my quim. It was over; now we could be happy; we had won.

Voices surrounded us, insignificant voices, the voices of people who sleepwalked through each day, never seeing the richness of life, the beatifying lifeforce. Neighbours with accents, police, a barking dog: 'He killed 'im widda golf club. No reason at all; just cold-blooded murder'; 'One minute he's sittin' on the sofa; next, *whammo!* and he's shtupping the girl.'

The handcuffs on us, the pain of my cracked shoulder blade returning, reality returning.

19

The sound of the church bells still peals cheerfully in my memory. This was the scene: I was the centre of attention at the reception at Carlton's understated pre-Revolutionary house in Connecticut.

There I was on my wedding day, with this kindly looking man on the lawn at the back of this wonderful house and I was wearing my wedding dress and to one side of me were leaves raked into a little hill by the gardener and it was fall and the man was smiling proudly at me. Somehow I'd always expected to live this life. Carlton was in a fall suit; I was in a brilliant, fluffy white wedding dress. My friends were there, rice had flown, it had been a beautiful wedding.

The wedding guests milled about at the reception. All sorts of people were there: Zoë and Jack, the Ketts, Jane Conch, a jazz combo under a tent in Carlton's back yard.

Carlton and I slipped inside the house to be alone for a moment. We didn't make it up the stairs. The kiss just went on and on halfway up the staircase and I became aroused. I sank to my knees hopelessly in love and delirious with passion.

'But Julia . . .' It was the voice of my husband speaking quite clearly.

'Now, Carlton Westergaarde, you'll always be my only true love.'

Carlton sat on the stairs and cradled my head in his lap. It made me feel comfortable. This is the man I love. This is the man I will always love.

Some stories do have happy endings.

Not long after Gavril's bound body was found floating in the East River, the FBI swooped down on a warehouse in Brighton Beach in a pre-dawn raid and recovered all of the Groves' stolen possessions – and my fur coat. Gavril and David had been involved in the art theft – they owed money to the Russian mob and David had told them how to steal the Groves' art.

Jane Conch uncovered documents that enabled me to recover most of David's wealth – free and clear of any claim by the government. In his paranoia and greed, David had hidden most of his net worth offshore – and he had always paid our taxes, so the IRS had no claim. He apparently thought he could lie low until things cooled off. He had no choice, seeing that law enforcement and the Russian mob were after him, and he had set up his offshore accounts so that he had no way to get at the money except to travel offshore, which he couldn't do.

Our Upper West Side flat – the one I had unequivocally walked out of on that frantic spring night – could not be recovered. Its seizure under RICO was final. I couldn't bear to set foot in that place again anyway. To this day I regret losing all my books and the few mementos I'd had of my late parents. All gone.

Oh! Calculus! was a smash hit on Broadway and Carlton and I received cheques for our share of the proceeds every week for many years.

Carlton and I had stolen our moment away from the wedding party. I looked into his eyes and I could not hold back the tears that ran down my face.

'It's OK now,' Carlton said, whipping the silk kerchief out of his suit pocket and dabbing my cheeks. 'You're here now. You're with me now. You're home.'

'That handkerchief is only supposed to be for show,' I pointed out.

'Well, right now we need it.'

We went back down the stairs and outside to the guests.

I felt such joy at so many people joining me on this my special day.

It is here that I close my diary, although this is not the right moment. This is the diary of my Manhattan passion. But it is at this moment, if the truth be told, that my passion opens up to the world for the first time. It is only now that my full passion begins.

LOOK OUT FOR THE ALL-NEW BLACK LACE BOOKS – AVAILABLE NOW!

All books priced £6.99 in the UK. Please note publication dates apply to the UK only. For other territories, please contact your retailer.

WICKED WORDS 6
A Black Lace short story collection
ISBN 0 352 33590 0

Deliciously daring and hugely popular, the *Wicked Words* collections are the freshest and most entertaining volumes of women's erotica to be found anywhere in the world. The diversity of themes and styles reflects the multi-faceted nature of the female sexual imagination. Combining humour, warmth and attitude with fun, filthy, imaginative writing, these stories sizzle with horny action. Only the most arousing fiction makes it into a *Wicked Words* volume. **This is the best in fun, cutting-edge erotica from the UK and USA.**

HARD CORPS
Claire Thompson
ISBN 0 352 33491 6

This is the story of Remy Harris, a bright young woman starting out as an army cadet at military college in the US. Enduring all the usual trials of boot-camp discipline and rigorous exercise, she's ready for any challenge – that is until she meets Jacob, who recognises her true sexuality. Initiated into the Hard Corps – a secret society within the barracks – Remy soon becomes absorbed by this clandestine world of ritual punishment. It's only when Jacob takes things too far that she rebels, and begins to plot her revenge. **Strict sergeants and rebellious cadets come together in this unusual and highly entertaining story of military discipline with a twist.**

Coming in July

CABIN FEVER
Emma Donaldson
ISBN 0 352 33692 7

Young beautician Laura works in the exclusive Shangri-La beauty salon aboard the cruise ship *Jannina*. Although she has a super-sensual time with her boyfriend, Steve – who works the ship's bar – there are plenty of nice young men in uniform who want a piece of her action. Laura's cabin mate is the shy, eighteen-year-old Fiona, whose sexuality is a mystery, especially as there are rumours that the stern Elinor Brookes, the matriarch of the beauty salon, has been seen doing some very curious things with the young Fiona. **Saucy story of clandestine goings-on aboard a luxury liner.**

WOLF AT THE DOOR
Savannah Smythe
ISBN 0 352 33693 5

Thirty-year-old Pagan Warner is marrying Greg – a debonair and seemingly dull Englishman – in an effort to erase her turbulent past. All she wants is a peaceful life in rural New Jersey but her past catches up with her in the form of bad boy 'Wolf' Mancini, the man who seduced her as a teenager. Tempted into rekindling their intensely sexual affair while making her wedding preparations, she intends to break off the illicit liaison once she is married. However, Pagan has underestimated the Wolf's obsessions. Mancini has spotted Greg's own weaknesses and intends to exploit them to the full, undermining him in his professional life. When he sends the slinky, raven-haired Renate in to do his dirty work, the course is set for a descent into depravity. **Fabulous nasty characters, dirty double dealing and forbidden lusts abound!**

THE CAPTIVE FLESH
Cleo Cordell
ISBN 0 352 32872 X

Eighteenth-century French covent girls Marietta and Claudine learn that their stay at the opulent Algerian home of their handsome and powerful host, Kasim, requires something in return: their complete surrender to the ecstasy of pleasure in pain. Kasim's decadent orgies also require the services of Gabriel, whose exquisite longing for Marietta's awakened lust cannot be contained – not even by the shackles that bind his tortured flesh. **This is a reprint of one of the first Black Lace books ever published. A classic piece of blockbusting historical erotica.**

Coming in August

DIVINE TORMENT
Janine Ashbless
ISBN 0 352 33719 2

In the ancient temple city of Mulhanabin, the voluptuous Malia Shai awaits her destiny. Millions of people worship her, believing her to be a goddess incarnate. However, she is very human, consumed by erotic passions that have no outlet. Into this sacred city comes General Verlaine – the rugged and horny gladiatorial leader of the occupying army. Intimate contact between Verlaine and Malia Shai is forbidden by every law of their hostile peoples. But she is the one thing he wants – and he will risk everything to have her. **A beautifully written story of opulent palaces, extreme rituals and sexy conquerors. Like *Gladiator* set in a mythical realm.**

THE BEST OF BLACK LACE 2
ISBN O 352 33718 4

The Black Lace series has continued to be *the* market leader in erotic fiction, publishing genuine female writers of erotica from all over the English-speaking world. The series has changed and developed considerably since it was launched in 1993. The past decade has seen an explosion of interest in the subject of female sexuality, and Black Lace has always been at the forefront of debate around this issue. Editorial policy is constantly evolving to keep the writing up-to-date and fresh, and now the books have undergone a design makeover that completes the transformation, taking the series into a new era of prominence and popularity. *The Best of Black Lace 2* will include extracts of the sexiest, most sizzling titles from the past three years.

SHADOWPLAY
Portia Da Costa
ISBN O 352 33313 8

Photographer Christabel is drawn to psychic phenomena and dark liaisons. When she is persuaded by her husband to take a holiday at a mysterious mansion house in the country, unexpected events begin to unravel. Her husband has enlisted the help of his young male PA to ensure that Christabel's holiday is eventful and erotic. Within the web of an unusual and kinky threesome, Christabel learns some lessons the jaded city could never teach. **Full of dark, erotic games, this is a special reprint of one of our most popular titles.**

Black Lace Booklist

Information is correct at time of printing. To avoid disappointment
check availability before ordering. Go to www.blacklace-books.co.uk.
All books are priced £6.99 unless another price is given.

BLACK LACE BOOKS WITH A CONTEMPORARY SETTING

☐ THE TOP OF HER GAME Emma Holly	ISBN 0 352 33337 5	£5.99
☐ IN THE FLESH Emma Holly	ISBN 0 352 33498 3	£5.99
☐ A PRIVATE VIEW Crystalle Valentino	ISBN 0 352 33308 1	£5.99
☐ SHAMELESS Stella Black	ISBN 0 352 33485 1	£5.99
☐ INTENSE BLUE Lyn Wood	ISBN 0 352 33496 7	£5.99
☐ THE NAKED TRUTH Natasha Rostova	ISBN 0 352 33497 5	£5.99
☐ ANIMAL PASSIONS Martine Marquand	ISBN 0 352 33499 1	£5.99
☐ A SPORTING CHANCE Susie Raymond	ISBN 0 352 33501 7	£5.99
☐ TAKING LIBERTIES Susie Raymond	ISBN 0 352 33357 X	£5.99
☐ A SCANDALOUS AFFAIR Holly Graham	ISBN 0 352 33523 8	£5.99
☐ THE NAKED FLAME Crystalle Valentino	ISBN 0 352 33528 9	£5.99
☐ CRASH COURSE Juliet Hastings	ISBN 0 352 33018 X	£5.99
☐ ON THE EDGE Laura Hamilton	ISBN 0 352 33534 3	£5.99
☐ LURED BY LUST Tania Picarda	ISBN 0 352 33533 5	£5.99
☐ THE HOTTEST PLACE Tabitha Flyte	ISBN 0 352 33536 X	£5.99
☐ THE NINETY DAYS OF GENEVIEVE Lucinda Carrington	ISBN 0 352 33070 8	£5.99
☐ EARTHY DELIGHTS Tesni Morgan	ISBN 0 352 33548 3	£5.99
☐ MAN HUNT Cathleen Ross	ISBN 0 352 33583 1	
☐ MÉNAGE Emma Holly	ISBN 0 352 33231 X	
☐ DREAMING SPIRES Juliet Hastings	ISBN 0 352 33584 X	
☐ THE TRANSFORMATION Natasha Rostova	ISBN 0 352 33311 1	
☐ STELLA DOES HOLLYWOOD Stella Black	ISBN 0 352 33588 2	
☐ SIN.NET Helena Ravenscroft	ISBN 0 352 33598 X	
☐ HOTBED Portia Da Costa	ISBN 0 352 33614 5	
☐ TWO WEEKS IN TANGIER Annabel Lee	ISBN 0 352 33599 8	
☐ HIGHLAND FLING Jane Justine	ISBN 0 352 33616 1	

BLACK LACE BOOKS WITH AN HISTORICAL SETTING

☐ DARKER THAN LOVE Kristina Lloyd   ISBN 0 352 33279 4

☐ STAND AND DELIVER Helena Ravenscroft   ISBN 0 352 33340 5   £5.99

☐ THE CAPTIVATION Natasha Rostova   ISBN 0 352 33234 4

☐ CIRCO EROTICA Mercedes Kelley   ISBN 0 352 33257 3

☐ MINX Megan Blythe   ISBN 0 352 33638 2

☐ PLEASURE'S DAUGHTER Sedalia Johnson   ISBN 0 352 33237 9

☐ JULIET RISING Cleo Cordell   ISBN 0 352 32938 6

☐ DEMON'S DARE Melissa MacNeal   ISBN 0 352 33683 8

☐ ELENA'S CONQUEST Lisette Allen   ISBN 0 352 32950 5

BLACK LACE ANTHOLOGIES

☐ CRUEL ENCHANTMENT Erotic Fairy Stories   ISBN 0 352 33483 5   £5.99
     Janine Ashbless

☐ MORE WICKED WORDS Various   ISBN 0 352 33487 8   £5.99

☐ WICKED WORDS 4 Various   ISBN 0 352 33603 X

☐ WICKED WORDS 5 Various   ISBN 0 352 33642 0

☐ WICKED WORDS 6 Various   ISBN 0 352 33590 0

BLACK LACE NON-FICTION

☐ THE BLACK LACE BOOK OF WOMEN'S SEXUAL   ISBN 0 352 33346 4   £5.99
     FANTASIES Ed. Kerri Sharp

To find out the latest information about Black Lace titles, check out the website: www.blacklace-books.co.uk or send for a booklist with complete synopses by writing to:

Black Lace Booklist, Virgin Books Ltd
Thames Wharf Studios
Rainville Road
London W6 9HA

Please include an SAE of decent size. Please note only British stamps are valid.

Our privacy policy
We will not disclose information you supply us to any other parties.
We will not disclose any information which identifies you personally to any person without your express consent.

From time to time we may send out information about Black Lace books and special offers. Please tick here if you do not wish to receive Black Lace information. ❑

Please send me the books I have ticked above.

Name ....

Address ....

....

....

....

Post Code ....

Send to: Cash Sales, Black Lace Books, Thames Wharf Studios, Rainville Road, London W6 9HA.

US customers: for prices and details of how to order books for delivery by mail, call 1-800-343-4499.

Please enclose a cheque or postal order, made payable to Virgin Books Ltd, to the value of the books you have ordered plus postage and packing costs as follows:

UK and BFPO – £1.00 for the first book, 50p for each subsequent book.

Overseas (including Republic of Ireland) – £2.00 for the first book, £1.00 for each subsequent book.

If you would prefer to pay by VISA, ACCESS/MASTERCARD, DINERS CLUB, AMEX or SWITCH, please write your card number and expiry date here:

....

Signature ....

Please allow up to 28 days for delivery.